M000250715

Nevermind

Richard Seltzer

Nevermind

Copyright © 2020 by Richard Seltzer

All rights reserved. No part of this book may be reproduced or transmitted in any form or by any means without written permission of the author and publisher. This is a work of fiction. Any resemblance to actual persons, living or dead, is purely coincidental.

ISBN: 9781734685589

Library of Congress Control Number: 2020951666

Cover Design by All Things that Matter Press

Cover photo by victor-freitas-B0zAPSrEcFw-unsplash

Published in 2020 by All Things that Matter Press

Never mind. Never mind.

Give me now my nevermind,

Happily-ever-after time.

To my wife Barbara (1950-2012)

Acknowledgments

I want to thank:

Rex Sexton, artist and author, and his widow Rochelle Cohen for their frequent helpful feedback and encouragement.

Diane Motowidlo for her feedback.

Jennifer Barclay and Leslie Wells for their editorial help.

thespunyarn.com for the feedback of their beta readers.

Gabi Coatsworth for her monthly Writers' Rendezvous meetup sessions, and her advice which led me to find my terrific publisher, All Things That Matter Press.

My parents and Uncle Adolph (who I never met but often heard of) for their inspiration.

My sister Raven for many long and helpful conversations.

My son Bob for his continuing support.

Prologue

Ruth, one letter shy of "truth," the sixth of seven children, grew up in a row house in East Falls, an immigrant neighborhood of Philadelphia, at a time of sharp social distinctions. The Kelly family lived in a mansion on top of a nearby hill. Grace Kelly, nine years younger than Ruth, grew up there. Sometimes Ruth would get a chance to play tennis on their courts, but, for the most part, that was a dreamland—near physically, but far away socially and economically.

The street where Ruth lived was paved with cobblestones. Once a week the horse-drawn ice wagon rattled by; once a month the rag-and-bone man. The row house was narrow and deep. From the street, you entered a long hallway that led to a staircase. The door to the living room was on the left. That room opened into the dining room, which opened into the kitchen, where a wash tub, a hand-cranked clothes ringer, and an ironing board were crammed together among the pots, pans, and cooking utensils. The kitchen door at the back opened onto a rickety porch which overlooked a patch of dirt yard. Upstairs were three small bedrooms; up another flight were three more. At the very top was the attic room where Ruth slept.

Money was scarce. The older kids took care of the younger ones.

Emily, the youngest of the seven, slept in Abby and Madeline's room on the third floor. Madeline and Abby had taken care of her since she was an infant and hadn't allowed Ruth to hold her, much less change her diaper or feed her. They insisted that babies are fragile, and that five-year-old Ruth was far too young to be so entrusted.

Ruth was her mother's favorite. Emily was Father's. But physically they were reversed. Emily, like all her sisters, except Ruth, and like their Aunties, resembled her mother. Ruth, alone, looked like Father.

Her mother, Mabel, half-Welsh, half-Irish, and a hundred percent Protestant, was short, with a round kind face, bright blue eyes, and shoulder-length curly black hair that she wore tied in a bun at the back. Her father, Philip, was the manager of the general store across the street.

Strikingly handsome, tall, and thin, with dark brown eyes, blond hair, and mustache, he dressed and acted like a southern plantation owner—wearing silk shirts and a tan suit while his children were all in hand-me-downs. At mealtime, Ruth's mother served Father first, separately from the rest of the family. He never talked to the children about his background. Ruth knew that he was from Tennessee, but she didn't know if he had any living relatives.

Ruth knew very little about Father, which she first realized when she was nine, a few months before her mother died. That night, at bedtime, her pregnant mother was slow to join her. She sat beside Ruth on the bed in her attic room where the sloping sides of the roof converged and told her stories, as she did every night. Not ones from books, but rather ones that she remembered or made up, telling them with dramatic flair, changing voices that spoke in sync with shadows she cast on the wall. That night, her mother had bruises on both cheeks, and drops of blood in her left nostril.

How could Father hurt Mommy this way? She thought. It was impossible, against nature, against his nature. It couldn't have been as bad as it looked. Mommy forgave him, always forgave him. And she repeatedly told Ruth, "It's nothing. Don't worry."

Ruth kissed her cheeks and wiped away the blood with a wet washcloth. "What happened, Mommy?" Ruth asked, as she always asked.

And her mother answered, "Never mind. Never mind. Give me now my nevermind."

"Happily-ever-after time," Ruth added, as she always did. And they laughed together, chasing away tears with laughter.

Nevermind was magic, her mother claimed. "When you say that, when you believe that, bad things that have happened go away. They never happened at all, and you're free to live a new life without them."

"Then why don't you say it all the time, Mommy, when the least little thing goes wrong?"

"The more you use it, the more it loses its power. Use it too often, and it will have no effect at all when you really need it. Save it up for years if you can. I've used it too often. So for me, it no longer works. But you, my love, I hope you never need it, never need to say it. And I don't mean just mouthing the words. I mean believing them with your whole heart and soul. I hope you'll never need such a spell, never need to wish for a fresh start, a new life, and a new world to live in."

Ruth understood that to make the nevermind work, just saying the words wasn't enough. She would have to pray them, like she said her prayers when she kneeled beside her bed at night—god-blessing everyone in her family and everyone whose name she knew. When she first saw a phone book with page after page of names, she knew it was her duty to memorize as many names as she could and god-bless them all. That was how she built her ability to memorize, which made it easy for her, later, to learn Latin and French and to quickly learn parts in plays.

Over the years, Ruth often wanted to use the nevermind, but she restrained herself. Believing that she had that power in reserve, as a last resort, and that she should only use it when she really needed to, she found ways to cope without it. Using it unnecessarily would be a waste, a sacrilege.

When she was tempted, she would run the words through her mind, sometimes even speak them aloud; but she never gave them the intensity, the oneness of will that could make them real. Before getting to that point, she'd realize that what had seemed so important was too trivial to waste magic on. She could deal with it. She could get over it. She could move on. She got used to coping and forgiving and making the most of bad situations. And over time, her belief faded as her ingenuity and determination grew. The more she believed in herself, the less she needed to believe in the magic of nevermind

PART ONE ~ Ruth's Education

Chapter One–Losing Mommy

February 1930, Philadelphia, PA

George was twenty-three, Edgar twenty-two, Abby twenty, Madeline eighteen, Ethel seventeen, Fran sixteen, Ruth ten, and Emily five when their mother died.

She died of slow, undetected hemorrhaging after the still birth of what would have been her eighth child, Phil, Jr. In those days, women gave birth at home and with a midwife rather than a doctor. And at death, the body was laid out for the wake not at a funeral parlor, but rather on the dining room table.

Ruth's mother was laid out in her Sunday best–an ankle-length black dress with white lace trim at the neck. All the children were expected to kiss the body, while in the background neighborhood dogs, smelling death, howled non-stop.

When her turn came, Ruth stared in disbelief. The hair was the same. The shape of the head was the same. But that was not her Mommy's face. The skin of the face was stretched tight to the bones underneath. The lips were rigid in a straight expressionless line. When she leaned forward to kiss, the heavily powdered cheek didn't taste like Mommy and, with no response, it wasn't a kiss at all—more like brushing her lips against a wall. She was bewildered, not frightened to learn that a body without a soul was so alien, so empty.

After Ruth had performed that duty, she retreated to the living room where she sat on the floor in the shadow of her father's empty armchair, which no one but he could sit in. There she sucked her thumb for the first time in years and whispered to a blue stuffed bear named Catfish Snail and to Gladys, her favorite doll, who had been her mother's before her. Gladys had a ceramic head and a cloth body. This morning, while aunties were dressing her mother's body, Ruth had carefully ironed her own dress and her doll's dress, and had talked make-believe to Gladys, as if they were getting ready to go to a dance where there would be princes.

Ruth's dress was brown and white. She didn't have anything black. Her aunts had been annoyed when they learned that. It was the same color as her doll's dress, which Ruth found comforting, at a time when any comfort was welcome.

As friends and neighbors paraded in to express their sympathy, Ruth alternated between brushing her doll's hair and brushing her own hair.

Her aunts were busy talking to guests.

Her two brothers, George and Edgar, stood stiffly, in second-hand ill-fitting suits, in the hallway near the front door. Supposedly, they were there to greet arriving guests. But standing there, it was easy for them to avoid talking to anyone but one another and to stay far away from the body.

Her older sisters were busy calming their youngest sister, Emily, who was sobbing convulsively. The aunts insisted that Emily, five years old, stay downstairs for the guests. So, she huddled on the lap of Abby at the far end of the kitchen near the back porch. The other sisters hovered near and tried to distract her with word games, having been forbidden to bring out playthings.

No one knew where Father was.

After the guests had left and Ruth's siblings had gone to bed, Father staggered in and went upstairs. The aunts left in disgust, muttering, loudly enough for him to hear, that they didn't want to be in the house when he was in such a state. They would be back in the morning to take care of the children since he didn't have a clue how to do that.

Ruth, unnoticed, stayed on the floor in the shadow of the armchair with Gladys and Catfish Snail, and, in whispers, recited to them stories her mother had told her many times: *Cinderella, Snow White,* and *Beauty and the Beast.* Fairy tales in which bad things were suddenly erased, poverty and grief were forgotten, and everyone lived happily ever after.

Then, dolls in hand, she climbed the many stairs to her attic room. There would be no story tonight. There had been no story for many days as her mother grew weaker. Now there would never be stories at bedtime.

Looking out her window into the dark, feeling very alone, she, on a whim, flipped the switch on the lamp on her nightstand off then on. Many blocks away, a light went off then on. She flipped her switch twice and that same light in the distance went off and on twice. She laughed. Some kid out there was just as lonely as she was.

Before her mother's illness, such contact would have delighted her, like an astronomer finding evidence of intelligent life in space. She would have tried to build a code with that stranger and communicate with him or her. She would have told her mother, and together they would have sent signals to that stranger blocks away and made up stories about him or her. But tonight, she had no one to share that fantasy with.

The day after the wake, her mother's unmarried sisters, Aunt Mathilda and Aunt Olive, moved in with the children in the row house. Ruth referred to them collectively as *Aunties* because they seemed to speak with a single voice. Small of stature and strong of will, round-faced but harsh, not kind, both women were proud to have never depended on a man. Aunt Olive worked as a secretary, and Aunt Mathilda ran the house.

Father moved across the street, above the store he managed. He minimized his visits to the children. The Aunties had always had a low opinion of him.

That morning, when Aunties chased the kids out of the house so they could clean up and rearrange the house as they saw fit, Ruth stopped short at the threshold, and Fran ran into her. "What are you doing?" Fran demanded.

"The pavement's full of cracks," Ruth tried to explain.

"So what? It always has been."

"But Mommy said, 'Step on a crack, you'll break your mother's back.'"

"Nonsense. That never bothered you before, and it shouldn't bother you now."

But Ruth, who had never paid attention to the cracks before, now stepped and jumped carefully to miss them—not that she thought that stepping on them could in any way hurt her mother, who was now beyond hurt, but because being careful that way made her feel her mother's presence, as a guide, a compass.

It was difficult adjusting to the Aunties. While they looked very much like her mother, their voices were very different. Mommy had said, "Know yourself." Now Aunties said, "Know your place." Mommy had told her children, "Know your strengths." Now Aunties said, "Admit your weaknesses." Mommy had told each of them, "You are unique." Aunties told them, "You are no better than anyone else and worse than many." Mommy promised, "Anything is possible, even magic." But Aunties insisted, "Accept your limitations."

A few weeks after the funeral, the two oldest, George and Edgar, moved out and lived together on their own, leaving their sisters and Aunties in the row house an all-female household.

A few months later, Abby married a prison guard and moved out, leaving Ruth and her four remaining sisters with Aunties.

2 ~ The Closet

Less than two years later, when Ruth was eleven going on twelve, at a birthday party for her friend Katie, Ruth was "it" in a game of sardines, a variation of hide-and-seek. She hid in the hall closet, in a corner behind the coats. Matt, Katie's brother, fourteen going on fifteen, was the first to find her. She liked him. She wished she were older so he'd take her seriously, and they might be boyfriend and girlfriend. Following the rules of the game, he joined her there in the closet; and they squeezed close together, to hide from the others.

She was shocked and confused when, in the dark, his hands reached out and held her, touched her. She didn't say a word. Others were walking by and talking. Ruth and Matt had to stay quiet or they would be found. The game must go on. But his touching wasn't part of the game. She had no idea what to do or say. She had never been told that this might happen. He held her firmly, but gently. His hands touched her here, there, and everywhere—echoes of her mother giving her a bath and sponge-caressing her back, her front, her legs, her everywhere. The warm water, the warmth of her mother's presence, her caring, her loving, extending from her fingertips. Is this what boys did when they liked a girl? Did this mean he liked her? Maybe this is what came before a storybook first kiss. Spin the bottle didn't count, nor did a quick kiss that a boy might snatch, uninvited, on a dare. Later, she realized those roaming hands of his were curious, not loving; that he was taking not giving, not caring what she was feeling and thinking.

It might have lasted seconds or hours. She couldn't remember where he had touched—one sensation cascading to another. It felt good, but she was scared. It was over before she had time to give it a name and decide to pull him closer or to push him away. It was cut short when Katie opened the door, found them, squeezed into the closet with them, and Matt backed off, without a word. Soon, one after the other, everyone found them, and the game ended.

Out in the light, with everyone watching, Matt didn't say a word to her. He avoided looking her in the eye. He joked and rough-housed with the other boys. But that hadn't been random contact. She thought, Why the silence afterward? Why didn't he acknowledge to the others that he liked her? Had she done something wrong? Was she supposed to have pushed him away? What did his avoiding her mean? What had she signaled by letting him do that? What was the code?

Hovering between images of Prince Charming and strict but vague edicts from Aunties to beware of men, she didn't give a label to that moment in the closet; but sometimes in bed at night or in the bath, she felt echoes of those sensations.

Two months later, she woke up wet between her legs, and the sheet under her was wet. Her first thought was that she had wet her bed, like a little child who hadn't been properly potty trained. Aunties would be outraged. She turned on the lamp on her nightstand. At first, she didn't register what she saw. It wasn't yellow. The liquid was red. Blood. She was bleeding between her legs.

Did she sin when she let Matt touch her the way he did? Was this punishment for that sin? Was she bleeding from an injury? Might she bleed to death like her mother? After these thoughts she screamed.

Her sister Fran ran to the rescue and hugged her and comforted her and explained as best she could that this was "normal," that she wasn't going to bleed to death. This meant that she wasn't a little girl anymore. She was a woman. And this would happen once a month. And this had something to do with how babies are made.

When Auntie Olive finally arrived on the scene, Fran greeted her with anger, "You should have told her, explained to her, prepared her as Mother did for me. Imagine the shock, knowing nothing about all this. As if she could sort it out on her own. And she's so young. Probably none of her friends have gone through this yet. Out of the blue, she bleeds."

"It's the curse. The curse of Eve is what it is," said Auntie Olive. "Thank God I've outlived it. And this is too soon. She's too young for this," Auntie Olive insisted. "What have you been doing?" she asked. "What have you let boys do to you? What brought this on? What unholy nastiness have you been up to?"

Ruth lay in the bathtub for over an hour, convinced that what she had let Matt do in the closet had brought this on, making it happen sooner than it should have. She was sinful and lustful—whatever that meant. She didn't dare tell anyone.

Fran had said that she wasn't a little girl anymore. Then what was she? And what was expected of her now? What could she say to her friends? How could she relate to them and play with them if she was a woman already, and they might not be for years to come? And boys, what would the boys who had been her pals think of her now—now that she was a —? Would they try to touch her like Matt had? And would they look down on her if she let them? She found herself in a new world and didn't know the language.

3 ~ As Good as Dead

February 1932 to 1934, Philadelphia, PA

A few weeks later, on Valentine's Day, two years after her mother died, Ruth once again sat with Gladys and Catfish Snail in the corner of the living room, in the shadow of Father's armchair.

"Father isn't here anymore," Ruth explained to her dolls. "Aunties will still take care of us, but we have no mother and no father. That means we're orphans, like Little Orphan Annie and Cinderella. Lots of special people have been orphans. That's not something to be ashamed of; it's something to rise above. Father is dead and gone."

Ruth was lying to her dolls. She knew that Father was "gone" and "as good as dead," not "dead dead." He was in prison, and she would never see him again, but she had to tell everyone that he was dead. She told her dolls that story and told it over and over again. This was practice. It wasn't easy to lie, even when that was the right thing to do, when the truth—whatever the truth was—was too nasty to talk about.

"We have to stick together, now, more than ever," she continued, "and study hard, do all our chores and be good. And we mustn't talk to strangers. We mustn't trust grown men, unless it's a very special man—the man—when we're older and the time is right.

"Something very bad happened across the street, but we mustn't ask about that. That's not for little girls to know about or talk about, even among ourselves. We must thank the Lord that we have been spared."

Ruth was tempted to use the nevermind to try to undo what had happened. But she didn't know what had happened, so how could she magically make it go away?

Father had done something to Emily and her friends. Years later, from the few clues she had gathered, she guessed that he somehow talked them into undressing and getting into the bathtub and gave them an intimate washing. Maybe it was nothing more than that. Maybe people over-reacted. Maybe he was given an unjustly harsh sentence. Then again, maybe it was something horrible, and he deserved even worse.

Aunties wouldn't talk about it. They were adamant that men were evil, that sex was evil. But they wouldn't say what sex was. Providing no details, they ordered that Ruth and her sisters never talk about what had happened to anyone, not even to one another. And seven-year-old Emily would never defy the Aunties and talk to Ruth about it.

The day Father went away, Ruth wondered, was what Father did to Emily like what Matt did to her in the closet? But she didn't talk to her dolls about that. Rather, she reminded them, "Aunt Mathilda and Aunt Olive are strict and no-nonsense. They know how to raise children properly. They know it's important to teach us to deal with facts; to learn our place; to follow God's wishes in all things. We need to stick to the straight and narrow; to avoid temptation; to respect our elders; to not clutter our thinking with fantasy; and to beware of men."

She held Catfish Snail tight with one arm; and with the other, she cradled Gladys and rocked her. The doll's eyes opened and closed, repeatedly, as if she understood and agreed.

"Remember, Gladys, don't talk to strangers. When you're older, you'll understand why. But for now, just obey and know that that's best for us. Men, and especially strange men, are evil."

Gladys blinked again and again, in agreement; she seemed to smile even more than usual. It was hard to smile on a day like this, but Gladys was cheerful, even in the worst of times. It was reassuring to see Gladys smile.

"There are no visitors for Father today. You remember how the house was swarming with people from the church and the neighborhood when Mommy died? Cousins came who we'd never seen before. Everybody came when Mommy died."

Gladys blinked. The memory was still fresh, and still hurt.

"Father was not well liked. That's what Aunties say. Father didn't have relatives, either, aside from us, none that we know of. He came from far away, from Tennessee. That's why he talked funny. So nobody is coming to say goodbye to him, not even the neighborhood dogs. He hated dogs."

Gladys blinked again in agreement.

"Aunties never understood him. Mommy, me, and you, we knew he was special and different. He was raised knowing he was better than everyone else. That would be his position in life one day, and he had to be ready for that. He was like a king in exile, but he died before his true identity could be revealed and before he could assume his proper role and position. You know how it goes in stories."

Gladys agreed.

"That means that I'm a princess," Ruth continued, "forced to live in poverty until my prince finds me and restores me to my rightful state. I'm special and beautiful, Gladys. Mommy always said I was. Someday my prince will come. Meanwhile, I need to study hard and keep my head up, knowing that I'm special.

"And I need to do what Aunties tell me to. They seem cold, but that's their way of preparing me for life—no matter how harsh life might be; that's their way of keeping me pure and god-fearing. When they nag me and yell at me more than any of the others, that's proof of how special I am."

Both Gladys and Catfish Snail nodded in agreement.

"Father, when he was home, would sit in this armchair, in the tan suit that Mommy washed and ironed every day, and read his newspaper while smoking his pipe, brushing his mustache with his fingertips. He'd pay no attention to what was around him, except if we were too loud, and then he'd bellow about these misbehaving kids, and couldn't she keep them quiet? Children are not to speak unless spoken to. They are to be seen, but not heard.

"Then, when Mommy died, he moved out and Aunties took over. They had to. Father did nothing to help around the house and just got in the way. That's what Aunties said, and, of course, they were right. So, Aunties moved in, and Father moved across the street, upstairs from the store he managed.

"Then, today, on Valentine's Day, he died. Remember that's what you're supposed to say—he died."

Now all the neighbors and even the kids, like Katie and Matt, who had been Ruth's friends, shied away from her. They didn't know what had happened, any more than Ruth did; but they knew that her father had been sent to prison—he had done something un-nameable, something evil.

A year and a half later, just before she started junior high, she had a growth spurt. Almost magically, she towered over her Aunties and her older sisters, a head taller than them. The others all had curly black hair and round faces, like they were made from the same mold. But Ruth was tall with bright blond hair, dark brown eyes, a long face, and high cheek bones—the very image of her father. And suddenly, she had a bust that couldn't fit in her sisters' hand-me-down clothes. She needed to wear a brassiere, but the brassiere that fit her last month didn't fit this month, and it felt awkward, uncomfortable, and itchy. And she dared not adjust it or scratch herself in public.

In another setting, she would have been deemed beautiful, but here she was freakishly out of place, or so she thought, having been suddenly transformed—not out of, but into an ugly duckling.

Her knees hurt when she walked. When she sat down, she needed to remember to keep her long legs together. And no one else in her class had noticeable breasts. Boys stared at her, and girls avoided her. Or so she thought at the time. She exaggerated her difference and awkwardness. She realized later that when she cringed to imagine what others were thinking of her, they weren't thinking of her at all.

Where did this body come from? she wondered. This wasn't hers. This wasn't her. This was no more natural than bleeding once a month. If this was "life," then life was crazy.

She needed her mother now more than ever. Walking home from school, she chose the path with the most cracks in the pavement and repeated the singsong superstition, as she focused all her attention on avoiding stepping on cracks, finding it relaxing to focus on anything but her looks and what others thought of how she looked.

Whenever she could, she escaped to the Germantown Branch Library where she read all the Bobbsey Twins books, all of Nancy Drew, then anything and everything, to get her mind off the everyday random humiliations and disappointments she faced at school and at home. She invented excuses to tell Aunties, who wouldn't approve of her reading so much fiction. In the books she read, girls her age had friends they confided in and shared experiences with. So she made up friends and events to tell Aunties about. These imaginary friends—Florence, Joan, Agnes, and Lillian—had triumphs and defeats, strengths and weaknesses. They gossiped and joked about others who weren't in their clique. They admitted to having crushes on boys and solved minor mysteries involving neighbors and teachers. Ruth would ramble on about these friends to Aunties while washing dishes, sweeping floors, and ironing clothes, talking so much that Aunties would tune out and not notice when she confused one plot line with another and contradicted herself.

Then one day, Ruth was no longer a freak, even in her own mind — not that she had changed, but that others had caught up with her. And on her first day of high school, the life she had imagined in the tall tales she had made up to tell Aunties became real, as if a fairy godmother had waved her magic wand.

4 ~ New Sisters

September 1934, Philadelphia, PA

High school was a fresh start for Ruth. It was with great relief and pride that, having passed the entrance exams and with the encouragement of Aunties, she went to Girls' High, escaping the social networks of her neighborhood where everyone distanced themselves from her as if her father's crime, whatever crime it was, had tainted her, as if she were guilty though she had nothing to do with it.

She didn't mind the long trek to and from Seventeenth and Spring Garden, by trolley and then on foot, even though she had to pass the Eastern State Penitentiary where her sister Abby's husband was a guard and her father an inmate. Going to and from school on the prison-dominated stretch of Fairmount Avenue, she carefully avoided stepping on cracks, as a distraction from thoughts of Father and as a reminder of what her mother expected of her and hoped for her—a daily dose of incentive.

Ruth never had the luxury of being a rebellious teenager as she had no mother or father to rebel against. Her Aunties were kind to her, in their own way, out of duty. She was obliged to obey and try to please them. Though they could never take the place of her mother, she could never imagine going counter to their wishes.

There were no boys at Girls' High—Aunties liked that. And the school's motto was *Vincit qui se vincit*—she conquers who conquers herself—in keeping with Aunties' emphasis on discipline and self-control. Fortunately, it was also one of the best public schools for women in the country—Ruth liked that. And there was a school uniform so she wouldn't have to compete in clothes, wouldn't need to think about clothes at all—she liked that as well.

There was just one little problem, as she learned on day one—all freshmen were required to pass a swimming test—four laps, non-stop.

Ruth had never swum before, never been to a beach, never been to a swimming pool. She had never even worn a bathing suit. She wasn't used to changing clothes in front of others, much less parading around in an outfit as tight-fitting and revealing as the standard-issue school swimsuit.

She still thought of herself as physically freakish. So, she quickly got into the water, despite her fear of drowning and despite the shock of the cold against her skin, never having been immersed in water, except warm bath water. She thrashed and splashed wildly, with the other girls laughing as if they thought she was deliberately clowning, and the instructor yelled at her for making a mockery of the class.

By chance, she leaned back and discovered that with no effort at all, she could float. Then she saw other girls floating on their backs and propelling themselves with their arms and legs. She imitated what she saw and slowly but steadily went the length of the pool. Then like the other girls, she pushed off from the wall and went back. She then did that again, and again.

"Enough," shouted the instructor. "You've passed. No need for any more fooling around. Let others have a chance."

She climbed out, delighted with her unexpected performance. In the full-length mirrors that covered the walls on all sides, she saw herself side by side with her classmates, and she looked normal. No, she looked better than normal—good, very good. And she could see in the eyes of others that she was admired and envied for her looks.

In the locker room, a girl who was even taller than Ruth approached her, arms akimbo. Pulling off her bathing cap, and shaking her long blond hair, this girl told Ruth, "You. Yes, you. You have the look. You're one of us. We'll meet in the library after last period."

This girl and the girls beside her were all blond and all tall, at least as tall as Ruth, but none taller than the leader.

"Are you sisters?" asked Ruth.

"Sorority sisters," the leader answered. "But more than that. The four of us, now five, are a sisterhood within that sisterhood, the creme de la creme. You are now a chosen one."

Thinking about that moment in later years, Ruth realized she was chosen like a piece of clothing—not for any personal qualities, but for how her looks would fit in with the rest of the group. And her sense of belonging with them was triggered by a coincidence. The girl who accosted her and recruited her and who became her best friend had the same name as Ruth's imaginary friend Florence—Flo for short. It was as if Ruth had been rehearsing for this moment with her fantasies. She knew her part and could improvise in character with the greatest of ease. Opening up and feeling close to these new sorority sisters felt natural to her, even though she had never been that close to anyone her age before.

Yes, there was a sorority social club. And this was a subset of that sorority. Ruth adopted their hair style, and, like the rest, wore a red ribbon in her hair and another around her throat—their marks of distinction, above and beyond the school uniform. Flo, Dorothy, Helen, and Diane were all freshmen, but from mothers, older sisters, and friends who had been sorority members before them, they, unlike most of their classmates, knew what to expect and operated with confidence from day one, with Ruth following their lead in lock step.

The five of them marched down the halls shoulder-to-shoulder from class to class and sat near one another in class and had their own table in the cafeteria, which was acknowledged as theirs by everyone else.

While in junior high, she had lied about her social life to her Aunties to avoid letting them know she spent long hours reading fiction in the library. Now she told them that she had to stay late at school to do her homework—which she did, in addition to socializing. And when she was invited to the homes of her sorority sisters on weekends and sometimes for sleepovers, she told Aunties she needed to work on group projects. The school emphasized social experiences and teamwork, she explained to Aunties, who were impressed with this fantasy theory of education as well as with the straight A's that Ruth consistently earned. Her friends understood that she was ashamed of her relative poverty, and that her aunts wouldn't have let her invite friends over if she wanted. Nevertheless, she was a member of their elite group. She was a close friend. That was all that mattered.

But while Ruth took pride in belonging and enjoyed the company of her new sisters, that didn't stop her from doing what she wanted when she wanted, on her own. Her mother, paraphrasing Polonius, had told her, "Never a follower or a leader be." And now those words made sense to her—for neither followers nor leaders were free to be themselves, to discover who they could be, on their own.

In free periods and after school, Ruth often returned to the pool for the sheer physical pleasure of swimming. She didn't swim the way the instructor told her to, with her face in the water. She didn't like water on her open eyes and didn't like goggles, either. So, she developed her own idiosyncratic style. Admittedly her way wasn't the fastest, but she wasn't going out for the swim team. She was swimming for herself alone. She enjoyed the sensations, immersed in water and moving through it at a leisurely pace. And she liked the physical weariness that came after half an hour of laps. It was relaxing to blank her mind of everything for such a stretch of time, erasing every thought, with all her body in motion, every muscle straining, stroke after stroke.

At other times, she delighted in stretching her mind, learning not just in class, but from her interactions with her new friends as well. Her mother would have been delighted that she had this opportunity to grow. But Aunties warned her not to think above her station. These girls she was socializing with came from a different social world—with different norms and goals and expectations. They came from families with money. They would go to college. They would marry men with money. Their lives would turn out very differently from hers.

Yes, she should do her best. Yes, she should make the most of high school. But when it ended, she'd be riding home in a pumpkin. College was out of the question.

5 ~ Crying Wolf

1934-1938, Philadelphia, PA

From the windows of the library, she could see the prison five blocks away, on Fairmount Avenue. She sometimes wondered if her father might, like Lear, be more sinned against than sinning, that there might have been some mistake, some misinterpretation, some miscarriage of justice. Without facts or evidence, she wanted to give him the benefit of the doubt.

She remembered him being selfish and being mean to her mother; but she wanted to believe that underneath that rough surface, he was a good man. He was her father. He deserved a second chance, a third chance, even a fourth chance. He couldn't be totally evil. How could she believe he was evil when she saw reminders of him every day when she looked in a mirror? Rather, she imagined him like Jean Valjean or like Edmond Dantes the Count of Monte Cristo—a good man suffering in prison.

Ruth suspected that her mother, who so readily spun stories for her at bedtime, had the talent to be a writer—a great one—and she hoped that she had inherited that gift from her. And perhaps her father, like Cervantes, was even now writing a masterpiece in his prison cell. Perhaps he had a talent for fiction in common with her mother, perhaps that brought them together in the first place. And perhaps that's what kept them together so long—their ability to imagine the best, regardless of actual circumstances.

She had no photo of him, no tangible reminder of him, except the prison that dominated the skyline near her school. Aunties had destroyed everything that had anything to do with him. But Ruth found his image in the library, in the person of William Faulkner—tall and thin, smoking a pipe, and dressed in a suit, with the air of a southern plantation owner. His hair and mustache looked white in the black and white photos on the backs of his books, but they might actually be blond, like Father's.

She stole the dust jacket from the library's copy of *The Sound and the Fury*, cut out the photo on the back, and taped it on the inside cover of the three-ring binder with her English notes.

As she explored the school library, she came to think of Faulkner and Woolf as her literary parents.

Her enjoyment of swimming prompted her to read *The Waves*, then *To the Lighthouse* and *Mrs. Dalloway*. She and Virginia Woolf almost had the same birthday—January 25 and 31. Woolf was the seventh of eight children, while Ruth was the sixth of seven. And if Phil Jr. hadn't been stillborn, there would have been eight. Woolf's mother died when she was thirteen, and Ruth's when she was ten. Woolf's father died when she was twenty-three. And Ruth's father was as good as dead.

Woolf loved water and waves, and must have been a swimmer, immersing herself in sensation. And reading her novels heightened Ruth's awareness of her own sensations, the sensual richness of the moment—with layer upon layer of thoughts and feelings interacting and heightening and enriching one another. She felt she was more complete, more alive, and aware for having experienced the flow of such prose. She wished that she could write like that and give her readers such a gift of self-awareness, to stimulate their minds as hers had been stimulated. She wished she had such a gift, to plunge into the depth of her self, and to thereby make contact with others—for we are all connected, not so much by sight and sound, as by inner events and emotions and hopes and fears and the warp and woof of our memories, how one thought or feeling evokes another, without our willing it so.

Ruth was amazed to discover in novels that the social world she had taken for granted—the world of her Aunties and of her mother—was just one of many. She could imagine what it would have been like to live in the worlds of Jane Austen or of Virginia Woolf. Class distinctions weren't just a matter of money and property and clothes. Your social world is what fills your days, what matters to you, what you value, what you expect of life, what makes you happy or sad, what you consider success or failure, how you might or might not find meaning in your life.

She realized that her father came from a different social world than hers. That was why he seemed so out of place among the row houses, cobblestone streets, and multi-cracked pavements of East Falls. Others sensed that he didn't belong, and he sensed it, too, and rebelled rather than trying to fit in. He insisted on dressing for dinner in his tan suit and insisted that it be freshly cleaned and pressed, not because he was mean and selfish, rather, he needed to preserve his self-image and his pride—relics of the social world he grew up in.

She concluded that it's possible to move from one social world to another, but the transition can prove difficult. Many of the stories she loved involved striving for such a change but stopped at the moment when that dream was fulfilled, when Cinderella married the prince. But the real drama started when Cinderella moved into the palace, and her habits and expectations and values all had to change.

Ruth would love to experience such an adventure and challenge—to explore different social worlds and not just as an anthropologist studying them, but to participate and by doing so to savor the experience of living not just one life, but two or more. And maybe she would, depending on who she married, for surely, she would marry and have children. Life wouldn't feel complete if it didn't include a man to love and children to love. She wanted to understand her life, not just live it, and to pass along to the next generation what she had learned. She wanted to be part of the chain of writers who talked across centuries, receiving and understanding messages from the past and sending messages into the future to help people make sense of their lives.

But she knew, from reading *A Room of One's Own*, that she would need to have money and a room of her own to be able to write her novel. First things first—now she must do her very best at her schoolwork.

It helped that Florence and her gang of sorority sisters prided themselves on their academic excellence, were near the top of the class in nearly all subjects and were highly competitive. Ruth exceled at English, Latin, French, and Elocution—winning prizes repeatedly in those subjects. She also joined the Drama Club, playing Helena in *Midsummer Night's Dream* and Rosalind in *As You Like It*.

Meanwhile, she was awash in story and drama. By gossiping about others as they shared their experiences and thoughts and feelings with one another, her sorority sisters heightened their sensitivity to emotional issues and learned how to manage relationships. Ruth often commented on what the others said and speculated on what that might mean and what might come of it. But she didn't offer stories of her own. She dared not.

Rather than turn to Flo or any of her other sorority sisters for advice and comfort, she deliberately stayed aloof and didn't unburden herself about anything, for fear that if she once started, by accident, some hint of her secret would come to light and they would relentlessly drag out the rest of the story, and she would be labeled as the daughter of a criminal in prison, convicted of child abuse or incest. No one would want to associate with her. She'd be a pariah, a social leper for life. She could never let down her defenses to anyone or she would be ruined. So, she became known and valued as a great listener, a sympathetic ear.

But on the written page, in the three-ring binder with Faulkner's photo taped inside, she vented her emotions and explored her concerns and aspirations, in the guise of fiction, like Virginia Woolf, for whom she now felt a special affinity, based on the rhythm of her prose, the flow of her thoughts and images, and the sensations she described and evoked.

On weekends, Ruth often went to Flo's house where there was a tennis court that was every bit as good as the courts on the Kelly estate, and where she saw Flo's older brother Ralph. She enjoyed listening to Flo talk about her brother's high school friends, and, later, his college friends from the U. of Penn. She especially enjoyed Ralph himself, who she had played with and against in mixed doubles, who she had never really talked to, nothing more than polite general chatter, never separate, never alone, never revealing—nothing worth remembering or recounting, nothing that could lead to anything between them.

Ruth held back because she was rational and level-headed and refused to delude herself, as well as because she wouldn't dare open up about anything for fear of what that might lead to.

But by senior year, Flo was dating her brother's friends, and her brother was seriously dating a girl her age, who Ruth had played tennis with and beaten.

Ruth couldn't help but wonder if she had opened up to Flo and admitted how she felt about Ralph, maybe Flo would have told him, and might he have looked at her differently and have realized that he was attracted to her as well?

6 ~ Graduation

June 1938, Philadelphia, PA

The Girls' High graduation was held not at the school itself, but rather at the Academy of Music, the oldest opera house in the U.S., home of the Philadelphia Orchestra. Ruth, in her academic gown, sat next to Flo and near Dorothy, Helen, and Diane. Aunties, Emily, Fran, Ethel, Madeline, and Abby all sat ten rows back from her on the other side, having arrived more than an hour early to get good seats.

"You can tell me now," Flo whispered.

"What?"

"The college you'll be going to. You can't keep that a secret any longer. Dr. Mayhew will be announcing everybody's college when he hands out the diplomas. So, fess up. Tell me now."

Ruth froze. She had never imagined that that would be the case. She had focused on her neck-and-neck competition with Flo for valetudinarian. She had finished three hundredths of a point behind her friend. But she was proud to be salutatorian. And if anyone was to beat her, she was glad that it was Flo. Ruth was to get senior year prizes in English, Latin, French, and Elocution. This was the crowning moment of her academic career, and her whole family was here to share it with her.

She hadn't wanted to admit to her friends that she couldn't afford to go to college. She didn't want to think about it. She enjoyed belonging to the group, and, to her mind, not planning to go to college would label her as an outsider. When her friends had asked about college applications and acceptances, she was evasive. She had joked, like it was a game.

No one in her family had ever gone to college. That was something rich people did; and as Aunties repeatedly reminded her, she was not rich. For her, high school was the be-all and end-all. And Girls' High was the "creme de la creme," as Flo would say. But, for her, college was out of the question.

Her last name was "Yates," so, alphabetically, she'd be one of the last called. That meant she heard the colleges of all the others first. Flo would be going to Bryn Mawr which she richly deserved. And the other three were going to U. Penn, Barnard, and Pembroke. No surprises, except Diane, who might have chosen Holyoke instead of Pembroke.

But nearly everyone else in their class was also going to college, even those who were notorious for their laziness and incompetence, who didn't take their studies seriously, and probably couldn't have done well if they had tried.

When her name was called—her name, but no college name—Ruth rose and walked to the podium with shame rather than pride. Afterward, standing with her classmates and throwing her cap in the air with them, she couldn't look Flo in the eye. But Flo wouldn't let her retreat to her family.

"For God sake, Ruth! Did you not apply? What the hell are you going to do? What was all this work for but to get into the best of the best, to get ready to have the best of the best life?

"So here you were a big fish in a little pond. That game is over now. Don't you understand that? You're not ready to go out into the world—the big world, the real world. What were you thinking? Once you leave the hallowed, sheltered halls of dear old Girls' High, you'll be just another woman in a world built for men. That's a world shaped by class distinctions, a world in economic depression. Do you have some 200-pound plumber or electrician you've never mentioned, who is going to whisk you away to domestic bliss—five kids, a dog, and a cat?

"You have no skills. You have no plan. You can't survive on your own. Are you going to stay at home and take care of your old-maid aunts until you're an old maid yourself? I can't believe that of you. That's not the gutsy, brilliant, self-reliant Ruth Yates I've known and loved for four years. Wake up and do something with your life."

Ruth had believed that going to college was a matter of social status, rather than economic necessity; and she wasn't into status. She had thought that for a woman it wasn't preparation for a career, but rather a place to find a mate, and she wasn't looking for a mate, not now.

Virginia Woolf was home-schooled. She went to college, but much of what she learned was on her own, in her own idiosyncratic way.

Ruth hadn't given much thought to her next steps, but she vaguely expected to continue living as before, for a while at least, without the responsibilities of schoolwork. She'd read and write what she wanted when she wanted—living a life of leisure. Now, hearing Flo, she realized she had missed the boat.

Two weeks later, sitting in her father's armchair, where she had never sat before, she explained her new plan to her Aunties. Emily, age thirteen, watched and listened in disbelief. Ruth spoke respectfully, but firmly. "Girls' High is a college preparatory school. It provides a good education, but what they teach is intended to lead to college, not the workplace. I can't afford to go to college. I have to work, but I have no work-related skills. The only kind of job I can get is menial—a maid in a hotel, a waitress—with low wages and no way to ever better myself except by marriage. And who would marry me except a man with a menial job—at best a plumber, an electrician, a factory worker? That's not the kind of life I want.

"I've decided to go to business school. Peirce, I believe, is the best. They offer a two-year program that will prepare me to be a secretary, so I can make a decent wage, so I can support myself without a husband. And my skills will be transferable and in demand. If I should want to, I could move anywhere and quickly find new employment.

"Yes, Peirce is expensive, but I'll pay for it myself. I'm not asking you to sacrifice for me. You've done enough for me, more than enough—I'm grateful.

"I need to do this, and I need to pay for it on my own. I'll waitress nights and weekends. I'll live in a low-cost but respectable rooming house, downtown, near school and near where I work. That way I'll no longer be a burden to you, and I'll be able to juggle a tight schedule—not having to trek back and forth to East Falls. When I finish at Peirce, I'll get a secretarial job and save up enough to put myself through college.

"I'll make it on my own. I'll build my own life. Please don't stand in my way. Give me your blessing and your prayers. I'll need your prayers. This path I've chosen as a single woman isn't an easy one."

Before she moved out, she looked through boxes of her mother's things, hoping to find diaries or stories or poems. She had imagined that her mother had written brilliant snippets but had never shown them to anyone, that she was a closet author, a modern-day Emily Dickinson and that her mother had talent and, by extension, Ruth had inherited that talent. But all she found was photos. She kept one that showed all seven children, arranged from youngest to oldest, one behind the other, one head on top of the other. All of them with round faces and curly black hair, like their mother, except Ruth, with the blond hair and long face of their father.

Then she went to her attic room, found a half-empty school notebook, and wrote down as many of her mother's made-up stories as she could remember.

"Once upon a space there was a time, a cute little time, her name was Now ..."

"Once beneath a time there was an Oops named Ker Plop ..."

"And despite everything the Little Princess did to make herself miserable so Prince Charming would come and rescue her, she lived happily ever after."

7 ~ On Her Own

1938 to 1940, Philadelphia, PA

That summer Ruth got a full-time job at an Italian restaurant two blocks from her new school. They made her a greeter/receptionist, obviously for her good looks. She wore a tight-fitting uniform with a skirt that only went to her knees. After she learned the routine, she was promoted to waitress, which meant the customers who flirted with her gave her tips; and the tips were good enough not just for room, board, and tuition, but also for membership at the YWCA, which had a swimming pool, where Ruth could unwind and forget the cares of the day.

In the fall she switched to part-time so she could go to class and do her homework. She had no time to socialize and lost touch with Flo and her other sorority friends, who were immersed in college life. She shared a room with another woman who she rarely saw since they worked different shifts. Ruth had the top bunk.

She didn't have money and a room of her own yet, but she was confident that she was on the right path, and one day would. In the meantime, she kept her dreams alive by sketching—not drawing but writing. She kept a notebook in her pocketbook, and, on breaks, she'd sit on a park bench and write descriptions of the surrounding scenes and the people who walked past or sat nearby.

She was inspired by a passage in *Waves*, "I have made up thousands of stories; I have filled innumerable notebooks with phrases to be used when I have found the true story, the one story to which all these phrases refer."

Sometimes, she deliberately arranged objects, like an artist working on a still life. She wrote and rewrote her sketches many times until she got them right, by her standards, preferably with metaphors. She didn't show her work to anyone. This was for her and her alone, not intended for publication. She knew full well that these meager but precise writings didn't fit into any established genre. No magazine would want them. But she felt they were a necessary part of her education.

After two years, in June of 1940, at the age of twenty, she graduated from Peirce at the top of her class—able to type at the astounding speed of 120 words per minute and do shorthand dictation at 100. She got a job as a secretary for a stockbroker and kept living at the rooming house, which was both decent and inexpensive.

At first, she kept her waitressing job as well, saving for college, thinking she might be able to start by the time her high school friends were graduating. She figured that once she was in college, she could work during vacations, getting temporary secretarial assignments through an agency, but when school was in session, she would need to devote all her time to her studies. So, she had to save in advance, which meant she had no time to socialize. With discipline, diligence, persistence, she could build the life she wanted. By following the precepts of her Aunties, she could achieve what her mother would have wanted for her.

Then she learned that Virginia Woolf had drowned herself, walking out to sea with rocks in her pockets. Her literary mentor, her mother substitute, whose ideas about women and writing had motivated her and guided her plans, hadn't just died; she had given up. So, this spartan life Ruth was living, working for college and money and a room of her own, was pointless. Virginia Woolf herself had said so eloquently—not in words, but in action—that life, even the best life that Ruth could imagine, wasn't worth living.

Soon after that, war broke out and, within a few months, the city was swarming with servicemen either passing through or getting specialized training at local schools. Every Friday and Saturday night Ruth went to the Stage Door Canteen, a USO gathering place for the military, under the Academy of Music, where her high school graduation had been held. There she could forget her work and her shattered dreams. There she could lose herself in music and motion, unwinding as she did with her swimming. There she could be admired for her looks rather than her diligence and intelligence. There she could hold handsome strangers and be held by them; whirling, twirling, laughing, wanted by all, free to dance with one and then another, to say what she pleased, to flirt as much as she wanted, without expecting to see any of these men again. It was the perfect escape for a curious but inhibited beautiful woman, with no experience in romance, much less sex.

Then she met Mark.

PART TWO ~ Coupling

Chapter Eight—True Love

November 1943, Philadelphia, PA

Mark was a soldier in wartime in Officer Candidate School, taking courses in German at the University of Pennsylvania. He would soon be sent to Europe, possibly for service behind enemy lines. He was going to die soon, and he had never really lived. Yes, there was God and Heaven and God's will, and dying for an important cause. But first he wanted to live.

Today, he was hoping to spend the night with a reputedly "loose" red-headed jitterbug star named Daisy. He had danced with her a dozen times before. A couple of those times, they had danced so well together that people around them stopped and stepped back to give them room and to watch.

He was sorely tempted by Daisy. At the same time, he was afraid to be so tempted. His mother would label her a "hussy," a "jezebel." She was the kind of woman his mother had repeatedly warned him about. He caught a glimpse of her thighs as she spun and her dress swung high, and a glimpse of her breasts as she bent low, moving this way and that. Her breasts pushed against her blouse, threatening to pop buttons and break loose from her black brassiere. She followed the strict dress code to the letter but managed to be suggestive none the less.

Mark had decided to take the plunge tonight. If they had another magic dance together, if she came on to him, tempting him as she had before, this time he would go along with it. He would enjoy the moment. If she wanted, he would "go all the way," as he had fantasized often these last two weeks. If she got pregnant, despite condoms, which he had never used before, but which he had bought from an Army buddy, just in case and which he hoped he'd know how to use, when the time came, he'd do the right thing and marry her. She was the sexiest woman he had ever met. Why should he be afraid of hitching up with her? And why gamble if you don't want to win? he thought.

She was dancing with a sailor now. Five minutes ago, she was with a marine corporal. She'd had a few beers and was warmed up from all the dancing. Light shimmered off the coating of sweat on her bare arms, neck, and cleavage. She might have a different partner for every dance, and any one of them might end up sleeping with her tonight. Better him than someone else.

He cut in on a slow dance, held her close and got an erection immediately. She smiled a mischievous smile that said she felt that stiffness pressed against her and knew damn well what he wanted, and that was fine with her.

Then a jitterbug started, and they swung apart then squeezed together over and over, the momentum bringing them closer, He had never before been with a woman who unashamedly made herself available like this; who seemed to want to enjoy herself physically with him and who showed no concern for what people thought of her.

He spun her forcefully, dramatically. He felt the rhythm in his bones. He was living the music. He was one with the music. He was totally in sync with her shapely body.

Then, as she spun back to him for another tight clutch, he realized that he was pressing against another woman who looked at him in shock, before he spun her away again.

He felt like he was in a square dance where you find yourself with another partner as part of some elaborate pattern. Only this time it was simply an accident.

Daisy was now in the arms of a heavy-set sergeant, just ten feet away, smiling broadly, as the back and forth of their dance moves brought them close together. Mark could cut in and have her again, and she'd be just as happy with him as she would be with anyone else.

But he hesitated. Who was this new woman, who he'd just held more closely and intimately than he'd ever held anyone?

Tall and dazzling blond, she could be a movie star. He was shocked by her beauty, and how she followed his lead. Her movements flowed effortlessly with his. It was as if they had been dance partners for years.

Then the band started playing a slow song, The Tennessee Waltz, and they stayed partners, without saying a word to one another, as if it was already a given. He realized that he wasn't leading, but rather his muscles were getting cues from hers, and neither of them had to think at all.

She must be unattached, or she wouldn't be at this USO canteen. He guessed that she was older than him by two years, maybe three. Physically, she was mature—a woman, not a girl. He had never danced with anyone like her before. He would never have dared to ask, knowing that he would be shot down. He was lucky that she had simply appeared in his arms. When she smiled—which was often—it wasn't the phony flirtatious smile of a woman who wanted to attract a man. It was the natural smile of someone who was enjoying herself, confident because the man she was with was obviously and unashamedly smitten with her, and she with him.

Another jitterbug and God, could she dance! As her skirt bounced up and down to the frantic rhythm, he caught glimpses of her beautiful thighs.

She laughed, and Mark heard her voice for the first time, despite the music, the stomping feet and all the loud talking. He could imagine her singing. He wanted to hear her sing, to sing with her.

He had never felt anything like this, and he sensed that she hadn't either.

They were made for each other.

This was fate, he realized.

This was true love.

There was just one small problem—not really a problem—he had told her a white lie. His age.

He hadn't intended to. But she was so sophisticated and mature. She was twenty-three, and he couldn't bring himself to admit that he was just twenty, not yet officially a grown man. So, he fudged a little. He told her he was twenty-one. She would laugh about it when he confessed it to her when the time was right. He was sure of that.

9 ~ The Ring

December 1943, Philadelphia, PA

Mark and Ruth both told the same story and told it to everyone. It was immediate, it was magic. They were made for one another.

Mark had dated a dozen other women in the year before he met Ruth. He was seriously shopping for a mate. In his diaries, he analyzed each candidate for compatibility, morality, and religious background. His mother had taught him that some women were morally upright, god-fearing homemakers and mothers, and others were jezebels, who led men astray. He needed to look beyond the surface and pick the right woman—the ideal wife and mother for his children.

In years, he was twenty—nearly an adult, but emotionally, he was younger. He had little knowledge of or experience with women, having grown up with three brothers. His mother brought him up to respect her, but to presume that, aside from Bible lessons and matters of morality and discipline, she had nothing of importance to say. A man had to take charge, make decisions, take responsibility, and be the wage-earner. A woman's place was in the home. His father was short and frail, but with an inalterable will. What he said was law. It took but a whisper for him to command immediate obedience from his dutiful wife who would never question him and his four sons who were twice his size.

In his diaries, Mark speculated on the nature of "true love" before he experienced anything of the kind. Now page after page was about Ruth, and how she differed from all other women he had met. They talked little, confident that they could read one another's thoughts. This was the kind of experience that they both had hoped for, and neither of them wanted to do or say anything that could put it in question. Mostly they walked hand-in-hand together through the crowded streets of downtown Philadelphia or sat on park benches, her head resting on his shoulder, smiling at squirrels and pigeons, laughing for no particular reason, oblivious of the winter weather, punch-drunk with love.

A week after they first met, sitting on a bench in Rittenhouse Square, they realized that they were alone. From where they sat, sheltered by bushes, they couldn't see anyone else, and no one could see them. When they stared into one another's eyes—hers brown, his green—each telegraphed to the other a tremor of anticipation. It would be easy to not just kiss and snuggle and hug, but to cross the unspoken boundaries, to grope with abandon. Mark wasn't sure what to do, what she might expect of him, what would be too much, and what would be too little. He hadn't had to deal with such questions on the dance floor or in a crowd. Now he was under the spotlight of her attention. What was she thinking of him? He was clueless what to do next. She was dear to him. This connection they had between them was rare and precious, but he had no idea how fragile it might be. He was afraid to do anything, or to do nothing.

Then she broke the tension by standing up abruptly and announcing with a laugh, "Let's run to Market Street and catch a trolley."

Delighted at this suggestion, he jumped to his feet and hugged her and kissed her.

The first trolley to come their way was standing-room-only. That was perfect. They had no choice but to stand pressed close to one another, proud to be seen with one another, proud that everyone seeing them knew that they were in love.

That became part of their regular routine—catching trolleys, not to go anywhere, just to be close together in a crowd, with none of the temptation and awkwardness of being alone together and all the gratification that came from the reactions of strangers, confirming to them what they hoped and believed—that they were ecstatically happy and that all the world should share their happiness.

Mark's life was just beginning. He had never really been alive before. He wanted to marry her; she was the one. But he needed someone to talk to about it—not his army buddies who joked about loose women, and not his parents who were far away in Silver Spring, Maryland. He needed someone older, who understood the world and who would talk straight to him. He needed to talk to his Uncle Adolph, his mother's bad-boy brother—a teenage captain in World War I, with a battle-field commission for reckless bravery, a wheeler-dealer with a

Harvard MBA, who knew more about racetracks than Wall Street. One day, flush with cash and showering his nephews with gifts; the next day trying to talk family and friends into investing in his latest scheme. Adolph was flashy and fun and the antithesis of Mark's parents. And to Mark, he was the fount of worldly wisdom.

So, a month after he met Ruth, Mark pounded on the door of a room at the Drake Hotel in Philadelphia at four in the morning. Adolph opened the door, bleary-eyed and in a red-and-white striped dressing gown. Rotund, mid-forties, but looking mid-fifties, he could have been type-cast as Falstaff. With a little makeup, including a more bulbous nose, he could be a stunt-man double for W. C. Fields.

Adolph stared in disbelief at this intrusion.

Mark blurted out, "I knew you were in town. I guessed you'd stay here. I convinced the guy at the front desk that it was an emergency, so he'd call up and wake you."

"No trouble. No trouble at all. I wasn't sleeping. I was entertaining a friend. I don't sleep much. Work hard, play hard. That's my motto. The Drake, Rittenhouse Square. You guessed right, kid. You've got to go first class for people to think you're first class. I've got a big deal in the works. I hit it big at the Hialeah trifecta. Flush with cash. Want to put that money to work. Not much happening at the racetracks with the war going on. Reduced schedule, no Flamingo Stakes this year. But wars don't last forever. And for folks with foresight, now's the time to invest. Now this is strictly on the QT, get me? Don't tell this to anybody. But Jack Kelly, the brick guy from here in Philly, is lining up investors—a who's-who set of players—Bob Hope, Frank Sinatra, Harry James. He's going to build a racetrack in Atlantic City. It'll be the only place running horses near New York and Philadelphia. A money factory. And I want in on the ground-floor. That's why I'm here. But why are you here at my hotel room at four in the morning?"

"I'm in love."

"Oh, shit. My condolences, kid. Nothing much I can do about that. Incurable disease."

"Seriously, Unc. I need your advice. I've never felt anything like this. All I know is what I've read in books and seen in movies, and that doesn't jive with what's going on."

"Okay, shoot. But make it quick, please. I'm entertaining. I need to get back to my guest, if you get my drift."

"Well it's a line from a movie that's bugging me."

"Glad it's not the woman who's bugging you. So, get on with it."

"Well in the movie, this guy says, 'She gets me. She lets me be myself.' In the movie, that means they're really in love. But what's happening to me isn't like that at all. Since I met Ruth, I feel like I'm a new person, and I like that new person. The trees are new and the grass and the birds, the smell of fresh toast, the way moonlight reflects off puddles. It's all new. I've never seen the world like this before. I'm on a different planet. There's a spring in my legs and I need to jump, dance, sing. I can still feel her in my arms. I walked all the way home the night I met her at the Stage Door Canteen. No, not walked, I ran, double-time—three miles, four. I don't know. Time and distance meant nothing. I danced with the lamp posts. I grabbed hold of each one as I went by and swung around and shouted 'Yes! Yes!' That was the only word that mattered. She had said 'yes'. Her eyes, her dark brown eyes said that she wanted to see me again and again—forever. Lightning had struck both of us at once. We were in love. Then the sun rose, and I sprinted to be in time for class. I wasn't the least bit tired that day, with no sleep, knowing I was going to see her again that night.

"Both of us had been in a fog, not knowing where we were going or why. Suddenly, the fog lifted, and the sun was bright, and life was brimming with joy. There was nothing to fear—not war, not death. We were together. We were meant to be together. Magic had happened."

Mark paused to catch his breath, and Adolph, smiling indulgently, lit a cigar and gestured for him to continue his story.

"I met Ruth nearly a month ago. We've seen each other every day since. I'm still manic—high as the Empire State Building, high as the moon and the stars. It isn't just a mood swing or wishful thinking. She's different from anyone I've ever known. I could never have imagined her. When she tells me what she's thinking, it's like I'm thinking it myself; like there's no need for us to exchange words, because we understand each other already. And my thoughts about history, about God, about destiny, about the future—my future, our future—it's like sparks are flying. I'm seeing connections I never saw before. It's electric.

Thanks to her, I have super-powers. I can do anything, become anyone. There's no limit to the possibilities of our life together."

"You sound totally obsessed," Adolph interrupted him.

"Yes, I am obsessed, and it feels wonderful. I want to marry her. I have to marry her."

"She couldn't know so soon," Adolph interjected.

"Know what?

"Pregnant. She couldn't know she's pregnant this soon."

"Pregnant? What's that have to do with anything?"

Adolph puffed on his cigar, and looked at his nephew askance, finding it hard to believe anyone could be this naive. "You said you have to marry her."

"I meant that I love her so much, I can't imagine life without her. And no, it isn't the way you are thinking at all. I've held her hand. I've hugged her close. We've kissed. But we've never ... I've never ... with anyone, nor has she. She's pure, innocent, and religious. She's Lutheran, would you believe the luck? We've talked about God, fate, and love. I've told her I love her. It feels so good to tell her that and see the way she brightens to hear it. It feels so good when she tells me she loves me, too, and that she sees the world through new eyes now, just like I do. I borrowed money from friends, and I'm going to buy a ring tomorrow— not that she needs an engagement ring. She isn't like that. But I want to give her one, as a tangible symbol of my love. I'm going to ask her tomorrow at the Stage Door Canteen, where we first met. I know she'll say yes—even though I'm unworthy of her. She could have any man in the world, but she loves me, I know that for sure."

"You've got it bad, kid. But you came to me, which means you still have some connection with reality. You have doubts. You must or you wouldn't have turned up at my door at four in the morning. Were the two of you drunk when you met?"

"Nothing of the kind. Not a beer. Neither of us. Not then, and not since. No appetite for alcohol. We're drunk on each other; bubbly drunk, all senses heighted. Punch-drunk happy."

"Well, just by chance, I may have what you need right now. I told you that I'm entertaining a guest. She's in the bedroom now, and all warmed up."

"What the hell are you suggesting?"

"Just something to relieve your stress, so you can think straight before you go jumping off a cliff. I know what your mother, that whacked-out sister of mine, has pounded into your head the 'no sex before marriage'. Sin, hell, and damnation. Like what we do and don't do matters to some cold-hearted dude up in heaven. Sex is not a big deal, kid. Maxine, my friend in there, enjoys sex. She enjoys it with me, and she could enjoy it with you. It would probably turn her on that you've never done it before. Besides, she's turned on already. You interrupted us in the act. I'm sure she wants to finish. With me? With you? No matter. Go for it. She'll thank me for it, and you'll get over this hang-up. You'll know if you love that woman or not—if you're just horny as hell, or if this girl is a keeper, the one and only. From what you say, this fairy-tale princess of yours was raised the same way you were. That means if you come on to her and try to get her into bed, she'll think that's all you want—you'll be just another sinful man. And if she lets you do it, you'll think she's slutty. So, get this out of the way with somebody who has a different outlook and who can enjoy you and give you pleasure, no strings attached. Take care of that, and you'll be able to see more clearly. Have sex with another woman so you can find out if you're really in love. How can you lose? It's a sure thing. Go for it."

If this had been Margery, Uncle Adolph's steady girlfriend, Mark could never have done it. But this Maxine was a total stranger who he'd never see again. He nodded to Adolph and went into the bedroom. Mark's time with her only lasted five minutes. She took care of him efficiently. For those five minutes, he suspended his moral sensitivity and felt so good he didn't want it to end. But it did end, quickly. Then as he got dressed, the guilt came rushing in, like wave after wave crashing on a rocky shore.

How could he have done this? How could Ruth ever forgive him? How could he ever forgive himself? Mark thought as he left the bedroom.

Adolph was sprawled comfortably in an armchair, still puffing on his cigar. "It's for the best, believe me," Adolph mused. "You finally got it out of your system. You're flesh and blood. Now maybe you can tell the difference between wanting to get laid and wanting to spend the rest of your life with a woman.

"Maxine is good, isn't she? One of the best I've ever had. But there's a lot like her. Maybe not as good, but plenty good enough, if you know what I mean. Sex is good—don't get me wrong—but it's not all that important. Get it when you want it. Order it a la carte. A little of this, then a little of that."

"But I love her," Mark mumbled. "I love Ruth. I still love her. And now she'll never forgive me. I've messed up big time. It's over."

"What she doesn't know won't hurt her," Adolph pressed on. "Grow up, already. It isn't like she's told you everything about her past."

"But she has. She's been totally honest with me about everything. That's essential to our bond—our total honesty to one another. The whole truth and nothing but the truth."

"I thought her name was Ruth, not Truth. What she doesn't know won't hurt her. Truth is overrated. Sin's nothing more than an idea in your head. A good story trumps the facts, any day of the week. So, your story is that you love her, and she loves you, and it was love at first sight. Great story. Stick with it. Don't let little details like Maxine get in the way.

"If a dude fucks in a forest and nobody sees, it doesn't really happen. No big deal. So now you know you love Ruth. Before, you had doubts. You'd have never come here to talk to me if you didn't have doubts. You did this for her, for your love. Where's the guilt in that? Since when is it a sin to test your love? If you didn't test it, how could you know it was real?"

Mark put on his coat, with a hang-dog look. He felt numb and tired.

Adolph tried to cheer him up. "So, you got laid; you got it out of your system. Now you know that it's not such a big deal, and you can hold off fucking her until your wedding night. She'll take your restraint as a sign of your respect. She'll love you all the more for it. And then you'll have some idea what you're doing when you finally do it with her, so she'll enjoy it more and you'll enjoy it more. You'll both love each other more and live happily ever after. You should be thanking me, not just for providing you with a first-class lay, but for helping your fairy-tale romance come true."

Mark couldn't bring himself to say thank you for a gift he had never asked for, that he already regretted accepting, and that might prove to be a disaster. "I need to get going," he mumbled.

Adolph stood up and gave Mark a hug, overdoing his look and tone of confidence, wanting his nephew to leave in high spirits, wanting to once again be seen as wise and generous. "You're going to buy a ring for her," he added. "Well, here's five hundred bucks. Add that to what you've got and buy a really good one; one that will wow her, that she can show off to her friends. That's an early wedding gift from me.

"Now get the hell out of here. Catch a cab. It'll be time for you to get up in an hour or two. And Maxine, I'm sure, needs my attention. Five minutes was enough for you to get what you wanted, but I'm sure you left her unsatisfied. Believe me, boy, you should never leave a woman unsatisfied. Remember that, and your fairy-tale romance will last forever."

The streets were nearly empty—few pedestrians, fewer cars. The one cab that passed was occupied. He walked all the way, staying away from the lamp posts that he had swung on with joy the day he met Ruth.

He used the money to buy the best ring he could. Ruth was delighted and showed it off to her friends. The two of them thought of the ring as the tangible symbol of their love for one another. But to Mark it had additional meaning, recalling Adolph and Maxine and the balance between the way of all flesh and fairy-tale aspirations. To him, the ring was a symbol of sin as well as of love—a reminder of his weakness and unconfessed guilt.

Guilt and gilt. Animal lust and sacred love. Sinner and saint. The moral lessons of his Protestant upbringing and the urges and curiosities of youth.

He loved Ruth with a pure and sacred love, but he also wanted her. He needed her physically, but he felt sinful for wanting her that way. He suspected that she, too, was torn. He dreamed of their wedding night, when they could let loose all that repressed passion, as they were meant to and as God meant them to.

10 ~ Engaged

December 1943, Philadelphia, PA

Horn and Hardart's was mobbed. Ninety percent of the clientele were young women on their lunch break, many of whom would never have had a job if it hadn't been for the war. But Ruth had no problem spotting her sister Emily in a black dress, waiting in the automat line leading to the ham sandwiches.

Not that long ago, this stunning, vibrant woman had been the baby of the family, the favorite of her older sisters who wouldn't let Ruth hold or care her because Ruth, at the age of five, was too young to be entrusted with an infant. Back then, Emily had been Father's "little girl," his obvious favorite. He let her, and no one else, sit on his lap when he was in his armchair. After their mother died and Father moved across the street, Emily was the only one of his daughters he invited over. She could bring her friends and he'd give them gifts of candy and toys from the general store he managed.

If this woman had been abused as a child—prison-worthy abuse— there was no outward sign of that now. Aunties' regimen of lying and forgetting appeared to have been effective, and Ruth would never bring the subject up with Emily, for fear of the painful memories that might unleash.

Now, at eighteen, Emily was the widow of a war hero—a beautiful woman with a tragic past and a promising future. She now wore black dresses every day, at home and at work, with the bronze star that had been awarded to Bill hanging from a red-white-and-blue ribbon worn around her neck. With round rosy cheeks, she still had some baby fat around the middle, which emphasized her youth and innocence, making her even more attractive.

Emily had grieved over Bill, crying uncontrollably for days. But then, aside from occasional nightmares, she had encapsulated the pain. She'd filed it away in a storage cabinet in the basement of her mind, almost out of conscious reach. The death of her mother was filed there too. The loss of her father was probably several basements lower, almost totally forgotten. Some things were better forgotten, as Aunties said. Don't talk about it, don't think about it, don't even dream about it. It never happened. Some day when someone asked what had happened, she wouldn't remember at all, and then she'd be truly healed.

After a week's honeymoon in the Poconos, Bill had left her with his parents in Bryn Mawr, and had shipped out to North Africa as a fighter pilot. He was shot down in the invasion of Sicily in July, five months ago.

The Aunties had been outraged when Emily eloped with Bill. But they consoled her in her grief, and would have welcomed her home, if she had wanted to return. But, instead, Emily got a job as a secretary. She had never been to secretarial school, but her face shone with a beguiling mixture of innocence and worldly-wise grief. She got special consideration as a war widow, an advantage she was quick to exploit. She moved to a rooming house in downtown Philadelphia, near her work and near the University of Pennsylvania. By eloping, she had graduated from the family row house, and now there was no way she was going to stay under Aunties' strict control.

Neither Ruth nor Emily wore lipstick—ever. That was one thing about which they agreed with the Aunties. Using artificial means to enhance your looks was an admission that you needed it; it showed a lack of self-confidence. Men seemed to appreciate their natural look. Besides, the sisters didn't like the taste of lipstick and face powder, so why should they think men would like it?

By now, all the sisters except twenty-three-year-old Ruth had married. She had felt the shadow of old maidenhood approaching. Having graduated from Peirce Business School, Ruth worked as a secretary for a stock brokerage, where the only men were fat, over fifty, and married. All the boys she had grown up with in the neighborhood were either married, in the military, or both. Emily teased her that she was too standoffish and too picky; that she needed to let go and let herself fall in love. Emily urged that there were lonely servicemen everywhere, looking for companionship and a good time. Some of them were handsome, fun, and easy to snare into a romantic wartime marriage. Ruth insisted that she would never just settle, never marry a man who was "good enough," just to get married. She believed in true love, and she would be satisfied with nothing less. And now she had found it in Mark. It was Emily who'd convinced Ruth to go to the Stage Door Canteen. It was Emily she had to thank.

"Okay, what is it?" Emily asked, after they squeezed into standing space at a counter near the window. "Out with it. You've got a smile like the cat who won the lottery."

Ruth raised her left hand.

"A ring. He did it! You did it! Congratulations!" Emily took Ruth's hand in her hands and held the ring up to the sunlight streaming through the window, admiring the sparkling diamond. "Lovely," she added with enthusiasm.

"Of course it's lovely." Ruth laughed and pointed at Emily's ring, which was identical to her own. "He told me you helped him pick it out."

"And I thought I was supposed to keep that a secret." Emily smiled broadly.

"How long ago did Mark ask you where Bill bought your ring?" Ruth pursued.

"He did more than ask. We went together to the jeweler and picked the same one. It was the day before yesterday," Emily said.

"And you didn't breathe a word to me?" Ruth pretended to be hurt.

"Of course not. There are times when not saying things, when lying by omission is the right thing to do. But tell me everything! Mark told me next to nothing. What's the date?" Emily demanded.

"We haven't decided yet."

"But soon?"

"Very soon. Of course."

"Church or civil?"

"We haven't talked about the details yet."

"And what do Aunties say?"

"I haven't told them yet. They don't even know that Mark exists. They're going to be furious."

"They will, but that'll make no difference at all. You don't need their permission; you're twenty-three, for God's sake. And I eloped at eighteen. They got over that, and they'll get over this. They have no choice in the matter."

"But they've done so much for us. They've devoted their lives to us. I feel ungrateful, selfish—almost sinful for having lied to them."

"For God's sake, all you need to feel is happy. This is fantastic."

"I dread telling them, knowing very well what they'll say. I can hear them so well." Ruth went into mimic mode, scrunching up her face and pinching her nose to make the sound nasal, "'This man, this stranger, this here-today, gone-tomorrow soldier boy. Don't let yourself get involved with a soldier in wartime. That's asking for trouble. Even if you're married to him, you'll be forced to live apart, and he'll be tempted here, there, and everywhere. All men are weak. Remember your little sister. Emily met a pilot, ran off and married him. He was shot down over Sicily. So, she's an eighteen-year old widow. Thank God she isn't pregnant. We have so little to thank God for these days. These are times that try our souls. Lord have mercy. Amen.'"

Emily laughed heartily. "That's them all right—either of them, both of them. Just remember that it's easier to ask for forgiveness than permission—that's what Bill always said. Go for it. Marry right away. Enjoy as much time together as you can. Live in the now and don't worry about tomorrow."

"You don't regret ..." Ruth started to ask.

"Don't get me wrong. I loved Bill. Of course. But I met him just six weeks before we married, and I only lived with him for the week of our honeymoon. I knew him less than two months before he shipped out. Without the help of photos—and I have precious few of those—it's hard for me to remember what he looked like. I can't really say that I miss him—the real him, the person, as opposed to the romantic idea of him. He sounded so brave and unselfish when he told me, 'If I don't come back, don't grieve over me. Move on. Find someone else. Live a full life.' And a week before he was shot down, he must have had a premonition, because he enclosed in a letter to me an old poem he had copied out. The poem began, 'Miss me, but let me go.' That was his final gift to me, telling me to start a new life. I had the minister read that at the memorial service, remember?"

Ruth nodded, and Emily continued. "Now everyone expects me to meet and marry someone else, even his parents encourage me to do that. I'll wear black for another three months—that should be enough to satisfy everyone's sense of propriety in wartime, even Aunties'. Then I'll date again. I thought I'd go hunting for a guy at the Stage Door Canteen together with you, but I guess it will be with my friends from the rooming house instead. Congratulations," she repeated warmly, squeezing her sister's hands. "I'm so happy for you." She paused, then plunged ahead, bursting with curiosity. "Tell me more. If you can't tell me anything about the wedding, tell me about him, about Mark. I like the look of him. Who wouldn't? He's movie-star handsome. But he looks so young."

"Yes," Ruth laughed, "he's a couple years younger than me."

"And you don't see that as a problem?"

"What's the problem? He's not a baby. He doesn't need his parents' permission."

"That never made sense to me," Emily noted, "that women are considered adults at eighteen, but men have to be twenty-one. In so many ways, the law treats women as second-class citizens. It was a long hard battle just to get the vote. Aunties helped fight for that. I can just imagine them picketing with their suffragette signs. But when it comes to marriage age, women have the advantage."

"That's probably a male thing too," Ruth offered. "Aunties explained that to me. Men like to marry young girls—younger than them, the younger the better. They want to shape and control their brides. It's for them, not for us, that they made the marriage age for women younger."

"So, you're going to give him a run for his money," Emily said with a smile.

"Me being older than him, rather than he being older than me? Yes, that sounds fair. I'll never be a little girl to him. I'll be at least his equal. Besides, women usually live longer than men. What sense does it make for a woman to marry a man older than her and be left a widow? We're just right. We'll age together, and we'll die together."

"Speaking of time, I've got to get back to the office. My lunch hour is only forty-five minutes."

"You mean they expect you to do more than smile?"

"There's always something that needs doing. But, yes, my boss says my smile perks up the office, like a fresh cup of coffee."

"Men," Ruth grouched.

"Yes, men," Emily agreed with a smile and a wiggle of the hips.

***

Ruth procrastinated telling Aunties about the engagement, hiding the ring in her pocketbook when she visited them. But when Mark asked her to go to meet his parents in Silver Spring, she had to tell the Aunties where she'd be going, and why.

They gave her the silent treatment, which was worse than their lecture mode. They continued eating their fried liver and asparagus dinner, saying little more than, "Pass the salt, please." They refused to react to Ruth's guilty revelations. They didn't object to the engagement, or her traveling to Silver Spring—they simply ignored her.

"Now I lie me down to sleep," she sobbed, when she went to bed that night. "Lie", not "lay." One lie after another. She had lied by omission to her Aunties; now she would have to lie by omission to Mark. She couldn't let him know that the Aunties objected to the marriage. He had to believe that they were delighted, otherwise that could sour his relationship with them forever. But the lie bothered her. Every little thing that she didn't share with Mark damaged their intimacy, which was precious to her. It created a minefield of things she couldn't say or allude to; a field that was growing. But telling him would hurt him even more than not telling him. She couldn't bear the thought of there being a rift between the man she loved and the two people who had been so important to her before he came along.

She also couldn't be open to him about her anxiety about travel, about leaving Philadelphia, her home. She couldn't mention that she had never left the city of her birth, had never even gone anywhere for summer vacation. Mark looked up to her as a mature "older" woman, and she liked that. She didn't want to admit to him that she still slept with her doll, Gladys, and her teddy bear, Catfish Snail, and that she still said her evening prayers, aloud, kneeling on the floor by her bed. It would be difficult going with Mark to Silver Spring. But that was all part of becoming a true adult, getting married, and starting a new life together.

But there was an opportunity here that she should seize. Her mother-in-law might become a new mother to her, taking the place of the mother she had lost thirteen years before. She remembered the Bible passage about the Ruth she was named after. A mother-in-law and daughter-in-law could be close, like mother and daughter. That was what Ruth believed. She loved Mark so much, surely, she would love the mother who had nurtured him and shaped him from his earliest days.

11 ~ Training

The world raced by. Ruth was disoriented. She didn't dare admit she was scared like a little kid. She had never been on a train before.

Riding in an automobile was different from this. The stop and the start. The sound of the engine. She could hear it go on and off, speed up and slow down. A car didn't go this fast—it couldn't in city traffic. As a passenger in a car, she could tell the driver to slow down, stop or turn a different way; she had some modicum of control.

Now she was sitting next to Mark in a train on a seat by the window, facing forward, with telephone poles, leafless trees, houses, and fields of frost-covered stubble racing by. She turned away from the window, though she felt drawn to it in a horizontal vertigo, as if the tightly shut windows were about to blow away. She could fall out and away into a world where fields and trees were alive and threatening. As in Disney's *Snow White*, she'd be lost in a malevolent forest. The window beside them was open a crack at the top, jammed so it couldn't be closed, and the whistling wind and the metallic rattle of the wheels on the tracks intensified her sensations of speed and jeopardy.

She tried to focus on Mark, who sat with a broad, childish smile, holding her hand and squeezing it repeatedly—as if taking her to see his parents and to introduce her as his bride-to-be were the most amazing experience he could imagine.

Ruth smiled back, trying to mask her terror of train travel. He kissed her on the cheek and squeezed her hand harder. He squeezed too hard, but she didn't want to tell him it hurt. He looked so happy that she didn't want to break the spell. It didn't matter that it hurt; she would do anything for him. But here she was lying to him by omission, by not telling him it hurt, and she was lying by omission about so much more. She turned away from Mark, toward the window, its vertigo pulling at her.

Then she turned back and broke the silence, asking "What do you want me to say?"

"Be yourself."

"And who is that?"

He laughed.

She explained, "I want so much to make a good impression that I won't be able to act natural. I wish I had a script, like in a play. I'm good at memorizing. I'm good at acting. When I'm on stage pretending to be someone else, I feel comfortable, safe. Then I'm not at risk because that's not me. The role shields the real me. Give me a role. Tell me who they want me to be. Describe to me their ideal daughter-in-law."

"You, simply you; the you I know and love."

"Indulge me, please. Tell me who that is. Tell me who you think I am."

"Beautiful."

"I don't mean physical looks. I mean personality, character."

"Modest, religious, respectful ..."

She cut him short, "Not intelligent?"

"Yes, intelligent."

"But that wasn't high on your list."

"That's not so important."

"To you or to them?"

"I never thought about it."

"You never thought about my intelligence? I did graduate from Girls' High, you know. Salutatorian, nearly valedictorian. Prizes in English, Latin, French, and Elocution. Star of our school plays. I couldn't afford to go to college, but I'm 'college material'—my teachers all said that."

"Of course. You're brilliant, and I love it that you're brilliant," he quickly corrected himself.

"So I shouldn't talk about education?"

"No, certainly not. My mother only made it to the eighth grade."

"And your father?"

"George Washington University. He's an architect. Remember?"

"Yes, of course. He designed your family home. But I shouldn't come on as too sophisticated, too much of a big-city know-it-all?"

"You've got it. Prim and proper. Humble and upright. A perfect helpmate and mother."

"Smile a lot?"

"Yes, definitely."

"I'll model my smiles on my sister Emily. She has great smiles."

"Your normal smiles will do just fine." He laughed.

"But I never see my own smiles, so I can't consciously make them. But I know what Emily's look like; so that's what I'll keep in mind."

"Whatever works for you."

At the end of the journey, when the train stopped suddenly, they lurched forward. Mark anticipated and held her tightly, saving her from falling. He was there for her when she needed him, as he had promised. He would always be there for her. He was hugging her and kissing her, oblivious of the other passengers who were all looking, though trying not to stare—not disapproving, rather smiling, sharing the joy of a uniformed soldier and his bride-to-be, so obviously in love.

Mark grabbed their suitcases from the rack above. She held his arm with both hands. He guided her through rush-hour crowds in Union Station and out onto the street, then three blocks to where a pale green two-door Nash was parked outside a Woolworth's five and dime.

A short, thin bald man with glasses opened the passenger door, pushed forward the front seat, and welcomed them into the back. "Hello. I'm Hank," he introduced himself, in a warm tone of voice. "Welcome home."

With traffic, it took an hour to reach Silver Spring. Mark's mother, Sarah, had supper ready for them when they arrived—meat loaf and mashed potatoes. Mark's favorite, she said.

The house was like something out of a fairy tale. Hank was an architect, working for the Veterans' Administration—an employment safe-haven during the Depression. He had designed the house himself, in Tudor style—masonry with dark wood trim, and a sharp roof sloping nearly to the ground.

The front doorbell rang with the tones and rhythm of Big Ben. They entered the living room. A grandfather clock, loudly ticking and wound once a week, stood to the left. There was a baby grand piano, the lid propped up, ready for play. The piano bench was strewn with sheet music, and half a dozen instrument cases were neatly arranged on the floor near and under the piano. Ruth also saw a sofa, with cushions, but hard wooden spokes for the back—comfortable if you sat up straight, but not meant for leaning back and relaxing. Sunlight came through a large bow window with leaded panes. Through that window, a ten-foot by ten-foot goldfish pond was visible. In the dining room, a mahogany veneer hutch displayed fine china, near a large mahogany dining table. A phonograph sat on top of a cabinet-style radio, and several boxes of records lay on the floor beside it. There was a large stone fireplace, such as would be found in a medieval castle. Above the mantelpiece were crisscrossed flintlock rifles, dating back to the days of Daniel Boone. Walking under the mantelpiece revealed alcoves with stone benches on either side of the hearth. Ruth imagined that you could sit there in private beside a warm crackling fire and hold hands and whisper.

Upstairs was the master bedroom. To the left and right were bedrooms once shared by the four sons, rooms constrained by the sharp slope of the roof so you had to duck your head to avoid bumping into the ceiling.

Hank, Jr., the oldest son, was in the Army, stationed in California and likely to be shipped to the war in the Pacific. The two youngest, Luke and John, were in high school. John had taken over Hank's room but for this visit, he moved in with Luke, leaving his room for Ruth. Mark would sleep on the sofa in the living room.

Ruth could see that this was a busy, full house She savored every detail. This house and these parents had shaped Mark. This was a model for what her life might be like after marriage.

The home was brightly lit, well suited for welcoming guests and sharing with them, as opposed to the cramped little row house where Ruth grew up, which had few windows and many shadows. There, meals were served and devoured separately, because there wasn't room enough at the table for all at once. That house was only open to guests for funerals. This one was always open and ready.

Hank was five foot four. His sons towered over him, but he was quietly in control. He never needed to raise his voice to command attention and obedience.

Sarah was an inch shorter than Hank, with a square face and a square body. She weighed twice as much as her husband. She paid no attention to how she dressed, except for putting on her Sunday-best frock and a feathered hat for church activities. She quietly went about the business of the house—cooking, washing, ironing, sweeping, dusting, repairing clothes, doing needlework, and playing the piano when the family gathered for music. Her hands were always busy, always accomplishing something. While talking to Ruth and giving her as full attention as she ever gave to anyone, Sarah would sweep or dust or prepare meals. Her meals were all bland, consisting of what were then considered healthy staples—meat, potatoes, and standard vegetables such as peas and corn. She made gravy from the meat of the day, but she used no sauces or spices.

Ruth's Aunties had similar ideas about healthy eating, but they boiled everything together in a big pot on top of the stove. Sarah baked and broiled and fried, giving taste and variety to the meals she prepared.

Sarah knew her role in life and stuck to it. When Hank and the boys talked about war, politics, school, work or sports, Sarah excused herself and got on with her next chore. On Sundays, there might be some talk about the sermon or about what they heard on the radio during the Lutheran Hour. But even then, Sarah would limit her contributions to moral truisms and Bible quotes, rather than venturing to express opinions of her own.

Sarah never seemed to rest. She believed that cleanliness was next to godliness and that her housework and childrearing activities kept her in close proximity with God. In fact, Sarah often hummed or whistled hymns while she worked.

At lunch, Ruth set the table and dried the dishes, chores she was used to from living with the Aunties. But she didn't volunteer to do anything else. It never occurred to her that she should. When Mark was outside helping his father and brothers shovel snow in the driveway, Ruth sat on a bench by the fireplace, reading *A Curtain of Green*, a collection of stories by Eudora Welty. When she reached the end of the first story, she looked up and realized that Sarah was sitting on the bench across from her, and patiently waiting for Ruth to acknowledge her presence.

"What are your favorite dishes? What do you like to cook?" Sarah asked. When Ruth hesitated, Sarah continued, "Would you like to cook dinner for us tomorrow night?" Her tone implied that this was a generous offer that Ruth should be delighted to accept.

But Ruth had never cooked a meal in her life and was ashamed to admit it. What would Mark think when he found out she couldn't cook? How could she learn? Certainly not from the Aunties who were terrible at it. After an awkward silence, Ruth said, "Spaghetti is my favorite. But there's no way I could cook it here, not without my recipe—an old family recipe, which is home in the family cookbook, handwritten, passed down for generations," she added quickly. When Sarah looked at her askance, Ruth added, "That's my aunts' favorite dish, as well. They cook it in large quantities, and then we eat left-overs for three or four days. It tastes even better as leftovers."

"And how do you make the sauce?" Sarah asked, patiently, warmly, as if trying to draw the young girl out, and to find common ground on which they could relate.

Ruth scrambled to remember what she had seen and tasted. "Canned tomato sauce and tomato paste, fresh tomatoes, too, when in season, ground beef, sausage, mozzarella cheese, onions, olives, and raisins."

"Raisins?"

Maybe it wasn't raisins. Ruth didn't know for sure. She never paid attention when the Aunties cooked. Meals were not very important in their house. Aunties would rather "eat to live, than live to eat." But it tasted like raisins in their spaghetti; and having said that, Ruth couldn't take it back, so she elaborated. "Yes, they, I mean *we*, use raisins to add a touch of sweetness to the sauce. The raisins swell as they're heated and absorb tomato sauce. They take on a unique taste of their own. I hunt for them and eat them separately first," she added with imaginative flair.

"Indeed." Sarah stared at her, in disbelief, then she suggested, "Please write down a list of the ingredients. Those I don't have, I'll buy at the market tomorrow, and you can cook it for us. I'm sure that would delight Mark, and for the rest of us, it would be an interesting adventure."

"But, like I said, that's a family recipe. It includes spices and herbs, and I don't remember how much of what. I always have to check our handwritten book of family recipes. The raisins are an extra touch of mine," Ruth added.

Ruth silently told herself, "I need to learn to cook, pronto." That would be one of her wifely duties. The Aunties didn't believe in wifely anything. They had recognized Ruth's intelligence and encouraged her studies. While her sisters had to help with household chores and with the cooking, Ruth was expected to study her Latin and French and Elocution. She was the straight-A kid, the only one in the family. The Aunties took pride in her academic success, and she took pride in it, too, as she did in her secretarial skills, as well, which made her very employable and enabled her to live independently. But she knew nothing about running a household. When the war finally ended and life went back to normal, Mark would be the wage earner, and she would be a housewife and mother, but she was totally unprepared for that. There must be a book, she reassured herself. There were books about everything.

Then, by chance, their eyes met and locked. Ruth realized that Mark's mother was reaching out to her. This was a critical moment and she needed to act quickly. "This is awkward," Ruth admitted.

"The spaghetti? There's no need for you to cook for us if you don't wish to. I just thought you might like to join in."

"Yes, I understand. I appreciate your kind gesture. But what is awkward is that I don't know how to address you. I don't know what to call you."

"My friends call me Sarah."

"But that sounds so formal. May I address you as mother or mom, as Mark does? Did Mark tell you—I'm an orphan? My mother died when I was ten, and I always hoped I would one day have another mother," she explained. That was hard for her to say, but she was glad that she had. Tears came to her eyes.

At the sight of those tears, Sarah stood up, walked over, threw her arms around Ruth, and hugged her tightly.

"Call me Mom, please."

***

At church on Sunday, Sarah talked freely with the other women about anything and everything, and proudly introduced her future daughter-in-law, her first daughter of any kind. As was usual for her, Sarah didn't mix with the men and their conversations. She knew her place.

"And where is this lucky lady who has won the heart of your Mark?" asked Sarah's friend Constance.

"Why she was just here." Sarah was surprised to realize that Ruth had wandered off to the other side of the church, where she was talking animatedly with Hank and Mark and a group of men, who were showing great interest in everything she said. It was natural for her to be with Mark, as his bride-to-be. But to make herself the center of attention of strangers, of men, including men her own age, that was unseemly. That simply wasn't done.

Sarah was hesitant about accepting this all-too-attractive stylishly dressed woman who was older and probably more worldly-wise than her son. But taking a Christian attitude and giving Ruth the benefit of the doubt, Sarah guessed that the girl had natural grace and innocence but had been raised improperly. Ruth was a city girl, with city ways, and she had been raised by old-maid aunts, not by a mother and father. With instruction and discipline, she could still become a good wife. But would Mark, as young and naive as he was, be able to properly train her?

***

After lunch, and after everyone had listened to the Lutheran Hour on the radio in the living room the men started talking about war news. Sarah took Ruth's arm and led her to the fireplace, where they could talk confidentially, sitting beside one another by the hearth.

Their eyes met again. Ruth felt a surge of joy that she would be loved and accepted by this woman she had only known for a couple days. This strict, judgmental woman who initially seemed reluctant to let a stranger into her heart.

Sarah began, "I'm trying to sort out the bits and pieces of your life story that I've heard from Mark and from you. I'm a bit confused about your father."

"He died."

"Yes, I understand that. But when exactly did he die?"

"When I was ten."

"But that's when you said your mother died. Your father died later, didn't he?"

"Yes, of course, how could I forget a thing like that?"

"How, indeed."

"It was years later," Ruth added quickly. That much she knew; but beyond that, her memory was suddenly blank. She felt like a senile old lady who had lost touch with her own past. She hesitated, awkwardly. Her mother-in-law-to-be looked puzzled by her silence.

"Well when was it?" Sarah prompted.

Ruth needed to say something, anything. She guessed, "1935?" Why had she said it like a question, rather than an answer? She said it again, this time without the questioning intonation, "1937." Then she frowned, confused. She had given a different answer, and it wasn't the right one, was it? She couldn't remember, and not remembering something so important to her made her feel insecure and threatened. She wanted to curl up and hide behind Father's armchair.

"Which was it?" Sarah pursued.

"1932," she remembered, finally. Yes, that was the answer she was supposed to give. "Yes, 1932. Valentine's Day, 1932. I had just turned twelve."

Sarah smiled a polite smile. Then she switched the topic to her four boys and their musical talents and sat down at the baby grand piano and played the hymn "A Mighty Fortress is My God." Everybody, including Ruth, joined in.

But Ruth felt uncomfortable. Something in her new mother's manner had changed. From that moment on, Sarah's eyes avoided contact with Ruth's. There was something ominous about her politeness. Whatever Ruth said was met with a smile, but it wasn't a smile of acceptance, rather it was an ironic smile of doubt.

***

That evening, Mark was spreading his sheets on the sofa, when his mother suddenly attacked with machine-gun rapid-fire words. He had never seen her this angry.

"She's lying. Lord only knows why, but she's lying about her father. He didn't die when she was twelve. She doesn't know when he died, or if he died—if she even knows who her father was. Better to be known as an orphan than as a bastard."

"Mother, how could you?"

"Ask her yourself. Ask her when her father died and check the look in her eyes—her hesitation. Look for a flash of fear. You picked a winner, Mark. Like my brother Adolph, you're great at picking winners. You gambled, and you lost. She's not who you thought she was. Dump her. The sooner the better."

"Because of the date of her father's death?"

"Because she's a liar. Because you could never trust her.

"Because she misremembered or misspoke one little fact?

"And raisins."

"What?"

"Nobody puts raisins in spaghetti sauce. There was that same lying look in her eyes when she told me that, too."

"So now you're a lie detector? An infallible lie detector?"

"I trust my instincts, and my instincts tell me not to trust that girl. She's a pathological liar."

"That's the woman I love that you're talking about."

"That's a big-city hussy I'm talking about—a fast-talking, deceitful Jezebel."

"Well, I trust my instincts, Mother. And as much as I respect you and value your judgment, that's the woman I love, the woman I'm going to marry. And I'm asking you to treat her with the respect she deserves."

"She deserves no respect at all."

"Enough. This conversation is over. I won't listen to any more of your insults. We'll be married within a month. No, within a week. As quickly as we can get a license and get it done."

Sarah laughed. "Over my dead body you will."

"I'll marry who I want, when I want."

"When you're twenty-one, you can do that. But not before then. Not without our permission, and your father is with me on this. Believe me, he's a hundred percent with me. When you're twenty-one, then it's your business. Then it's on your head, and the Lord be with you. But for now, you're my responsibility, and I will not condone this marriage."

"But, Mom, that will be five months from now."

"Yes, only five months. Not long to wait if you're in love, the way you say you are. She isn't pregnant, is she? Is that why you're in such a hurry?"

He blushed. "No. Nothing like that."

"Then show some restraint. Show some Christian dignity."

"But it's wartime, Mom and I'm in the Army. Anything can happen in five months."

"That's in the Lord's hands. Far be it from me, or you, to try to go counter to His will."

"Okay. So, we'll wait until my birthday, and not a day beyond it. But you won't say a word to Ruth about this. You'll be civil to Ruth. You'll come to the wedding, and Dad will come. If we wait that long, you'll give us your blessing."

"Bless your marriage? I could never bless it. But I'll keep my peace and pray hard for your souls."

"Then don't say a word to her about this," Mark pleaded. "If she knew that you had tried to break us up, she'd be crushed. Just yesterday, she was delighted to have bonded with you, to have found a new mother, and now this emotional whiplash. Don't do that to her. She's vulnerable."

"Vulnerable? She's a grown woman, older and wiser than you. But for your sake, I'll hold my tongue, for now."

12 ~ It's a Date

January 1944, Silver Spring, MD

The next morning, after breakfast, Ruth took Mark's arm and led him out the door. She said she wanted to talk to him in private about something important.

"Well, I have something to tell you, too," Mark said as they walked. "And I get to say mine first."

"What?" Ruth asked, welcoming an opportunity to postpone telling about her father.

"June 5."

"What?"

"The date of our wedding."

"But that's five months from now."

"Yes. That will give you time to plan the kind of wedding you've dreamed of."

"But this is wartime. I thought we'd be getting married right away, as soon as possible. People don't plan weddings when they can't plan anything else in their lives. You could get orders at any time. They could ship you to another city or overseas. You could be killed, God forbid."

"Don't talk that way."

"But you know about my sister Emily. I can't help but think of that."

"Think it if you must, but don't say it. It's a superstition thing. "

"But that's reality. We need to face it and get on with our lives despite it. Carpe diem."

"June 5."

"But I can't wait."

"Believe me, we'll enjoy the wait, the anticipation. And that will give us time to get everything ready."

"But we don't need to be 'ready'. This is an adventure. Let's take the plunge. Then we can figure things out and muddle our way through together, as a married couple. I don't want to wait. Let's get married as soon as we get back to Philadelphia and as soon as we can get the license."

"But there's no need to rush. I love you the way you are. I love us the way we are."

"I don't understand. Why do you want to wait?"

"But how would it look if we rushed into it?"

"What do you mean?"

"People would talk. People would jump to conclusions."

"Did your mother say that? I can't imagine you coming up with that notion. Is she turning you against me? I thought she had welcomed me. I thought we had bonded."

"No. That's not her idea," he scrambled to reassure her. "It occurred to me when we were at church, and Mom was introducing you, and you were wowing everybody. I was the envy of every man there. For years, every Sunday, Mom and Dad would parade the four of us boys at church and say that we would all someday be Lutheran ministers. I was proud of that. We all were."

"You never told me you wanted to be a Lutheran minister."

"No, not now. I see the world differently now. But that's not the point. We all—the whole family—have held our heads high, beyond reproach, beyond suspicion of any kind. Why race to get married and prompt people to speculate?"

"But why should we worry about what people think or say? I'm not pregnant, for God's sake. You mean people would think that of me? Your parents would think that of me? Or they'd be embarrassed that their friends might think that? Don't be ridiculous. This is wartime. Everybody who is going to get married does it in a hurry. There's no shame in that. It's love."

"Please don't say that."

"Say what?"

"Things like 'for God's sake'. Mom and Dad are sensitive about using the Lord's name in vain."

"For God's sake, Mark. Don't change the topic. Why do you want to put off the wedding until summer?"

"June 5. That's still spring, officially."

"You're absolutely maddening."

"Think about it. Get used to it. You'll love it. But let's not obsess about it now. You said you had something important to tell me."

She looked left and right, as if she were lost, facing one dead-end street after another, and couldn't find her way out. Then she spotted a lone oak tree on a nearby hilltop and started running toward it. "You can't catch me," she shouted. "I'm the gingerbread woman"

Mark was caught by surprise. By the time he started running, Ruth had an unbeatable head start.

Seeing she had won, she deliberately fell in his path, and he fell over her. They hugged and rolled on the grass and kissed. She held him close, wrapped her legs around him and shifted her position so his hands brushed her breasts. She didn't pull away or push him away then, as she always had before. She was willing to do anything not to have to tell him now what she had decided she had to tell him.

He was the one who pulled back this time. He stood, and took her hands, and walked the rest of the way to the tree, where they sat down.

"You're different here," she realized. "Being here, where you grew up, with your parents, makes you think differently, act differently. It's like you feel someone's watching you, even when no one's watching you."

"And you don't like that side of me?"

"It's different, that's all. I didn't expect that of you. Here I am, ready to roll in the grass with you and not caring what anyone thinks. I could never feel free like that back home where I grew up. We're two of a kind but we're from two different places."

"And that's okay?" he asked, uncertain.

"Of course, you handsome fool." She kissed him quickly, giving him a provocative flick of the tongue.

***

That afternoon, when Mark and Ruth were about to climb into the backseat of the Nash and head to Union Station, Ruth hugged Sarah warmly, but Sarah hugged back formally.

"Goodbye, Mom," Ruth gushed.

Sarah cringed, but covered that up with a formal smile. "It feels awkward, when you call me that," she said. "All these years that's what my boys have called me, and it doesn't ring true hearing it from anyone else. Please call me Sarah. That's what all my friends call me."

"But that feels so distant—just friends. I was hoping ..."

"I understand. The orphan who wants a mother. That's a lovely story," Sarah held her smile, rigidly. "Then please call me Nana. When you have children, I'll want the children to call me Nana, like I called my grandmother. You can start calling me that now. That's warm, but appropriate. It feels right."

13 ~ True Confessions

January 1944, on the train from Washington, DC, to Philadelphia, PA

On the train going back to Philadelphia, their car was nearly empty—no one within earshot. The motion of the train gave Ruth feelings of vertigo again. She focused her eyes on Mark to avoid looking outside; to avoid thinking about the train and the speed. Seeing him, loving him, she wanted to tell him about her father, as she had wanted to before he dropped the bombshell of the wedding date. It wouldn't be easy. She had never told anyone. But if she wanted total intimacy with this man, he needed to know everything about her. On the other hand, she needed to know everything about him, as well. And the muscles of his jaw were tense, as if he were holding something back.

She took a pocket calendar for 1944 out of her purse.

"What are you doing?" asked Mark.

"Checking June 5. If you insist on that date—and I have no idea why you would—I'd like to know what day of the week it is."

"Oh," grunted Mark. He hadn't checked.

"Monday. For God's sake. It's a Monday. Why in the name of God would you pick a Monday, a workday?"

"Please don't swear."

"You're driving me to it."

"It's a good day. Believe me. It's the right day."

"Are you a closet Hindu or Buddhist or something, and is that supposed to be a lucky day for weddings? Did some fortune teller say that's the day you're supposed to marry? What's so f-ing special about June 5?"

"Your language!"

"Your bullheaded stupidity."

On the spot, Mark invented a lame excuse. "I want my Uncle Adolph to be there, and that's the soonest he can."

"Be honest with me, for God's sake," Ruth pleaded. "We have to be totally honest with one another. I don't care what skeletons you have in your closet. You could tell me anything, absolutely anything, and I'd still love you. But lying to me—I can't take that." She was surprised to realize that tears were dripping down her face; tears of remorse for what she still hadn't told him.

"I was kicked out of school," he quickly babbled. "I meant to tell you, but I was too embarrassed to admit it. At Gettysburg College, I was pre-ministerial, I was going to become a Lutheran minister, like my parents expected and I expected. But I could remember jokes and tell them better than anyone else. I could play pop tunes and dance tunes on my saxophone. I knew everybody and everybody knew me; I was a big man on campus. Friends expected me to hang out with them, to drink with them. I joined a fraternity, and everybody expected me to write the skit for the spring bash. I did, and I did it too well. It was too racy. It was a big hit with my buddies, but the dean was outraged. And I hadn't been studying. My grades were borderline. I wasn't 'college material', the dean said, as he booted me out. I'm not the man you thought I was. I'm a loser. You won't want to get hitched to a loser like me."

She hugged him tightly and kissed him. This time, the first time she had ever done this with anyone, she inserted her tongue in his mouth, and then he inserted his in hers. It was electric, exhilarating. Total acceptance. No boundaries. They belonged to one another.

The footsteps of the conductor startled them. He was walking up the aisle to check tickets. By the time he got to their row, they were sitting sedately—Mark looking out the window, Ruth flipping through her pocket calendar.

When the coast was clear, she asked, "Do your parents know?"

"I never told them. I told them what I told you—that it was my patriotic duty to serve my country. Uncle Adolph's the only one I told the real story to, before now."

"The man you want to come to our wedding?"

"Yes. He's special to me. I've always been able to share things with him that I couldn't with Mom and Dad. He's a character and a war hero from World War I. He makes a living as a gambler. Would you believe we have a gambler in the family? He was always there to cover for me when I got into a scrape. He told me not to tell my parents about Gettysburg, and he was right about that. He told me to volunteer for the

Army, rather than wait to be drafted, and to apply for Officer Candidate School and the Army Specialized Training Program—all of which turned out right, because otherwise I would never have wound up in Philadelphia and met you. His advice may even have saved my life, because if I hadn't gotten into that program, I'd be with my old company in England now, waiting for the invasion, But best of all, he told me that, yes, I should marry you—and he was dead right about that, too."

"Thank you, Adolph," she declared. She kissed Mark again and again.

The kissing ended when the train stopped in Baltimore, and more people boarded. Constrained by the eyes of strangers, they held hands, and, with forehead touching forehead, looked deep into one another's eyes, oblivious of the world rushing by. When the train swayed as the tracks curved, their heads bumped, and they laughed.

"Thank you for forgiving me," Mark whispered.

"Thank you for sharing that with me," Ruth whispered back. "Secrets aren't bad, in and of themselves; they're only bad when we keep them bottled up. When we share them with one another, and no one else knows, secrets can bring us closer together." She hesitated. "I have a skeleton in my closet, too," she admitted.

"Out with it," he insisted with a smile. "Anything at all. Tell me anything. It will just make me love you more."

"It has to do with my sister Emily."

"The war widow?"

"Yes, my kid sister—five years younger than me."

"You two are close, from what I can tell," Mark ventured.

"Now, yes. But when we were very young, it was different. When she was born, she became the baby of the family, and I was jealous. Everybody made a fuss over her—Father and my sisters, but not Mom. Mom still held me close. Thank God, she never knew what I did to Emily when she was almost two.

Mark wiped away a tear from the corner of her eye.

"Emily had just learned the alphabet song, and she was proud that she knew it. Everybody made a fuss about how bright she was. She was singing it in the kitchen, and I sang along with her. Only I messed up the order of the letters, deliberately; and I got her to say it the way I was saying it. Then Abby and Mom came into the kitchen, and Emily started singing it again. I backed off and didn't say a word. She sang it the way I had sung it, with all the mistakes. Emily could see how surprised and disappointed they were, though they didn't say a word. So, she tried again—the way she had learned it in the first place. Only she couldn't remember it right and messed up again and again. I was struggling hard not to break out laughing. Then Emily got mad at herself and banged her head on the kitchen floor. Mom picked her up and hugged her, kissed her, and comforted her. She said that it didn't matter if she was bright or not bright. Mom loved her very much and would always love her, no matter what. Hearing that, I ran up to my room and cried for hours. I was so ashamed. It was another year before Emily could recite the alphabet song right."

"Is that what you needed to confess?" Mark asked incredulously. "That's all? Never mind. Never mind."

Ruth broke out in tears, "Don't say that."

"What?"

"*Never mind*. Don't say never mind."

"What do you mean?"

"That's something my mother said at special times, terrible times, when things happened like what I have to tell you."

"Never mind?"

"Promise you'll never say that again."

"Sure, I promise. I'd promise anything for you. But please explain."

"When something happened that shouldn't have happened, something that she didn't just want to forget, that she wanted to unmake, like it had never happened, Mom would say, no, she'd pray: *Never mind. Never mind.*

Give me now my nevermind,

Happily-ever-after time.

"To her that was more than just words. That was magic that one generation passes on to the next, magic that you hope you will never have to use, but that if you do use it, not just speaking those words, but focusing on them intensely, what has happened can be undone and the world changed. But you can't use the words loosely. It's like your mother and not taking the name of God in vain. And you shouldn't use that spell for trivial matters, things you can deal by ordinary means, with your own resources, because the power diminishes each time you use it, and then you wouldn't be able to use it when you really need it."

"Have you ever used it?"

"No. Never. But I've thought the words and said them aloud when I was tempted to use it."

"And do you know of any time that it worked?"

"No. Mother claimed that she had used it so much that, for her, it had lost its power. Maybe that was before I was born. She never talked about that. Maybe it was something so terrible that she didn't want to tell me or something she thought I was too young to understand."

"And you believe in this magic?"

"Yes. I believe in it, like your mother believes in God. I know you think I'm silly, superstitious. Of course, you do. Saying this aloud, it sounds silly. Anyone would think it's silly. It's not something to talk about and reason about. But to me, it matters. And I'm asking you to please respect my wishes. Don't use those words."

"Of course." He comforted her, hugging her, and rubbing her back. "But what's the terrible thing you said you want to tell me?"

"I don't know the whole story. It happened when I was too young to understand it. Mom was dead then, and Aunties wouldn't talk about it. Emily told the police and the jury. But then she was supposed to never say a word about it to anyone."

"Police?" Mark whispered back, eyes wide, but otherwise keeping control of his expression. No one sitting across the aisle would have guessed that he had just been hit with an axe.

"Valentine's Day, 1932."

"That's the day your father died."

"That's the day my father was arrested."

"Arrested for what? That was at the worst of the Depression. Did he steal? Did he need to steal for the family?"

"That, I would understand. But what happened, I don't understand at all. And Aunties didn't want me to understand—they were clear about that. Thinking about it now, I realize that seven-year-old Emily didn't know what was wrong about what father did. But when her friends told their parents what had happened, she confirmed that he had done it with her. Then she had to tell the police and say so in court. But she couldn't tell us, her sisters. She had no idea what was wrong, but the grownups took it very seriously. Father was convicted and sent to prison—the Eastern State Penitentiary. That's where Abby's husband, my oldest sister's husband, worked as a guard. When I was at Girl's High, I had to walk past it every day on the way to school, and on the way home. But we never visited him there. From the day he was arrested, I never saw him again. Aunties wouldn't allow it. They said he was as good as dead; that we should tell everybody that he died that day. And the sooner we forgot that it had happened, the better."

They sat together in silence, foreheads still touching, eyes still locked, as the train clattered on and on.

"What was the crime?" he finally whispered.

"I don't know. They never gave it a name. But it was serious—serious enough for prison, and serious enough for a sentence of ten years or more."

"God," he moaned.

"Watch your language," she giggled nervously. He hadn't flinched. He hadn't even blinked, but he was holding her hand more tightly than before.

"You must have some clue," he persisted.

"It was something to do with sex; something men are never supposed to do with young girls, and certainly not with a daughter. Maybe it was child abuse or child rape or incest. Aunties wouldn't talk about it. They believe that men are evil, that sex is evil. But they never said what sex is, and what men can do that's evil. The best I can guess is that Emily and some of her friends visited Father in his apartment over the store, across the street. He talked them into undressing and getting into the bathtub, and played games with them, touching them and maybe more. Maybe Emily's friends over-reacted, or maybe their parents over-reacted when they heard, and maybe the jury over-reacted when Emily described what had happened. Maybe he was given an unjustly harsh sentence. Then again, maybe it was something horrible, and he deserved even worse."

By this point, Ruth was sobbing, shaking. "I always felt that Father didn't love me as much as he loved Emily, didn't love me at all. I envied her. Then, suddenly, it was a blessing that he didn't love me."

Mark took out his handkerchief and dried her tears. She kissed his fingers, then his lips, gently, appreciating his sympathy.

"And Emily," she continued. "you've met her—she's beautiful and innocent and child-like, but also headstrong and passionate. Who would ever guess that she was a victim of child abuse, of incest? Then she fell in love, suddenly, and eloped. Soon after that, the man she loved was killed in battle. And now she's still innocent and child-like, as if nothing had happened. She has this ability to forget what's bad and start her life over again. I admire her for that. She's good at forgetting, and forgetting is hard, but she's very good at it. Forgetting is like that Buddhist thing—Nirvana—not having to relive the past over and over again. Sometimes I imagine Father getting old that way, staying away from me and Emily and the rest of us, forgetting what happened, forgetting what he did, finally freed from the past."

Mark hugged her again and again. What she had said felt unreal. In any case, this wasn't something that she had done. He wouldn't judge her for the deeds of her father, though his mother certainly would. His mother could never hear this tale. What mattered to him was the effect of this on Ruth. The sincerity of her confession, her evident pain and embarrassment in telling him made him feel protective. She had trusted him with this story that she had probably never told anyone outside her family. That made him feel close to her. "Is he still in prison?" Mark ventured.

"He should be out by now, but I don't know for sure. I don't know what the sentence was. I don't know what they called the crime. I don't know if he's alive or dead or where he is. If he ever tried to see Emily or any of the rest of us, Aunties would chase him away with a meat cleaver and call the police. Maybe that was a condition for his release—that he never contact us again. But wherever he is, I feel his shadow, even now."

"How's that?" he asked sympathetically.

"Your mother asked me when my father died, and my mind blanked out. I didn't know what to say. She must have thought I was the village idiot. She must have thought I had something to hide, and she was dead right about that. I could never tell her this. I could never tell anyone but you about this. But she probably thinks I'm a terrible person, a liar and I don't know what else. It was after that that she took it back."

"Took back what?"

"That I could call her Mom. Now she wants me to call her Nana. She distrusts me. She hates me. I'm surprised she didn't try to break us up."

"No," Mark scrambled to reassure her. "You're over-reacting. She'd never think ill of you. She's slow to warm up to people, but she'll warm up to you. She'll love you. I love you so much, she'll have to love you, too. That business about your father must have been terrible for you, and then having to hold that secret and hide it. Thank you for telling me. I feel closer to you now that you've told me. I'm here for you—now, and until death do us part."

14 ~ Monkey Business

January 1944, Philadelphia, PA

"We're as good as married," Ruth thought as the train pulled into Philadelphia. She didn't say it out loud but after the proposal, the ring, the visit to his parents, setting the date, and the confession of her darkest secret, she was tempted to venture into new territory. She didn't know the limits of Mark's moral code, but if he were to try to get physical, very physical, she might not resist.

"What's the name of the hotel your Uncle Adolph stays at?"

"The Drake."

"That's a nice hotel, right? But does it cost a lot?"

"Five dollars a night."

"Let's do it."

"What?"

"Let's stay there tonight. It will be a dress rehearsal." She laughed. "You don't have to be in class, and I don't have to go to work until morning. We could talk all night in private, in a room of our own. We could talk about the wedding and our future together. Or we could just hold hands and cuddle."

***

Mark felt uncomfortable going to the Drake, where he'd had sex with Maxine. He hoped Maxine didn't frequent the place, that he wouldn't run into her in the lobby. But it was the only hotel in town that he was familiar with. And he couldn't turn down an opportunity to spend the night with Ruth, even if it meant no more than necking and talking. He had to be careful with her. Given her history, she probably distrusted men, all men. Besides, he didn't have a clue how to advance to more physical contact. All he knew about seduction was what he had seen in movies, where the lights went out or the scene ended abruptly before details were revealed.

They registered as husband and wife, which gave them both a thrill. Then he carried her over the threshold, to the bed, where they hugged and kissed, caressed, and groped.

***

Ruth felt waves of sensation—echoes of swimming, of strange handsome men pressing against her on the dance floor, of Mark and her making out under the tree in Silver Spring. There was nothing to stop them from going farther than they had gone before. She might let him do anything he wanted. But he stopped abruptly.

She wasn't sure how to react. She wanted more, but she couldn't tell him that. She didn't want him to think that she was forward and loose. He had to make the next move. But he was probably as excited and as scared as she was. He was probably afraid of going too far too fast and offending her. His hesitation was a sign of his love for her. He didn't want to take advantage of her, even when she made it easy for him to do so.

That was part of Mark's charm—she could surrender to him in full confidence that he wouldn't take advantage of her, wouldn't ask her to do anything she would regret. It was like letting him lead when they danced. It was amazing how he could be so confident and so much in control when he was just as naive and inexperienced as she was.

She relaxed. There was no hurry. They had the whole night ahead of them. She cuddled, resting her head on his shoulder, and playing with his ear.

"I'll tell Aunties the wedding date tomorrow," she said.

"You want to invite them?"

"Of course," she said.

"I was hoping it would be a small intimate affair."

"Well, June 5th is five months from now. We could do lots of preparing in that time. And my Aunties have to be included."

"I understand, honey. But the problem is I'm not sure my parents will be coming."

"What? I thought one of the reasons for waiting so long was so your parents could save face, that they wouldn't be embarrassed with people thinking this was a shotgun wedding. If we're going out of our way for them, why won't they come?"

"You saw Mom when we left. You heard the tone of her voice. I didn't want to say this, I don't want to hurt your feelings, but I don't want to set false expectations, either. I think she's dead set against the wedding."

"She said that?"

"Not in so many words, and I'll do whatever I can to get her to change her mind. But I doubt that she'll budge. Once she's set her mind to something—"

"She hates me," Ruth sobbed, her tears dripping on his shoulder.

***

Mark scrambled to find an explanation that she could accept, that seemed plausible, that wouldn't hurt her, "No, it's not that. It's not you. It's someone else."

"There's someone else?"

"Not for me. Not someone I ever cared about. Someone Mom tried to set me up with, repeatedly. You have no idea how controlling she can be. Loving, but controlling. She wanted me and my three brothers to all become Lutheran ministers, and she decided that Betty would make a perfect minister's wife for me."

"You never mentioned Betty."

"Because she meant nothing to me. She was Mom's choice, not mine. She went to our church. Her mother's a good friend of Mom's. I'm sure the two of them shared fantasies about the future that Betty and I would have together, and our children and grandchildren. It doesn't matter how wonderful you are. You aren't Betty."

"Then I can't invite the Aunties," she conceded.

"That's why I told you now. If my parents didn't show up and your aunts did, your aunts would wonder why. You'd be embarrassed in front of them."

She gave his arm a quick, emotional squeeze. "You understand me so well. Thank you for being honest with me."

"Of course, I'll invite Uncle Adolph. He'll be my best man."

"Of course."

"And he'll probably bring Margery and her daughter Judy."

"And I'll invite my sister Emily. She'll be my matron of honor."

"That's probably enough."

"But what should I tell the Aunties? They know we're engaged. They'll presume they'll be invited to the wedding, no matter how small it might be."

"There's no need to give them a date. Tell them that we want to wait until the war is over. Then we'll tell them we eloped. We'll say I got orders and had to ship out, and it was sudden and passionate."

"You're a terrible liar," she chuckled and cuddled closer. "I'll think it out later. I just want to minimize the problems. And I don't want to hurt their feelings. In the long run, the details won't matter."

"So that's settled." He sighed in relief.

"Yes."

"So, we can save our money for the honeymoon and for starting our life together."

"Except the wedding gown. And the cake."

"Of course, whatever you feel is necessary."

"I'm sure I could fit in Emily's gown, but it would be bad luck to wear the gown from a marriage that ended tragically. I guess all we need to do right away is the blood test and the license."

"Blood test?"

"Yes. I looked it up. There's a three-day wait after the blood test, to get results, before you can get the license. We should get the blood test now, then pick up the license. We can fill in the date later. That way we'll be all set, in case you do get orders, heaven forbid." She squeezed his arm again.

"Blood test?"

She laughed. "You silly. Are you afraid of needles?"

"No. I just hadn't considered .... Do you think I might have a disease or something?"

"No, it's the law. I'm not worried about venereal diseases, for God's sake. Neither of us has ever done it with anyone. It's the Rh factor that matters."

"The what?"

"Rh, for 'rhesus monkey'. Monkey business. Very serious monkey business. I've been reading about it. It doesn't affect the first baby, but if there's bleeding during the first birth, and there usually is, the blood of the baby and the mother can mix. And that spells trouble for any children after that. When we go for the required test for venereal disease, we should ask to be tested for the Rh factor as well. I want to have four children—no, five. Seven, like my mother, is too many, but four or five is a good number. So the Rh factor matters. I love you. You come first. Test results won't change that; I want to marry you and only you. But I do want to know if our blood matches, so we can have as many children as we want, or if we'll just have one very precious, much loved child."

Mark tried hard to shut out the thought of the blood test, and the possibility that he had never considered before: that he might have caught something from Maxine in this very hotel. He changed the subject to discussing imagined details of their future life together.

They would both go to college. They would both become high school teachers—no, college professors. She would teach Latin or literature. He would teach American history. She would write novels, and he'd write history books.

Maybe they would go to Hollywood and become actors. Or Mark would become a cartoonist for Disney, and she would become a singer and dancer. Maybe, after that, he would go into politics, and she would become the CEO of a major charity.

"But promise me you won't become a minister, " Ruth insisted, "regardless of what your mother says. I don't want to be married to an Elmer Gantry. Aunties wanted me to read that book because they see it as proof that all men are evil, especially the ones who pretend they aren't."

"That's fiction." Mark laughed.

"Fiction matters. Now I've got that idea in my head, I could never marry a minister. Promise me you won't become one," Ruth insisted.

"Of course, my love."

On an emotional high, super-sensitive, tender, and alert, they fell asleep in one another's arms.

Nevermind

***

They had the test results sent to Ruth's rooming house. She wanted to see them as soon as possible. But when the envelope arrived, she didn't want to open it alone. She called Mark and met him at Horn and Hardart. It was the middle of the morning on a Saturday and the place was empty except for them.

Reading the paper, Ruth's face dropped.

Mark panicked. He imagined she was reading evidence that he had syphilis or gonorrhea, or any of a dozen other contagious diseases. It was incurable. She had caught it from him. They would never be able to have children. She would never forgive him. The wedding was off; his life was over.

"It's bad but we can live with it," she concluded.

"We can?" he asked, desperately wanting to believe that despite his having had sex with a prostitute, despite his having a venereal disease, she could still love him.

"Why are you so upset?" she asked. "We knew this was a possibility. I'm Rh positive, and you're negative. We can only have one child. But we can have that one child and love him totally—because I know it will be a boy, I just know it. But why is your face so white? Why is your jaw so tense? Why are you trembling? Why do you have such a look of guilt? Your blood type and my blood type are no fault of yours. But something else is your fault, isn't it? For God's sake—and I will use the name of God in vain—what the hell aren't you telling me? What the hell did you do?"

"I'm sorry. I'm so sorry," he blurted out. "I never should have done it."

"Done what? This Rh thing wasn't caused by anything you did."

"Please forgive me."

"Forgive you for what?"

"Adolph tempted me. He made it so easy. And I didn't think twice. My moral shield vanished. I was just a horny bastard, and she was naked. She opened her legs and welcomed me. And it was all over in a minute or two. It was nothing; it meant nothing. But now I'm so, so sorry."

"What the hell are you talking about?" Ruth demanded.

"When I saw Uncle Adolph at the Drake Hotel, he was with a loose woman, and I did it with her." Ruth recoiled and got up off the bed. "I was afraid I might have caught something awful," he continued. "That's why I was so anxious about the blood test." She backed up, staring in disbelief. "But I didn't catch anything, and you didn't catch anything from me," he said. "We have reason to be glad, don't we? Yes, we'll only have one child. But that mistake of mine is over and done with. There are no consequences from that. I was lucky. We were lucky. Please forgive me."

She stepped back and leaned forward, staring at him, her nose touching his nose. "Are you kidding? Is this real? You bastard!" She spit in his eyes, then kneed him in the groin.

He wiped the spit from his face, leaned over to relieve the pain, then reached toward her.

"Don't dare touch my hand. Don't dare touch any part of me. Don't dare get near me. I hate your guts!"

"I'd do anything, absolutely anything to undo that," he pleaded. "I'm so sorry."

"Get your sorry ass out of here. How could you? You aren't the man I thought you were. Here I was, upset that our Rh factors aren't a match. Compared to this, that was no big deal. So we could only have one child—one precious child—who now will never come into existence. No, you don't have a venereal disease. You can tell your next whore that you have a clean bill of health. But you're a filthy man, with a filthy mind. I don't want to have anything to do with you. Get out. No. Stay put. I'll leave. You just sit right there and think about what you've done to me, to us, to our future. Let the pain sink in. You're nothing but a ... a man!"

She grabbed her coat and stormed out.

Mark was paralyzed in shock.

On the train, Ruth had confessed to him about her father's crime, something that she hadn't done, but that she felt she needed to tell him to be totally honest with him. And that confession had brought them closer.

Now Mark had confessed to something that he himself had done, but that he hadn't needed to tell her. If he had kept his mouth shut, he would have learned that there was nothing to worry about—he was healthy; that was all over and done with. One little lie of omission, and they would still be in love, engaged, and on the brink of a wonderful life together.

Mark tried to call her at her rooming house and was told repeatedly that she was "out," and no one knew when she'd be back or if she would be back. He hand-delivered a letter, and the young woman who opened the door took it, tore it up, and threw it in his face, with a laugh. He would have intercepted her on her way to or from her work, but he had to be at class at those times.

He needed advice, but he couldn't talk to his parents about this, and couldn't talk to his brothers because that would be the same as talking to his parents. And his army buddies thought nothing about going out with loose women; their morals were very different from his.

He decided to talk to Uncle Adolph. Even though Adolph had gotten him into this mess, he was the only person he knew who might understand his predicament and might know a way out of it—a way to salvage his future with Ruth.

The next weekend he caught a train to Baltimore. Adolph was at the Pimlico Racetrack. It was a long shot, that was Mark's only bet.

15 ~ The Proverbs of Adolph

January 1944, Baltimore, MD

Uncle Adolph was a flamboyant, up-and-down wheeler dealer and gambler with a persuasive carnival pitch and an earthy, cynical view of life. A photo of him in uniform, on a camel in front of the pyramids, hung on the living room wall of Mark's parents' house. That was originally meant as proof of Uncle Adolph's larger-than-life heroic personality—a nineteen-year-old captain in World War I, with a promising future ahead of him and a reminder of what it was possible to achieve in life. But over time, that photo came to serve a different purpose, as a reminder of his downfall—a cautionary tale that Mark heard from his parents whenever a letter arrived from Adolph, bragging of great success soon to come, and asking for money to tide him over in the meantime.

During his lucky streaks, when Adolph showed up, unannounced, at the house in Silver Spring, he brought gifts for the boys—sleds and bikes and toy guns. The kinds of things boys would wish for at Christmas, and that frugal Depression-era parents couldn't afford. He delighted in spoiling the boys, taking them out for ice cream and movies. He loved playing the rich uncle.

Adolph distributed gifts equally, but Mark was the one he talked to the most, telling war stories and boasting about his business ventures. Mark was also the only one he corresponded with. Mark would check the mailbox before his parents did in case there was a personal note from Adolph. This communication had a thrill of the forbidden, in a strictly run house where everything to do with Adolph was subject to moral criticism. As a teen, Mark felt he could confide in Adolph about his hopes, his dreams, and the girls who caught his attention. Adolph was the worldly-wise adult he could turn to for advice and encouragement.

When Mark met Adolph at his hotel room in Baltimore, he didn't waste time blaming Adolph for what had happened—he was responsible for his own actions and should have had the gumption to withstand temptation. Rather, he explained his dilemma and asked, "What should I do? How can I win her back?"

Adolph puffed on his cigar, then intoned, "Your trouble stems from you're being a compulsive talker. Keep your mouth shut. A tongue is for inserting in the mouth and other parts of a beautiful woman. Speech is a secondary function. The less you say, the more time she has to think and imagine. Let her finish your sentences. Let her guess your thoughts before you say them. Let her guess thoughts you've never had. The less you say, the more she'll be able to convince herself that you two are on the same wavelength and that you're soulmates."

He brandished his cigar with confidence, then continued his lecture. "Shit, you have the looks of a Clark Gable. Let those looks work for you. Let nature take its course. Let the broad seduce herself with what she imagines you're thinking. For someone with your looks, that's good advice. For me, with my paunch and this face of mine, that wouldn't get me anywhere. So, do as I say, not as I do."

He paused to puff his cigar again and settled in an armchair. "What you don't say can be far more powerful than what you do say. When you go to the movies, watch for the pauses in dramatic scenes—what's implied by a look or a gesture. There's a long moment of silence right before the first kiss. If you're talking all the time, you'll never get there. Hold your tongue, then hold the woman, then you use your tongue as it was meant to be used."

He stood and put an arm around Mark's shoulder. "For you, this kind of change won't be easy. It will be like a chain-smoker stopping cold turkey, like a drunk going on the wagon. You need to become a man of few words. Then people will pay more attention to what you say. They'll value you as a good listener. Guys will seek you out as a friend, and girls will want to see you again and again—even if you have no lines and no moves. Let them imagine you the way they want to, and you'll become the man of their dreams."

Mark frowned, "I know you mean well, but this kind of advice doesn't do me any good. Not now. This is a crisis. I need marching orders, not the Proverbs of Uncle Adolph. What can I do?"

Adolph looked him in the eye and put a hand on each of Mark's shoulders. "Okay, let's presume Ruth loves you. Then the way she's acting, raised by old maids, is no surprise. She's a scaredy cat. Treat her nice. Be patient. She'll come around. Don't argue with her. Let her argue with herself. The less you say, the better. What she doesn't know, she'll fill in herself and it's likely to be far better than what you might make up. Play her, let her swim away a bit, then pull her back in. Take your time. You've got until June, for God's sake."

Mark looked away, trying to decide what of this to believe, hoping there was a way back, a way to undo what he had done.

"Above all, don't say another word about Maxine," Adolph continued. "Maxine doesn't matter. Get Ruth's mind off the old and onto the new. Tempt her. She has a good imagination and a good singing voice; you said she wishes she could be an actress. You can work with that. Make her a dream offer, an offer she can't refuse. Take her to New York City. There's a musical that just went into rehearsals for Broadway. 'On the Town' with Leonard Bernstein, the youngest guy to ever conduct the New York Philharmonic, wrote the music for this show. And the stage manager is a friend of mine. He can get the two of you into rehearsals. Not to try out for parts, but to watch, to see how things are done on Broadway, to give her the itch, to get her caught up in the fantasy. I have the lyrics and the sheet music to a great song from it — 'New York, New York.' Sing it with her."

"You've got to be kidding." Mark laughed nervously, hoping this wild plan could be real and doable.

"Stay at the Empire Hotel at 63rd and Broadway. I know the night manager. I'll give him a call. He'll set you up with a great room at a low price. She spent a night with you at the Drake, so this won't be that different. She doesn't live at home, and what the aunts don't know, won't hurt them.

"All you'll talk about is the show, right? Get it? Nothing about Maxine and how sorry you are. The less you talk the better. Let her do the talking. Focus on the show and on getting her into bed. Yes, it's high time you laid her. A babe like that, with her sense of what's right and wrong, you do it with her and you've got her — she's committed, for better or for worse. Most guys try to avoid that. They don't want to get trapped into marriage, so they stay away from dames like that. But you say you want her for keeps; use that to your advantage. Get her clothes off, get down to business, and you're home free."

Mark shook his head as if he didn't believe this was possible, but his imagination was fully engaged, visualizing the scene.

"One thing you've got to keep in mind, though—don't shoot your wad too fast, like you did with Maxine. You couldn't have been more than two minutes with her. That won't wash. Okay, so she turns you on so much you can't hold back, or you think you can't. That's not physical, kid. That's in your mind, and you can control it. If you feel you're about to come, think about something else until you cool down."

"What?"

"Try baseball. That's a natural."

"And why's that natural? What's baseball got to do with sex?"

"Plenty. Her name's Ruth, isn't it? And she's a babe. And here we are in Baltimore, Babe Ruth's birthplace. And it's time you stopped fiddling around with first and second base. You need a home run, kid. Give it all you've got."

16 ~ A Night on Broadway

February 1944, Philadelphia, PA and New York, NY

While he wanted to try Adolph's advice, Mark had no way to communicate with Ruth. She refused to talk to him on the phone, and her roommates tore up every written message he delivered. He went to the Stage Door Canteen on Friday night, but she didn't show up there, and he had no desire to dance with anyone else. He sat and watched until closing, then wandered home, slowly, taking a detour that led past her rooming house. Then he remembered the story she had told him about the day her mother died, about her loneliness and then the flashing light she saw blocks away, and the possibility that with a code she could make contact with a stranger in the night. He caught a cab home, fetched his flashlight, then took another cab back to her rooming house.

Standing on the sidewalk in front of her third-story window, he flashed over and over: dot dot dot, dash dash dash, dot dot dot—SOS.

The light went off in her room, but the shade didn't go down. There was a shadow by her window. She was watching.

She was into codes and she had been since the night her mother died. Mark signaled—"Music Hall. Tomorrow." He signaled it over and over. No response. Then, as he was about to walk away, the light in her room went on and off in a pattern—dash dot dash dash, dot, dot dot dot. "Yes." She had coded, yes.

***

The next night, Ruth showed up at the Music Hall above the Stage Door Canteen before the dancing started. There was no way she was getting back together with this bastard, but she wouldn't mind making him squirm and hearing him beg. Then she could dance all night with strangers, making him jealous, and start her new once-again-single life.

Much to her surprise, Mark didn't say a word. Rather, he sat at the piano and started playing and singing a hypnotic song she had never heard before, "New York, New York."

She stood beside him and read the lyrics as he sang. Then they sang together, verse after verse. Then they sang in harmony.

They had talked about their love of music, but they had never sung together before. And Mark was good; his baritone resonated with her soprano.

When the dance music started in the Canteen, he took her hand and led her down, and they danced until closing. He didn't say a word all night, not even when walking her to her rooming house. He kissed her quickly, not giving her time to kiss back. Then he smiled and left.

Before going to bed that night, she called him and suggested that they meet at Horn and Hardart's for dinner the next day so they could talk. He said, "It's a date," and added nothing more, no excuses, no apology.

At dinner, she opened with, "And what do you have to say for yourself?"

He replied, "New York."

"You mean the song?"

"I mean the city. I'm offering it to you. Saturday, two weeks from now."

"What are you driving at?"

"Let's go, together, by train. I've reserved a room at the Empire Hotel. My uncle can get us into rehearsals for 'On the Town'—that's the show that song is from. It's going to open on Broadway at the Adelphi in a few months. The rehearsals have begun. That's one of your dreams—acting on Broadway or in movies. Well, this will be a taste of what that's really like."

"After what you did, you expect me to share a hotel room with you? That's ridiculous. It's over between us. Over. Do you understand? I shouldn't even be here talking to you. I should never see you again, never talk to you again."

"Saturday morning, seven o'clock. I'll meet you at the information booth in the main concourse at Thirtieth Street Station. Wear your walking shoes. We'll get in at Penn Station on 34th Street near

Broadway. The Adelphi is on 54th near Broadway; the hotel's at 63rd. It'll be your first time in New York and mine, too. Let's walk up Broadway and spend the day watching rehearsals."

He left before she could say "no."

She almost ran after him to yell at him for being so rude. But then she felt a shiver of delight.

***

On the train ride to New York, she forgot that she was afraid of trains. She forgot that she had vowed to herself that she would never see Mark again. She talked non-stop about Broadway and Hollywood, about Clark Gable and Humphrey Bogart, and about the high school plays she starred in—*A Midsummer Night's Dream* and *As You Like It*. And she told Mark that two years ago, she had a part in a semi-professional production of *Don't Feed the Animals* at the East Falls Old Academy Players. She didn't get the lead because that part was for a young girl. Grace Kelly got that—the twelve-year-old daughter of the rich folks who lived on the hilltop a few blocks away. When Ruth was growing up, the Kellys let her and her sisters play tennis on their court. Ruth rambled on about how precocious and talented and unpretentious Grace was, and how she couldn't help but envy Grace for the opportunities she'd have.

As they walked up Broadway, she delivered a running commentary on the people they saw, imagining their life stories, like in the sketches she used to write. She was animated, delighted, and delightful. Mark felt a tingle of pride walking arm-in-arm with this beautiful and brilliant woman, and he was sure that everyone was staring at her and envying him.

Mesmerized, they sat through six hours of rehearsals. On smoke breaks, Ruth mingled with the girls in the cast. When offered a cigarette, she tried one. She coughed so they patted her on the back and coached her on how to inhale. She caught on, feeling a bond of camaraderie as she imitated their gestures.

On the way to their hotel, she bought a pack of cigarettes and smoked one after another. She felt sinful smoking. She felt sinful dreaming of an acting career. She felt sinful spending the day with this bastard who had betrayed her.

But when she inhaled, deep, it felt good to be sinful. After a lifetime of restraining herself, it felt good to let loose a little.

Why not take a shot at being an actress? She could catch the train to New York for auditions and, if she got a part, she could move there. It was her life, not her Aunties'.

And Mark was different now. She had loved him when she thought he was innocent and naive and unsure of himself. But today she had seen another side of him—a bad boy, yes, but confident, competent, a leader. Not a sensitive and compassionate Ashley Wilkes from *Gone with the Wind*, for her to respect, protect and mother. Rather a Rhett Butler to take charge of her and sweep her off her feet.

She still had her reservations—the hurt ran deep. But she wanted to get rid of those reservations and end this wonderful day with a wonderful night.

Walking from the theater to the hotel, she went into a wine shop. Mark followed. She hesitated and said, "I don't know a thing about wine, I've never tried it."

She imagined that he was as ignorant as she when it came to wine. But he didn't show it. He picked three bottles without hesitation—red, white, and rose. He bought a corkscrew and a pair of glasses as well. Then he took her arm and led her up the street. He knew what he wanted, and he knew how to get it. And knowing that he wanted her gave her a thrill she had never felt before—visceral, not emotional. She was drawn to him physically, despite the anger she still felt.

***

As for Mark, he had been afraid that the sales clerk in the wine shop would doubt his age and ask to see his ID. Fortunately, he was in uniform and with his air of self-confidence, the clerk wouldn't want to embarrass him in front of his girl by asking. Only later did he remember that while the drinking age in Pennsylvania was twenty-one, here in New York it was eighteen. That was a close call, but thinking he was at risk, he had kept a poker face.

Why had he lied to her about his age when they first met? Vanity? He didn't want to be three years younger than her. Two was better. Twenty-one was a man, an adult. And when he told her that his mother didn't want him to marry her, why didn't he end the farce and admit that the date he had chosen was because of his age, so he wouldn't need his parents' permission? Stupidity and cowardice. Having repeated the lie many times, it had become more of a lie. It was now all the harder to correct it and apologize, especially after the Maxine business. He needed to build Ruth's confidence in his trustworthiness. The littlest thing, like his age, could remind her of that other betrayal. He wanted her to think of him as forceful, decisive, mature, and confident. He didn't want her to once again have second thoughts about marrying him. He would tell her after the wedding that June 5 was his birthday, his twenty-first birthday. Then, they would already be man and wife, and they would laugh about this. It would become an anecdote they would laugh about with friends years later.

This day was going well. He was coming on as a manly man, worldly wise. He sensed she was under his spell. Adolph had been oh so right. Mark was determined to follow this through to the end, to stay in character, to be the man he needed to be to win her back. She wanted to be an actress someday. Well he was playing the role of his life right now and playing it to perfection.

***

Going up the elevator to their hotel room, Ruth realized that she might actually have sex for the first time tonight with this bold Clark Gable look-alike. She hadn't forgiven him, but his new forceful manner aroused her curiosity and her lust. She wanted sex with him even more than she did the last time they were in bed together, but she couldn't admit that. Maybe after some wine, she might go through with it. She wouldn't make the first move, but if he did, she might let him have his way with her.

He carried her over the threshold and placed her on the bed. Then, as if he were reading her mind, he opened the red wine and poured. They drank and drank again, neither of them saying a word, and he not making a move. He opened the white wine, but this time, before pouring, he reached over and brushed her neck and her ear lobe with the tips of his fingers. A moment later, they were hugging and kissing, and he reached inside her blouse for her brassiere strap, but he couldn't release it with one hand or even with both hands, so she reached back and unhooked it herself.

***

His hands brushed the sides of her breasts, then her nipples. He was at such a peak of excitement that he forgot to think of baseball, and before he got any further, he came. It was like a balloon had popped—his intensity, his urgent insistence deflated abruptly. He felt foolish, embarrassed. He forgot Adolph's advice and said too much. He withdrew his hands and apologized profusely. He didn't mean to insult her. He knew she wanted to wait until after they were married, and he would respect her wishes, though he was sorely tempted. They shouldn't play with fire. They could get carried away and have a moment of pleasure that they would later regret—one platitude after another. He was embarrassed to hear himself say such things.

***

Ruth had no idea why he had stopped so suddenly. She was ready, but now he wouldn't do it. She thought he had second thoughts. She felt guilty that *she* didn't have second thoughts. She felt wave after wave of guilt, then she over-thought and concluded that he was only pretending to have second thoughts. He was a man; he was an Elmer Gantry. He was playing her. He didn't just want to have sex with her. He wanted to corrupt her and control her. He wanted to drive her to the point where she would be willing to do anything he wanted, whenever he wanted.

She loved him, as much as she could ever love any man. But she couldn't trust him—not completely.

They drank another glass of wine, then fell into a deep sleep, her head on his shoulder.

17 ~ 'Til Death Do Us Part

March to June 1944, Philadelphia, PA and Fayetteville, NC

"Is this who you are?" Ruth asked herself. "Is this who you want to be?"

Her reactions confused her. She had good reason to never trust this man, but she melted when he put his arms around her, and she acquiesced when he stroked her breasts with his forearms as they hugged and kissed. He acted as if it was a foregone conclusion that they were back together, and the wedding was back on—no discussion. And much to her surprise, she didn't object, and not having objected, the upcoming wedding became an accepted fact. Only the details remained to be decided and about those, he agreed with her on everything, and let her do all the talking.

It wasn't going to be a full-blown church wedding because his parents wouldn't come, and hence she couldn't invite her aunts, and hence it had to be as small as an elopement. But it would have none of the spontaneity of an elopement and all of the anxiety of knowing that any day he could get orders sending him to Europe. She could get him to agree to anything she wanted, except the wedding date. How could he be so stubborn about something so insignificant? It was infuriating.

His excuse for waiting was weak. Why should it matter so much to him that Adolph be able to go to the wedding? The same Adolph who had set him up with Maxine. But Mark seemed closer to this uncle than he was to his father. And it was Adolph who had arranged the Broadway excursion which brought them back together.

Thanks to that June date, they were in a holding pattern, with far too little holding. Her rooming house prohibited male visitors, and his military lodging excluded women. They had blown the little cash they had on the New York excursion so another hotel stay was impractical even if they could get past their virginal awkwardness. Eating dinner together at the automat, dancing and getting refreshments at the Stage Door Canteen, and going around town by trolley was all they could afford.

They sang together at the piano whenever they were free, and the Music Hall was empty. They entered a dance contest and came in second to Daisy and a sailor. Ruth went to a meeting of Army wives and wives-to-be but left early when the conversation centered on pregnancy and caring for infants. Their high point during this time came at the Canteen, when the band's saxophone player fell sick, and Mark volunteered to fill in for him, and Ruth got to sing with the band.

But having to watch their money carefully, day-by-day, was deflating. It was hard to imagine their future life together when they could barely scrape along in the present. In addition, they were at the mercy of military decisions that had nothing to do with them as individuals. They fell into a routine and became numb to the situation.

The days dragged by slowly, but the months disappeared fast. Now it was May, and, for Mark, school ended early. He graduated at the top of his class. With his Pennsylvania Dutch background, having heard his father and grandfather speak it, the accent and sentence structure came naturally to him. And the song that, as a child, helped him learn the names of body parts was "Schnitzelbank," which for German-American kids was what "Alouette" was for French-Canadians. There was an urgent need for German-speaking officers, and most of Mark's class shipped out immediately. So, he expected to get his orders soon. But the Army being the Army, he was left in limbo, without assignment.

When Mark met Ruth, he was a corporal and made just $60 a month—far less than Ruth made as a secretary. At that point, marriage was a romantic dream, not a practical reality. She hadn't thought about money when she said "yes" to him. When soldiers got married in wartime, often the brides stayed with their parents and kept their jobs, knowing that real married life would start after the war.

In late April, with graduation from the Army Specialized Training Program, Mark got commissioned as an officer—a second lieutenant making $150 a month. Everyone in the program had been promised they would get commissions, but he didn't know anyone other than himself who actually did. Maybe coming out at the top of his class helped. Every day he heard of assignment screw-ups—people trained in German sent to the Pacific. Maybe promotion was random, and he was lucky.

In any case, it would be at least a month and a half before he saw the additional money in his pay. And not knowing where or when he would be sent was nerve-wracking for both of them. At this point, the odds of him staying in Philadelphia until June 5 were zero.

On May 15, Mark got orders to Fort Bragg in Fayetteville, North Carolina. He was assigned to the 82nd Airborne for parachute training. The implication was that during the upcoming invasion, whenever and wherever that happened, he would be air-dropped behind enemy lines. His survival—if survival was possible—would depend on his German language skills.

Ruth had been procrastinating and not taking the wedding seriously. Mark had kept her at an annoying and frustrating distance. He had seen her as often as possible, introducing her as his fiancée, going through all the motions, but without the passion, the uncontrollable desire that she had sensed when they first got together. How could he be so controlled? Though she hadn't said so to him, she wasn't sure if she would go through with the wedding, so she hadn't made the few preparations they had agreed on and hadn't even shopped for a dress.

Now he had one day to pack and leave. He seemed so wrapped up in his concerns about the war and the logistics of getting to Fort Bragg on time that he wasn't thinking of her at all. He said there was no time to get married right away. She knew very well that they could catch a cab to City Hall and wait in line for a justice of the peace and maybe get married in a couple hours if they were lucky. But he didn't even consider that possibility. She thought he was backing out. He probably had known that these orders were coming, and he welcomed them This was his excuse, his way of jilting her.

Then he called from the airport and confessed that he was only twenty; that June 5 would be his twenty-first birthday. That was why they had to wait until then. His parents wouldn't give permission. He was ashamed to admit that, but he was even more ashamed that he hadn't told her this before.

He sounded so vulnerable, so sensitive, so apologetic—so Ashley Wilkes. She loved both the men he had it in him to be—both Ashley and Rhett Butler.

His baritone voice, as he once again pledged his love for her, gave her a thrill. She let loose her pent-up enthusiasm over the phone. She would quit her job and catch a train to North Carolina. The train was far cheaper than air, and they needed to watch their expenses. It was good he had gotten his commission; the pay increase would make a big difference. She could type and take shorthand far faster than an ordinary secretary. With her skills, she could get a job anywhere, even in North Carolina. She could make $80, maybe $90, maybe even $100 per month. They needed to be frugal, to budget, to avoid unnecessary expenses. She should have saved. *They* should have saved but hadn't. They had been caught up in the emotion of the moment, wanting to enjoy one day at a time. But they were going to be married now, in just a few weeks, and practical considerations were paramount. They were on their own now, together. She would borrow Emily's dress—there was no need to buy a new one. Emily could take time off from her job, and the two of them could go to North Carolina on the same train. She'd prefer not to have to ride in a train alone, certainly not that long. And Emily could stay until the wedding. June 5—that damned date, that blessed date. And Mark should let Uncle Adolph know, so he could come, too. No need to worry about the Aunties showing up; that was too far for them to consider going. That was a blessing. Would Mark be able to get a few days leave so they could have a honeymoon? She had heard good things about Myrtle Beach in South Carolina. Maybe that was close enough. She would research that before leaving. And she would locate and reserve a place in a rooming house in Fayetteville. No point in looking for an apartment; there was no telling how long he'd be stationed there. If and when he shipped out, she would head back to Philadelphia and wait for him there until he got back. As an officer, once he was married, he would be entitled to free married housing on the base, or a housing allowance so they could pay for a place to live off base. There was so much to do, and so little time. Just twenty days until June 5. She would pack everything she could in two suitcases and put everything else she needed in a trunk that she'd ship ahead. Anything else she would leave with Emily. It might take as long as a week to deal with everything. Expect her and Emily to arrive around May 22.

And when he got out of the Army, the GI Bill would pay for college for him, and then he would be able to get a good job. Then they would be able to pay for childcare while she went to college. This was a relay race, and Mark would have the baton first. They would get a typewriter, and she would do secretarial work at home, and he would work weekends and maybe nights. They would both get college degrees and good jobs. And they would live happily ever after.

During that frantic week of preparations, Ruth started to smoke regularly, a reminder that she was no longer the good little girl from East Falls, who did everything her Aunties wanted.

***

Most army bases were dominated by draftees and recruits. The latter volunteered knowing they would be drafted soon and wanting to have some choice in what they would be asked to do. They didn't want to wind up in combat surrounded by undependable, ne're-do-well draftees.

But Fort Bragg was the home of the 82nd Airborne—gung-ho military men who loved military life, its structure and discipline. They took pride in their service and their rank and didn't want to leave the Army, at least not until they had put in twenty years and were guaranteed retirement income. When the war ended, the citizen soldiers would go home, but these professionals hoped to be among those who were asked to stay and serve as the backbone of the peacetime Army.

Mark and a handful of others fresh from German-language training felt out of place here. They had no dreams of becoming airborne rangers. They hoped to never be in a kill-or-be-killed situation. They had no desire to "see action." They would prefer if they could luck out and spend the duration of the war behind a desk state-side. If called upon, they would do what they had to do, but they hoped they would never be called on.

Mark was afraid of heights. He felt queasy looking out a tenth-floor window. Every night after he got his orders, his sleep was interrupted repeatedly—not by nightmares of combat, but rather by nightmares of falling from a great height with a parachute that didn't open, toward rapidly approaching sharp rocks already strewn with mangled bodies. He didn't tell Ruth, not wanting to alarm her even more than she was alarmed already. On the flight from Philadelphia, the first time he had been in a plane, he'd kept his eyes shut, clenched his teeth, and prayed that he wouldn't throw up. Until they were married, he'd live on base, and she off base.

During the interminable two weeks before the wedding, Ruth shared a bed with Emily in a rooming house in Fayetteville.

They needed to get a new blood test and a new marriage license for North Carolina.

"Maybe the results will be different this time," Ruth suggested. "Maybe they made a mistake the first time, and our Rh is compatible."

"Impossible," Mark concluded.

"Improbable, not impossible. Human error."

"Don't get your hopes up," he dismissed the thought, also wanting to dismiss the possibility that the clean bill of health for venereal disease might have been in error.

Fayetteville was in the middle of nowhere: scrub pine, flat, and desolate, with military planes flying low overhead. Trucks and armored personnel carriers on the street, the sound of artillery and rifles on the firing range. Housing was hard to find and expensive. They couldn't afford a car or taxis. Mark hitchhiked back and forth from the base, and the general store was a mile and a half away from the rooming house. She wore an army surplus backpack to carry the groceries home. Emily was around very little. She hung out at a bar, where there were many soldiers and few women. She enjoyed the attention as she danced with one after another. For her, this was a merry holiday.

The days dragged on, then suddenly it was the morning of June 5. Mark hitchhiked to the rooming house, then walked with Ruth and Emily to a clapboard Baptist church a few blocks away. Just in time, Uncle Adolph, Margery, who he had finally married , and Margery's daughter Judy arrived in a brand-new red four-door convertible Oldsmobile.

As Ruth walked up the aisle, a platoon ran by outside shouting, "I wanna be an airborne ranger, live the life of guts and danger! Airborne ranger, life of danger!"

Ruth looked scared and uncertain. Mark wasn't sure if she would go through with it.

He was scared, too.

For all the waiting they had done, it felt like they had run into this precipitously.

When the preacher asked her if she would take Mark Brehm Hocker as her husband, "for richer or for poorer, in sickness and in health, till death do you part," another platoon marched by shouting in cadence, "Shout out, one two; shout out three four; shout out one two three four; shout out!" The preacher waited patiently for the noise to die down, then repeated the question.

She looked like she might have second thoughts, that she'd never say, "I do," so Mark lunged forward and kissed her, and the preacher said, "I now pronounce you man and wife." They laughed, and now they were married.

PART THREE ~ Married Life

Chapter Eighteen—Invasion

June 1944, Myrtle Beach, SC

Adolph was exuberant. He would pay for the honeymoon suite at the best hotel in Myrtle Beach, and he would drive Mark and Ruth there so they could have their first night in style. They left right after the wedding.

With normal traffic on the country roads, the 120-mile trip would take about four hours. But this was wartime, with gasoline tightly rationed, so there were few cars on the road. Uncle Adolph, as usual, was an exception. He had won ration coupons at poker and wanted to use them while they still had value, figuring the war would end soon. After vacationing at Myrtle Beach for a week, he, Margery, and Judy would drive back to Miami.

The car was crowded, but crowded could be fun, as Ruth soon realized. She sat on Mark's lap, although she could have squeezed into the seat beside him. As the car hit bumps on the country road, and as she periodically adjusted her position, they enjoyed contact and pressure in intimate realms, which they acknowledged with quick hungry kisses. The ceremony had conveyed to them society's permission to enjoy pleasures that before had been forbidden. Ruth looked forward to being alone with him, flesh to flesh, and learning what their bodies were meant to do. She was very happy to be married to this man.

They arrived in time for lunch at the Ocean Forest Hotel—marble-columned entrance, crystal chandeliers, extensive garden, stable with horses, large swimming pool, golf course, and a beach that stretched as far as the eye could see. The structure stood alone, its central tower visible for miles, clad in white paint like a character from "The Great Gatsby" clad in a white tuxedo.

They took three rooms—Adolph and Margery, Ruth and Mark, and Judy and Emily.

Judy and Emily, who were eighteen and nineteen, had bonded on the ride. They quickly changed into bathing suits and headed to the beach, which was swarming with unattached muscular young men with GI haircuts. They hung out there and at Pawleys Island Pavilion, a wooden structure, among the dunes, for dancing and drinking.

When Ruth and Margery went to the ladies' room together, Adolph gave Mark some last-minute advice. "Believe me, Ruth wants it as much as you do, but you're both too uptight and self-conscious. Loosen up. Buy a bottle of rum at the bar. Charge it to my room. Drink and get her to drink. Then get naked. I wouldn't be surprised if the two of you have never seen each other naked before. Take her clothes off and then yours, with the lights on. Then nature will take its course. And don't forget to use a condom." Adolph handed him a fistful, which Mark awkwardly stuffed into his pocket.

After Adolph and Margery left for the nearby Washington Park Racetrack, Mark and Ruth went to their room. There they drank rum, kissed, and groped. Neither of them had had hard liquor before. The rum was sweet; they liked the taste and drank quickly.

They ducked under the covers to take off their clothes—touching and being touched was far less intimidating than seeing and being seen. Mark dug a condom out of his pocket. He had read about them in marriage manuals and back when he was interested in Daisy, he had carried one in his wallet, just in case. But he had never opened such a package or tried to use such a thing. He held it up and stared at it in amused disbelief. "It's a balloon." He laughed, and she laughed, too.

Then he blew it up like a balloon, tied it shut, and they bounced it back and forth between them on the bed, like a beach ball.

Then he jumped up, modestly pulled his trousers on, took more condoms out of his pocket, ran to the bathroom, and filled them with water. Ruth wrapped a sheet around her, and the two of them went onto the balcony, where they tossed the water balloons, one by one, to the ground, fifteen stories below. They landed, with loud splats, on the patio by the pool, and soaked the sunbathers, who stared up at the sky, through their sunglasses, amazed that it was raining on such a sunny day.

Mark and Ruth laughed hard, hugging and kissing, and rolling on the floor, until they fell asleep, exhausted from the emotional stress, and woozy from the rum.

They slept through supper and didn't wake until morning when their phone rang. It was Adolph, "Have you read the headlines?"

"What?"

"You're famous."

"What?"

"You're page one news. 'Invasion successful.'"

"What?"

"Oh, come on, wake up, kid. You've had your fun. And now it turns out to be a cosmic joke. You guys are in sync with the universe. The invasion. _The Invasion._ They're landing on the beaches of Normandy, wave after wave. They've broken through. They're calling it D-Day. Congratulations."

Mark admitted on the phone, "Our invasion didn't quite make it."

"Good god! How is that possible?"

Ruth wrapped herself in a sheet and ducked into the bathroom to put on her bathing suit.

When she came out, Mark stared in surprise and delight. This was the first time that sober and alert, he had seen her nearly naked. She looked so good that he felt intimidated. This was like waking up and finding himself married to a pinup model or a movie star.

In the lobby, on their way out to the beach, Mark bought a sketch pad and pencils. As they sat on lounge chairs under an umbrella, he drew her repeatedly—first cartoon style, then realistic. After a while, he didn't need to look at her to draw a recognizable likeness of her.

"I didn't know you were that good," she said, admiring his work.

"I didn't know you were that beautiful."

Ruth had never been to a beach before. She had never swum in salt water. She had never even seen the ocean or the curve of the horizon. But she lay listless, idle, and happy, covered in suntan lotion, basking in the sun. The thought, Is this who you are? Is this who you want to be? flitted through her head. She shrugged that thought away, savoring her laziness. She was tempted to swim but didn't have the energy or the will to stand up and walk toward the waves to get her feet wet, much less to swim. And watching Mark as he sketched her, she was tempted to write-sketch him, which she had never done of him, and which she hadn't done at all for several years. But the waves made her think of Virginia Woolf, and there was even a lighthouse in the distance, and the rocks scattered along the beach made her think of Woolf's weighted-down pockets as she walked out to sea to kill herself. "Carpe diem," she told herself. "Carpe diem and nightem. Carpe Markem." She chuckled, shut her eyes, and enjoyed the sun.

The two of them spent the morning deliciously idle, soaking up the sun, holding hands, punctuated with drinks and snacks delivered by white-uniformed beach waiters. They watched the waves as the tide came in. Brown pelicans soared high, then dove for fish. They watched passing ships of all sizes and talked about one day taking a cruise together. Ruth said she'd like to go around the world.

They joined Adolph and Margery for lunch in the hotel restaurant.

When Ruth and Margery headed to the ladies' room, Mark told Adolph, "No more advice, please. I'll do it my own way. I'll take it slow and easy. Maybe I'll sketch her nude and, sooner or later, instinct will take over, and we'll do what people have been doing forever. There's no need for an instruction manual. We'll do what comes naturally, when it feels natural to do it—no rush, no pressure."

Meanwhile, in the ladies' room, Margery lectured Ruth. "Tell him what you want."

"And how am I supposed to know what I want?"

"Come on. You can't be that naive."

"My mother died when I was ten. A girl needs a mother at a time like this."

"Well, you could read, for God's sake."

"My Aunt Olive gave me *How to Cook a Husband*, but that book explained how to avoid having sex with your husband, not how to do it. I think it was supposed to be funny."

"And you've had no practice?"

"That would be immoral." Ruth was taken aback.

"Oh, bull. You wouldn't play baseball without practice. Do you even know how to put a condom on him? You can be damned sure that he doesn't know how to do it himself. From what Adolph tells me, he's as clueless as you are."

"We were born for one another."

"Born to drive one another crazy."

Margery tipped a waitress to get a banana, then she demonstrated how to put a condom on it. She explained that the first time, they should make a game of getting naked. "Take one another's clothes off one item at a time, pausing to appreciate the body parts as they're revealed, appreciating with words and with your hands, then your lips, then your tongue. Yes, your tongue should go everywhere, and his should as well. And if he doesn't catch on, tell him, for God's sake. When he's in the state he's going to be in, he'll do anything for you. Enjoy it but go slowly. One step at a time. You've got to train him. Two steps forward, then one step back. The backing off is important. Watch the meter."

"What meter?"

"The built-in one. You want it to get hard so it can do its business. But this is a rookie you're dealing with. Don't let him get too hard too soon or he'll just squirt on the bed."

"How am I to control that?"

"Baseball. Talk baseball."

Ruth laughed, "Mark started talking about baseball when we were getting into bed in New York."

"I'm not surprised, Adolph coached him on that. He wanted to teach him how to self-regulate. I guess that didn't work. So, it's up to you, kid, until the two of you get some experience together and find your rhythm.

Rhythm's important, all kinds of rhythm. Figure you're learning to dance together and play duets and sing in harmony, the music of love."

"Do you talk this way to your daughter?"

"Most definitely. And believe you me, she's well prepared to take on any man."

"But she's only—"

"Eighteen. Plenty old enough to do it and to know what she's doing. She won't let men get away with anything she doesn't want them to get away with. She's got the upper hand. In fact, she's got both hands, and she knows how to use them."

"I wouldn't want to compete with the likes of her."

"Well, right now, you don't have to compete with anyone. You lucked out. Not knowing what you were doing, you hooked him good. If you were surrounded by naked beautiful women, he would see only you. But that starry-eyed trance won't last forever. Haul him in. Enjoy, and let him enjoy. Get him good and addicted to you."

"Okay. I'll try it tonight."

"For God's sake, don't wait until night. Take him to your room and do him now. And don't get uptight if he blows his wad too soon again, which he probably will. Act like that's natural. Act like it's sexy, like everything about him is sexy."

***

Ruth forgot the condom. She forgot everything she had been told, everything she had imagined. They did it three times before supper, with luxurious, sensuous pauses.

The first time was awkward and painful for Ruth, but she didn't dare tell Mark when it hurt. Was she doing something wrong? Was she good at this? Would she ever be good at this? Then, far sooner than she had expected, it was over. She had done it. What a relief.

The second time, she was able to relax, to stop thinking so much, to enjoy the sensations. She got into it, like swimming—the visceral muscular pleasure of it, the carefree forgetting. She enjoyed the sheer physicality, the luxury of being nothing more or less than a physical entity. Then came the high of caressing him as well as being caressed, electricity in her fingertips, in his fingertips; she an object of his pleasure, and he an object of hers. She enjoyed the high, the heightened sensitivity, the back and forth of touching and being touched; then release and the relaxing warm aftermath of cuddling,

The third time, they went slowly, and the intensity grew as they became more familiar with one another and with the needs and capabilities of their own bodies and of their bodies together—lust feeding on lust. They learned, without deliberately trying to learn, how to heighten one another's pleasure and stamina—not wanting it to end, swimming farther and farther, with ease and strength and delight, immersed in sensations, their own and one another's.

Living the moment, enjoying the moment. Visceral, all-consuming, then climax and tender touch, still high and happy together. "This is what I am alive for," she thought. "Nothing else matters. Life is good. God is good. Amen. Ah, men."

They skipped supper that evening—neither of them was hungry. They bought matching straw hats in a shop in the lobby, then stretched out on lounge chairs on the beach, holding hands as the sun set and the stars rose.

Ruth now saw the world differently than she had before. Some men were good. Mark was very good. It was natural for people to hunger for physical love. Sometimes that led to mistakes but sometimes to love when your body-mate was your soulmate. She and Mark were incredibly lucky.

She wondered, did her mother ever know this kind of happiness? Did she have a clue it was possible? God did a good job making people this way. Praise the Lord.

19 ~ Inconceivable

Summer 1944, Fayetteville, NC

Adolph, Margery, and Judy drove back to Miami. Emily went home to Philadelphia. Ruth and Mark returned to Fayetteville.

Now that they were married, they were on the waiting list for married officer housing on the base, but the list was long. So, they squeezed into the room that Ruth had rented before the wedding.

Ruth wanted to learn how to cook. She tried to make spaghetti with raisins, the way she thought her Aunties did. She bought the ingredients, as best she could remember, but she only had a double-burner hot plate and two small saucepans. She failed miserably. They ate it anyway and laughed about it, although she had spent a week's food budget buying what she thought she needed in far greater quantities than she needed. For the rest of their stay in Fayetteville, she limited her cooking to heating canned foods—such as Dinty Moore Stew, Spam, and vegetables—and making coffee.

She wanted their tiny room to feel like it was uniquely theirs. But this wasn't their furniture, and the room was so small, they couldn't turn the bed sideways, and they weren't allowed to put nails in the wall to hang pictures. They taped to the wall sketches of her that Mark had drawn at Myrtle Beach, and snapshots of the two of them that Judy took with the Brownie camera she gave them for their wedding.

Then she took a different approach, creating habits, rather than depending on the physical environment to make their little room feel like a home and make them feel like a couple—truly connected, and fated to be together, not just randomly joined. She started the ritual of saying grace before meals. The household she grew up in had been helter-skelter, with too many kids to all sit together at the little kitchen table. But she remembered the family meals at Mark's parents' house and wanted that kind of stability and regularity in their life. They even sat down and said grace at breakfast, and took turns on who said it, holding hands for it. And immediately after each meal, they did the dishes together—she washed, and he dried.

At night, before getting into bed, they both kneeled for prayers. Then they took turns reading out loud to one another from novels. The challenge was to see how many pages you could read before your bedmate seduced you into physical pleasure. Ruth held the record—two full pages. She also chose the novels.

A few weeks after the wedding, Ruth's period was late. She both hoped and feared that she might be pregnant. It was important to her that she have a child, even if she could only have one, and she would be anxious until she knew for sure that they could conceive. And the only way to know was to get pregnant. But, as Margery had pointed out, pregnancy would abruptly change their lives, and this was a difficult time—learning to live together and without the support of family or friends. And, they were stationed in this North Carolina wilderness, where every day logistics were difficult being three miles from Fort Bragg and a mile and a half from the nearest general store. She wondered how could she cope if she were pregnant? And if and when Mark got shipped to Europe, she'd have no choice but to move back with her Aunties, who were furious with her for her lies and her elopement. She'd never hear the end of it. In addition, the Aunties had no idea how to deal with pregnancy and newborns. But, heaven forbid, if Mark were to die, the baby would be all she had left of the love of her life. She wanted and needed to have their child, despite her total ignorance about caring for a baby.

Mark was protective, nurturing, and rational. After the first invasion at Myrtle Beach, even in the heat of passion, he used condoms even though Ruth tried to distract him. He couldn't be convinced to dispense with protection. Above all else, he wanted to take care of her. As long as the war went on, and he could be forced to leave her on short notice, it would be irresponsible to get her pregnant. But he couldn't stop himself from wanting to make love with her.

Every morning, Mark left at 5:30 and hitchhiked to the base. He had to leave early enough so he could arrive on time. If he didn't get a ride, he had to walk all three miles. Fortunately, that didn't happen often, and people went out of their way to pick up GIs in uniform.

For Ruth, the days were long and lonely. Aside from laundry and straightening up, there was nothing she needed to do, nothing she wanted to do. So, without telling Mark, who wouldn't want her wandering alone on country roads, she walked—and refused all offers of rides—to the base and stood outside the chain link fence around the area where trainees practiced jumping out of planes with parachutes. She took pictures with the Brownie camera, not knowing which one of the men drifting down to the ground in full army gear might be Mark. This activity helped relieve her anxiety since she saw hundreds land with nothing worse than twisted ankles. She'd surprise Mark with the photos when they were developed. After the war, those snapshots would be valued souvenirs of this time. They'd show them to their son—she was sure they would have a boy—and would tell him what it was like living through wartime.

On her second day taking pictures, she was arrested.

After a two-hour wait, she was led to a small room where a woman in an army uniform was waiting for her on the other side of an unpainted wooden table.

She didn't have ID on her. Why should she? She didn't drive; she didn't have a car. Why should she need to prove that she was an American citizen? What else could she be but American?

"German," replied the agent.

"As I told you, I am Ruth Hocker, born in the U.S. of A. on January 31, 1920. I'm an American, an English-speaking American with no accent at all."

"Your name is Hocker, a German name, and you do have an accent, ma'am, an accent the likes of which I've never heard before. And you've been observed near the perimeter of Fort Bragg, staring through the chain link fence for hours, taking photos of training exercises."

"But I'm an American citizen."

"We'll see about that."

"My husband is training in that field."

"So you say."

"I'm the wife of Second Lieutenant Mark Brehm Hocker."

"The letters in your pocketbook are addressed to a Miss Ruth Yates."

"That was my maiden name. We were married just a few weeks ago."

"Do you have a marriage certificate?"

"Not on me. Why would I carry my marriage certificate with me?"

"And why would you take photos of training exercises at a U.S. Army facility during wartime?" The agent pulled dozens of photos from her briefcase and placed them face-up on the table in front of Ruth.

"You had them developed?" Ruth asked.

"Of course. Now take a good look."

"Yes."

"You can read English?"

"Of course."

"And that sign that appears in photo after photo, what does it say?"

"Photography of any kind prohibited."

"Well done. And you should think hard about the meaning of those words while sitting in your holding cell."

"Can I call someone?"

"Who?"

"My husband."

"Does he have a phone?"

"He's on duty now, in training exercises."

"And will he have a phone when he gets home tonight?"

"No. We don't have a phone in our rooming house. There's a public phone a block away."

"So, who are you going to call?"

"Can I call his superior officer?"

"Do you know that person's name?"

"I don't remember."

"Do you know his unit?"

"Yes, he's attached to the 82nd Airborne."

"Congratulations. Two-thirds of the men on this base are in the 82nd. We need more than that. But I'm sure your memory will sharpen while you sit in your cell."

"Surely you must have a list of who's stationed here."

"This is the Army, lady. Don't take anything for granted in the Army. Do you have any idea how many men ship in and out of here every day? We're human, lady. The Army is human. We don't have some big machine keeping track of everybody and everything—just people like you and me, busy people. We'll make inquiries. We'll go through channels. Just sit tight."

"How long might that take?"

"A day or two, maybe three."

"This is inconceivable," she muttered.

A soldier with "MP" on his shoulders led her away.

"But I'm pregnant," she shouted back at the agent. "I'm pregnant. I can't sleep in a jail cell. It will be bad for the baby."

She never got her Brownie camera or her photos back.

Arriving home that night, Mark had no idea what had happened. After looking everywhere, in case Ruth was running an errand or had gone for a walk, without leaving a note—which would be totally out of character—he called the local police and tried to file a missing persons' report. But he was told he couldn't do that until the party in question had gone missing for forty-eight hours.

After two frantic, sleepless nights, Mark got a message from his battalion commander that his pregnant wife had been mistakenly detained on suspicion of spying. When Mark retrieved her at battalion headquarters, she was disheveled and penitent.

"Why didn't you tell me you're pregnant?" he asked, while an MP drove them home in a jeep.

"Not now," she pleaded. "Just hold me tight. Hold me tighter than tight."

Alone in their room, she admitted, "I lied. I thought they would pay more attention to me if they thought I was pregnant."

"You thought lying to MPs was a good idea?"

"It was a white lie, a well-meaning lie."

"Jesus."

"You never swear."

"Now I do"

"You're disappointed in me."

"I'm disappointed you aren't pregnant. And at the same time, I'm relieved you aren't because this is no time for that. And I'm relieved that you're safe and we're back together again. I just lived through the worst two days of my life. Do you have any idea how worried I was?"

She didn't say she was sorry; she didn't need to. It was written on her face and in her every gesture. She led him by the hand to the bathroom down the hall where she started the water for the bathtub. She stripped and took off his clothes as well, and they squeezed into the tub together. She wrapped her legs around him. He scrambled out and got condoms. Then they fell asleep, together in the tub, with him inside her.

Two weeks later, before she had a chance to tell him that her period had finally come, he told her, "I'll be shipping out on Monday."

"To Europe?" she moaned in fear.

"To Minnesota."

"What?"

"The Military Intelligence Service Language School at Fort Snelling, St. Paul, Minnesota. The invasion in Europe went better than expected. That was what I was training for. No one knows how long the war in Europe will drag on, but the tide has turned and there's not as much need for German-speaking officers. The focus is shifting to Japan. They must figure I'm some sort of genius with languages, and I've already had the parachute training. So, they're sending me to the language school at Fort Snelling. In eighteen months, they plan to teach me enough Japanese to help in our invasion of Japan. They'll parachute me behind enemy lines."

He hesitated. Her face was blank. She didn't answer.

"Wake up, honey. This is good news."

"Good news that you're going to be air-dropped behind enemy lines in Japan?"

"One thing at a time. Lots can happen in eighteen months. What matters for now is that we're getting out of here. We're going to a city … a real city. And I hear chances are good we can get married housing on the base. Pack your bags, lady. Minnesota, here we come."

20 ~ Second Honeymoon

September 1944, Fort Snell, MN

The language school was moving from Camp Savage, fifteen miles south of Minneapolis, to Fort Snelling in St. Paul. Mark would have three weeks of free time before the school reopened.

"Shall we check out the club?" Mark asked, when they finished moving in.

"The club?" Ruth replied.

"The O Club."

"There's a club on base? Hallelujah!"

When they got there, she asked, "How is this possible? Fort Snell has thousands of soldiers and this heavenly little club isn't crowded. That doesn't add up."

"The O Club is the Officers' Club. I thought you understood that."

"Just officers?"

"Of course. It's off-limits to enlisted men."

"And there was something like this at Fort Bragg?"

"Of course. Bigger and better. But we couldn't walk three miles each way to get there and back. And taxis would have cost too much. This one's two blocks from our house."

"So, this is a class thing? Only for the privileged?"

"Yessiree, and now we're the privileged."

"That sounds like East Falls."

"And what do you mean by that?"

"Where I grew up, the rich folks lived in mansions on the hilltop, and the poor folks lived down below in row houses on cobblestone streets. Different classes; different worlds. I had no idea the Army was like that. It doesn't have to be that way. I think that's morally repugnant."

"You really believe that? And when we were at Myrtle Beach at the swankiest hotel around, thanks to Uncle Adolph, should we have shared our room with the poor? Was it morally repugnant for us to luxuriate like that while the poor suffered?"

"That was different."

"And when you were growing up in East Falls, should the Kellys have shared their wealth with their neighbors? Did you expect that of them? Or did you envy them and wish you were in their place?"

"But this isn't fair."

"I'm sorry, honey. That's the way things are. We were down; now we're up. Let's enjoy the privileges we're lucky enough to have."

"But isn't there some way to make it all fair?"

"People have been asking that question for a long time. I'd rather enjoy what we've got than think about how to fix the system. Do you want to dance, or shall we eat first?"

"Eat? They serve food here, too?"

"As long as we're stationed here, there's no need for you to cook."

"The Lord be praised!" She mockingly brought her hands together as if in prayer and looked to Heaven.

"Amen," answered Mark.

"But it still bothers me that the enlisted men are excluded. I'd think it would be important for everyone to eat and play together, to build camaraderie, a sense of brotherhood."

"It's deliberate. The powers-that-be don't want officers fraternizing with enlisted men. An officer who goes out of his way to do so can get in trouble."

"But that makes no sense."

"Well, the rationale is that in battle, an officer who is friends with his men might hesitate to give the orders he needs to because that would put his friends in jeopardy. He wouldn't want to be responsible for them getting killed."

"That's even more morally repugnant."

"You'd rather not eat or dance here? And you don't want to use the tennis courts or the swimming pool, either?"

"Swimming pool?" she lighted up. "Oh, what the hell."

"Hell it is then. Let's eat, drink, and be merry."

This fort was known as the country club of the Army. Officers had access to a golf course, tennis courts, and a swimming pool. Its offices, warehouses, rail yards, barracks, parade ground, and recreational facilities extended over a fifteen-acre site. Many of the buildings were solid brick and stone structures, some of them dating back to 1820 on land bought from the Sioux. Streetcars ran frequently between the Fort and St. Paul and Minneapolis, the two largest cities in the state.

The golf course was carefully designed and immaculately maintained, a refuge of green in the midst of the city; a delight to the eye even for those who didn't play. For Ruth, the tennis courts called up memories of the Kelly estate on the hilltop in East Falls where she'd learned to play tennis as a guest. She had been one of the poor neighbors graciously allowed an occasional taste of what it was like to be born into wealth.

As an officer's wife, the courts and the pool were hers, as much hers as anyone else's.

Class distinctions hadn't bothered her before. She took for granted that the way things were was the way they had always been and always would be. She was one of the have-nots, and she'd have to make the most of what she had. Now, with Mark's military promotion, she had been promoted to a new lifestyle and a new social world. That was unexpected and disorienting. She wished that everyone could be so lucky, and she felt sorry for those who weren't. She also felt guilty that she enjoyed these new privileges so much. But she did enjoy them.

The officer's pay had finally kicked in, plus they had a three-bedroom townhouse apartment for free. They could walk up the street and pick up free furniture from the sidewalk; furniture that other families, suddenly reassigned, had no time to sell and that they left for others. The O Club was two blocks away, and the PX, with merchandise of all kinds at far lower prices than in city stores, was three blocks in the other direction.

"God," she exclaimed as they slow-danced to "Thanks for the Memories" at the O Club on their first night at Fort Snell.

"Please don't swear," he chuckled, giving her a quick kiss, and nuzzling her neck.

"That's not a swear. That's a prayer of thanks. This is like a second honeymoon. We'll have three weeks together here before you have to do anything. And then we get to live in this place for a year and a half. This is the closest to heaven I've ever seen."

For the first time, Ruth and Mark made friends as a married couple.

Rachel and Frank Liebowitz, who lived in the other half of their duplex, had a five-month-old daughter. Short and round, Rachel was always carrying her daughter, either slung over her shoulder or in a papoose pack on her front.

Ruth found it reassuring that an experienced mother lived nearby who could give advice, if she needed it, on pregnancy and care of newborns. When they first met and Rachel recognized Ruth's intense interest in the baby, she let Ruth hold her. That was the first time Ruth had ever held a baby. Rachel also lent her the new book that was the current bible of new mothers—*The Common Sense Book of Baby and Child Care* by Benjamin Spock. Ruth hadn't had a friend to confide in since Girls' High, and that was six years before. Talking about babies and married life made Ruth feel grownup and intimately close to her new neighbor.

A few days after they had moved in, as they were dragging home a nearly-new blue velvet three-cushion sofa they had found a block away, Ruth and Mark were greeted and helped by their neighbors on the other side—Eileen and Max Dombrowski. "Do you play tennis?" was the first question Eileen asked.

Eileen was over six feet—a couple inches taller than her husband Max, and half a foot taller than Ruth. She had long thin legs and her tennis skirt scandalously only reached half-way down her thighs. Her black hair was cut short. Eileen was an imposing figure in tennis shoes and even more so in high heels, which she wore whenever she was at the Officer's Club. Penetrating dark brown eyes. Prominent nose and jaw.

By wartime standards, the Dombrowskis were an old married couple, having linked up before the war when they were in college at Oberlin. Eileen had majored in fine arts and Max in Asian languages. He had guessed Japan was going to be important and that was why he chose his major.

Max was muscular, self-confident, and very much in control of his life. Thanks to ROTC, Max had been an officer for over a year. Because of his knowledge of Japanese, he hoped to cut short his course of study here, get a fast promotion to first lieutenant, and get to choose his next assignment. He hoped to serve the rest of the war in or near Washington, D.C., dealing with Japanese documents.

Eileen was vocal about not wanting children. She didn't want to bring a child into a world like this—with all the death and destruction of war. "Besides," she said, "Ours is a marriage of convenience. We get along fine, but we aren't in love. Nothing of the kind. Romantic love is a myth, a fairy tale. It's self-delusion. Sex and reproduction are real. True love is as much a lie as Santa Claus, the Easter Bunny, and magic. There is no magic and never was."

"But you seem like the perfect couple," Ruth objected, "like you were made for one another."

"Yes, we bought into the romantic love thing back in college when we got married. Then war broke out on both sides of the world, and Max was in the Army, and I knew damn well that despite all his grand plans about a safe desk job in D.C., he was going to be killed. And the more I believed in love and believed I loved him, the more that would hurt. That's when I realized that I didn't love him—not really, not starry-eyed romantically. As a practical matter, we could have fun; we could have sex. But he isn't irreplaceable. When he's gone, I'll hook up with someone else and have fun with that guy. That's what life is all about—having fun while we're here."

"That's so crass and clinical. I couldn't live that way," objected Ruth.

"That's the way of the world. That's the way people are made. Romantic love is a recent invention. Marriage used to be arranged by parents—a practical matter, a business transaction. Now we delude ourselves that there's a special someone we're drawn to magically, that that's the one we should live with and partner with and have children with. People need to believe in something bigger than themselves, something magical that gives meaning to their lives. So, when faith in God faded, people started to believe in true love and soulmates, as a substitute for religion, a new opium of the people. That's all nonsense, total nonsense."

The first time Ruth played tennis with Eileen, Eileen insisted on going straight to game play, with no warmups. She rushed the net with an intimidating grin, daring Ruth to try to get anything past the reach of her long arms.

Ruth missed her first dozen shots. She didn't even touch the ball with her racket. It wasn't that Eileen was that good, but the court had an asphalt surface, while Ruth was used to the Kellys' clay courts. The ball bounced higher and with a different spin. It took her a while to adjust. She was down five games to none before she got the feel of it. Then she figured out how to deal with Eileen's height and reach and learned to ignore her intimidating grimaces. She fought back with lobs over Eileen's head and well-placed taps to her right or left; never a hard put-away shot. Her shots barely cleared the net and just stayed in bounds. She sent Eileen racing and lunging from one side of the court to the other. After two hours, Ruth won the set 20-18.

That became the pattern of their future matches. Technically, Eileen was, by far, the better player, with a more forceful stroke, and with form that came from years of lessons, plus the advantage of her height. But Ruth won consistently, often by the smallest of margins. It was gratifying doing a David-and-Goliath and defeating her Goliath time after time. That success made Ruth more confident in other aspects of her life, more willing to defend her opinions and stand up for what she felt was right.

21 ~ Military Just Is

September 1944, Fort Snell, MN

In a very short while, the privileges accorded an officer's wife became a normal part of Ruth's world. She took them for granted, as if they had always been hers, as if this new social world she found herself in was hers by right and forever, and the world of East Falls was a temporary aberration in the distant past, fading quickly from her memory.

The rituals that had given her comfort in Fayetteville were forgotten here. There were no dishes to wash and dry, aside from an occasional glass or cup. They ate their meals at the O Club, where it would have been awkward to hold hands and say grace. All the little habits that she had built as a bridge to the world of her childhood disappeared.

She was a lady of leisure now. She went swimming shortly after Mark left for class in the morning. The pool was empty then, which was the way she liked it—a time alone, with no need to talk, no need to think, pure relaxation. Then she went to the post library and read best sellers like *Forever Amber*, and Agatha Christie mysteries. She was tempted to write. She intended to get to that eventually. But there was no hurry. If she had a personal slogan, it would have been "Never do today what you can put off until tomorrow." She was feeling deliciously, luxuriously lazy.

Mark got home soon after five p.m. Happy hour, with low-priced drinks, started at the O Club as soon as the workday ended. That's when most officers headed to the Club for drinks, then dinner, more drinks, and dancing. Mark and Ruth spent their happy hours in bed together. After that, they ate and danced at the Club. Then they went home early to go to bed again; and they were in so much of a hurry to enjoy one another that they didn't pause to kneel and say their prayers.

On her fifth day of leisure, Ruth woke up on a sofa in the library and realized that she had slept the afternoon away. This wasn't working out as she had expected. There was no direction or purpose to what she was doing. Such reading was enjoyable as a break from doing something else—but she had nothing to do that this was a break from. Much as she had envied people rich enough to laze away the day, she wasn't temperamentally suited for such a life. She needed to be doing, accomplishing something, making progress of some kind.

Eileen worked as a copywriter at a Minneapolis ad agency. With Eileen's recommendation, Ruth got a part-time job there as a secretary. She worked afternoons so in the morning she could swim and do whatever else she wanted. She would be a lady of leisure mornings only.

At the ad agency, Ruth met fellow secretary Jane Hayashi whose husband was going to the Army language school. Jane, Ruth, and Eileen rode the streetcar together to and from work.

From talking to Jane, Ruth learned that at the language school, some, like Mark, were learning Japanese from scratch. But many more already knew Japanese and were learning how to use it for the benefit of the military—translating documents and listening to intercepted radio transmissions.

"The officers, both students and faculty, are all Americans," Jane explained, over sandwiches at lunch. "The enlisted men who teach Japanese or who are learning to translate for the war effort, are all descendants of immigrants from Japan. They were released from internment camps in exchange for their service. Their wives and parents and children are still being held in internment camps in California, too far away for them to visit. My husband, George, is fourth generation Japanese. I am second-generation. I was born in Minnesota where the internment order has not yet been enforced. George and I met and married when he was at Camp Savage before the language school moved here."

When Ruth met George, her surprise was evident—he had blue eyes and blond hair.

"One eighth Japanese," he explained, with a smile.

Jane was raised as an American, with little knowledge of or interest in Japanese language or culture or history. George knew the language because his parents had gone out of their way speak it at home, to maintain the family tradition from nearly a hundred years ago. When his family was forcibly moved to an internment camp, his knowledge of Japanese enabled him to get out of there.

Ruth was puzzled. Up until now, her attention had been focused on the war in Europe. She didn't blame all Germans for Hitler. And she didn't see any reason to blame all Japanese for Pearl Harbor. If America had interned everyone of German descent, Mark would be locked up in such a camp now. And her son, if she ever had one, would be subject to that as well.

One Saturday night, Ruth and Mark, Eileen and Max, Rachel and Frank went bowling at the O Club. Ruth had never bowled before. The group reserved a lane two days in advance.

Ruth had natural talent or beginner's luck. By the fifth frame, she was leading by two pins. Then she recognized the pinsetter—George. This was one of the chores that enlisted men got assigned, providing services to support the officers in entertainment as well as in work. Not only could they not belong to the Club, but they also had to perform servile chores like this as well.

After that, Ruth threw her balls in the gutter, pretending to be terrible at the sport so George wouldn't have to reset her pins and so the others wouldn't ask her to go bowling again.

That night, in bed, she confided to Mark, "If nevermind were real, I would undo all that."

"You mean your mother's secret all-powerful magic?"

She nodded and smiled. She didn't take that story her mother had told her any more seriously than Mark did. She knew this was just wishful thinking.

"And what would you undo, oh great and powerful wizardess?"

"The Japanese internment, the class system in the military, all social injustice everywhere."

He laughed, and she laughed with him.

"Of course I can't make that happen. I'm not that naive. But it bothers me when I see injustice, and I wish I could do something about it."

On Friday nights, after the O club, Ruth, Mark, Rachel, and Frank gathered in the living room at Eileen and Max's house. That was when the men had a chance to vent freely about their issues with the Army and the language school.

Eileen's husband, Max, thanks to what he learned in college, had passed the language tests without having to go through the coursework. That was what he had been hoping for. He expected to get training in document translation, which should land him a stateside assignment, probably in or near D. C. But instead, they put him in intercept training, listening to recordings of Japanese radio traffic. That was very difficult for someone who wasn't a native speaker, and, worse still, that could lead to him being shipped to the Pacific for combat duty.

Rachel's husband, Frank, had a Ph. D. in chemistry, but the Army had him doing accounting in the paymaster's office.

Mark, Frank, and Max had been lucky to get commissions in the midst of changing rules about who got such promotions and why. They all were second lieutenants, but none of them had a clue as to what to do if they were ever put in command of troops in combat.

"The Army's just one screw-up after another," complained Frank. "The needs, the talents, and the interests of the individual get lost in the maze of bureaucracy. We're treated like statistics, not people. They need X number of men trained in Y, but they have no regard for what that means to the individuals. Repeatedly, they put people in the wrong jobs, wasting their talent and their training."

Max countered, "Imagine what it must be like to be in charge of this massive operation—the challenge, in a democracy, to enlist, to train, to supply, to deploy ten to fifteen million civilians; to get them ready for combat and to make them willing to risk their lives. And you don't know how long this might last, or if you might need double or even triple that number. You must be prepared for a war that ends quickly, and also for one that drags on for years. You have to be prepared for success on the battlefield, and also for disaster. You must have the ability to recover from disaster.

"How do you get people who have learned to think for themselves to shift gears and obey total strangers? People who were taught, as kids, to not even speak to strangers. And how do you teach those strangers to know what orders to give in a multitude of situations, and to command obedience to the death, if necessary, while at the same time obeying orders from above?

"It's a complex dance. Imagine trying to choreograph a performance with fifteen million dancers? You need to get the right people with the right training and the right equipment to the right places at the right times."

Ruth spoke up, with an ironic laugh. "The Army? Are you kidding? When we were at Fort Bragg, they didn't even know who was on the base. They were drowning in paperwork."

"Yes," Max continued. "We've all seen screw-ups here state-side. Just imagine what it must be like in a war zone. The unexpected is happening every day everywhere. People are dying and getting wounded all the time. The wounded have to be taken care of. Replacements must be ready to fill the empty slots. The effort must go on despite losses. Survival in one area of the front depends on the others holding firm. Interdependence, not independence is what's needed.

"And those ten to fifteen million men are coming from very different backgrounds—rich and poor, educated and ignorant, with different religions and political views, who up to now have had prejudices and hatred against other groups in the nation, based on geography and race and belief. Now they now have to live together and fight side-by-side, their lives depending on one another. They have to go through that transformation as well as learn the skills necessary for combat in a matter of months.

"Would you want that job?" he asked. "Making sure all of that happens and pulling all those pieces together?"

"Count me out," Eileen piped in. "That's not my idea of fun."

Max went on, "And think of the people necessary to support the combatants at the front so they have food and water, and fuel and weapons, and ammunition, and the means to go from one place to another. It takes nine non-combatants in the background to put one soldier in the field.

"Justice and fairness are luxuries for peacetime. In wartime, you do what you've got to do and pass the beer."

Ruth objected, "If that's what war is like, and nothing can change that, then don't go to war in the first place."

Max countered, "Just wave your magic wand, sweetheart."

The men laughed. None of the women did.

22 ~ Arigato for the Memories

Fall 1944 to spring 1945, Fort Snell, MN

After three weeks of classes, Mark started having severe headaches and dreams that left him sweating, freezing, and shaking. He had been assigned to the language school because he came in at the top of his class in German, which led the military to presume that he was good at languages. But he was good at German for the same reason that George was good at Japanese—family tradition. Mark's father and grandfather spoke to one another in Pennsylvania Dutch and swore in that language. A German accent came naturally to Mark, and the vocabulary sounded familiar. In contrast, the characters and sounds of Japanese were totally foreign to him. The Japanese had three writing systems, not just one, and he couldn't make sense of any of them. For eight hours a day, he heard nothing but Japanese. That was the teaching method at this school—immersion. Whether you understood or not, you heard nothing but Japanese. It was like a sledgehammer to the brain. And all he could remember was the pain.

He broke down in tears and admitted to Ruth that he couldn't learn it. Those scratch marks weren't language. That noise wasn't language. This home, this life, they would lose it, all because of his stupidity. The Army would give him a gun and send him to the front as soon as he flunked out. He was as good as dead.

"Don't give up," she coached him. She was impatient at his weakness. "Show some backbone. I'll learn it too and drill you in your dialogues. I learned Latin and French. I can learn this. And you can, too, for God's sake. I'll invite Jane and George over often. You can practice speaking with George. And you're an artist, or you have the talent to be one. Don't let the foreign-looking writing get in your way. Think of it as art. Doodle it anywhere and everywhere. We're a team now; this matters to both of us. We'll work together and do it right."

He bit his lower lip, looked up at the ceiling, then looked her in the eye. "I'll try," he conceded.

"You're damned right you'll try. How do you say, 'I love you' in Japanese?"

"I don't know."

"Find out. Learn *kiss me*, and *hold me*, and *make love to me*. And learn to say whatever else you want to do with me or have me do to you. The only way you'll get it will be by asking for it in Japanese."

Ruth got copies of Mark's language manuals and phrase books from the post library. In Minneapolis, she bought a cheap cotton kimono at a costume store, so she could role-play as a geisha at night. She also got plastic replicas of Japanese swords so they could play samurai.

It turned out that Ruth was much better at Japanese than Mark was. Ruth took to it immediately. She was motivated. She couldn't let him fail. Studying Japanese together became another way for them to relate to one another; and for Ruth, it was also a matter of pride.

She went outside the curriculum to stimulate his interest. She memorized haiku in Japanese and helped him to memorize them. They made up tunes for the haiku and sang them together. Language study became part of their love play.

Ruth hadn't paid much attention to the war in the Pacific. The war in Europe was the imminent threat, where Mark would be sent and could die. Now her focus shifted. She needed to know what was going on over there. Who were these Japanese, and why was the United States at war with them? George gave Ruth a reading list. She found the books at the St. Paul Central Library. They included: *Tales of the Genji*, works of Lafcadio Hearn on Japanese culture, history books about the sudden opening of Japan to the modern western world. Ruth, whose concerns had rarely reached beyond her family and friends, found herself at the intersection of her personal life and the history of the world.

She read Ruth Benedict's *Patterns of Culture*, comparing systems of custom and belief of people she had never heard of before. Her own way of thinking, the way she was raised, the way she would probably raise her son, was not the only way. Right and wrong were relative to the values of a culture, and there were many cultures. She read *The Races of Mankind*, which Benedict wrote for U.S. troops, so they could understand the belief system of the enemy and understand that this was not a war of one race against another and that despite the war, all men were brothers.

Ruth Benedict. Margaret Meade. Women could become scholars and professors. When it came time for Ruth to go to college, she might take courses in anthropology. Being married and having a child, she wouldn't be able to go on research expeditions. But she was concerned about the damage being done to native cultures on South Pacific islands. Maybe one day she would be able to go there, maybe on a world cruise. And she imagined that Mark would study history, and how people made mistakes, based on misunderstandings and lies.

They would be a team.

23 ~ Death Wish

May to August 1945, Fort Snell, MN

On May 8, 1945, VE Day, the day when the war ended in Europe, Ruth and Mark got drunk and didn't use condoms.

Two weeks later, when her period didn't come, Ruth started to pray again before going to bed at night. She wanted a baby. She was ready for a baby. When she told Mark, he admitted that he was ready, too. So, they deliberately tried for her to get pregnant.

Now the entire war effort shifted to the Pacific, and the timetable for the war there was speeded up. Some courses were cut short. Max got orders, as a radio intercept translator. A battle was raging over Okinawa, and that was where he guessed he was going, though, officially, his destination was a secret.

Mark could get orders any day.

Six weeks after VE Day, Ruth still hadn't had her period. She didn't want to get the rabbit test, it cost too much, and why kill an innocent rabbit? She knew in her gut that she was pregnant, and soon a gynecologist would be able to hear the heartbeat.

The Battle of Okinawa ended on June 22, and that very day, Eileen got a package from Max—a silk kimono that he had sent to her from wherever he was stationed. She wore it, and Ruth wore her cotton one, and they all went to the O Club for a celebration of the victory at Okinawa, like the VE celebration—only this time Ruth didn't drink because she thought she was pregnant.

Eileen drank more than usual and was unsteady on her feet, so Ruth and Mark walked her home. There was an envelope taped to her front door—a telegram. She opened it distractedly. She was trying to remember a joke she wanted to tell, one that Max told all the time, about a bunch of guys marooned on an island.

When her eyes focused, she screamed.

Max had stepped on a land mine. He was dead.

"The fucking Japanese! The whole race should be obliterated."

Ruth and Mark stayed with her that night; Ruth in bed with her, and Mark on the sofa.

When Ruth woke up, Eileen wasn't in the bed. She found her in the bathroom. Eileen had slit her wrists. Mark called for an ambulance. There was lots of blood, but Eileen had botched it— she would pull through. Mark donated blood for her.

Ruth sat by Eileen's side at the hospital for three nights in a row. When Eileen was released, Ruth and Mark insisted that she sleep on their sofa. She shouldn't be alone. They heard Eileen scream in anger and sob in grief repeatedly throughout the night.

Ruth found it ironic that Eileen, who had claimed that romantic love was a fake, was so deeply in love that she couldn't bear to live now her mate was gone. Her skepticism must have been an act, a defense mechanism, a way to deal with a possibility she couldn't face.

Eileen stayed with them day after day, incapable of functioning on her own, moping and moaning, both awake and asleep—a continuous reminder of her loss. This was the first time someone they knew well, someone their own age, had died. It made their own mortality real to them, especially Mark's mortality, as rumors persisted of another wave of orders to the Pacific.

They didn't talk to one another about that fear—talking would make it real. But Ruth knew very well that, given his role in the Army, Mark would probably die soon. She couldn't think about the practicalities of the matter—what she could and should do in that eventuality, and what she should do now to get ready for it. The enormity of the possibility that he would be dead—not here, absent forever, a part of her ripped away—was more than she could deal with. To avoid thinking about it, she buried herself in household tasks like Mark's mother did—going from one chore to another, non-stop. She didn't take breaks. She avoided opportunities for idle chatter that could remind her of the likelihood that loomed so near.

Fortunately, there was little chance for chatter. Eileen wouldn't talk to anyone, just muttering to herself. And Rachel was focused on her toddler daughter. For her and Frank, everyday life was too hectic for the luxury of worrying about anything else.

As for Jane and George, they never complained about their own plight. Rather, they were wrapped up in worries about his family in an internment camp in California, doing whatever they could to earn extra money to send there. They were busy all the time, and they found it was good to be busy all the time.

Ruth went to Dr. Jones, Rachel's gynecologist in St. Paul, and he confirmed that she was pregnant; he could hear the heartbeat. She got him to prescribe sleeping pills that wouldn't hurt the baby. Using the pills, she didn't have to lie awake and think of the imminent danger and in the back of her mind the thought lingered that the pills could be her way out, if need be. No, she couldn't do that. She loved Mark, and he loved her. And they both were looking forward to the baby. How could she have such contrary thoughts at the same time?

She was always in motion. She ate less than normal and by rote, forcing herself to eat even though she had no appetite. She lost ten pounds in a week. Mark worried about her health, and she couldn't make him worry, not now. So, she forced herself to eat more, and she made sure he saw her eat healthy portions. But her body couldn't take it, and without him knowing, after meals her stomach would convulse, and she'd throw up, alone in the bathroom.

Mark buried himself in his studies, not just as a distraction, but because when he was air-dropped in Japan, his slim chances of survival would depend on his language skills. He was so immersed in study that he didn't realize the degree to which Ruth was on edge and suffering. They talked little, and her new routine of using sleeping pills precluded sex in the unlikely event that either of them might be in the mood.

Prompted by Eileen's angry outburst, Ruth, too, wished that all fire and damnation be unleashed on Japan. She wanted that nation to be utterly crushed, devastated to the point that total surrender was the only option. To save the man she loved, the father of her unborn child, she wished the deaths of hundreds of thousands of Japanese.

She said aloud the nevermind words, and she was all set to say them again and again, to pray them, even though she knew that was futile. She knew she had no such power, but if she did, this was how she would wield it.

At that moment, when she was about to let loose her wrath, Mark rushed in the door with the news—Hiroshima.

They celebrated that night, and the next day, and the day after that. The war was as good as over. Mark was safe. Their real, civilian life together could begin soon.

Then came news that Nagasaki had been hit as well.

Then came the estimates of the casualties.

On August 6, over a hundred thousand died in the atomic blast on Hiroshima.

On August 8, another eighty thousand died in Nagasaki.

Other victims were suffering from burns and radiation sickness, and likely would die soon.

Ruth visualized the horror of the massive death and maiming. Even with sleeping pills, she couldn't sleep without nightmares.

"I'm guilty," she insisted to Mark. "I wished it. I neverminded it. I made it happen. All those people dying and suffering was my fault."

"No!" He put his hands on her shoulders and looked her the eye, trying to talk sense into her. "That wasn't your doing. The bomb was dropped hours before we got news of it here. And the chain of events that led to the development of the bomb and the decision to use it started years ago."

"But if I could have made it happen, I would have."

"There's no way you could have. You are not responsible."

"But I feel the guilt."

"Pull yourself together, Ruth. We can't change the world for better or for worse. But we can change diapers, and in six months we'll be changing lots of them."

24 ~ Pregnancy and Panic

August 1945 to spring 1946, Fort Snell, MN

With the end of the war, draftees all over the country were mustered out in droves, but not Mark. Having volunteered rather than being drafted, he was committed for a three-year hitch that wouldn't end until May 1946. With his Japanese language skills, he might be needed for Civil Affairs as part of the Army of Occupation.

Eileen cleared out and went to stay with her sister in New York. She took one suitcase with clothes and left everything else to whoever wanted to scavenge it. She wanted nothing that would remind her of Fort Snell and the man she had loved.

Frank got an early discharge. His services were no longer needed so he and Rachel left.

The radio intercept program ended. Jane and George headed to California where his parents and siblings and extended family had just been released from internment.

By the time Mark would finish the language course and know Japanese well enough to be useful to the Army of Occupation, his three-year hitch would be nearly up. There was no point in keeping him here; he should simply be discharged. But no such luck. He appealed but got no response.

Ruth had felt secure at Fort Snell, flanked by neighbors who were friends. Now the Fort was becoming a ghost town. Half the married housing was empty with no prospect that anyone new would be coming.

She worked full-time, realizing that they needed to save for the upcoming expenses of the birth and the newborn. But at the beginning of the fifth month, she was asked to leave her job. No matter how she dressed, it was evident that she was pregnant, and management considered that unseemly in an office.

To supplement their income, Mark started selling his blood once a week at six dollars per pint. His rare blood type, which in its incompatibility with hers limited them to one child, could help pay for the expenses of that child.

Without a job and without her friends, it was lonely for Ruth during the day while Mark was at class. She continued to drill Mark on Japanese, but less often and less urgently. He was over his initial jitters and was now at the top of his class.

It helped that Mark was so attentive and loving. He found her pregnant body beautiful and sexy. He insisted on drawing her nude. When he got home, he asked, "What's nude today?" And she stripped and assumed a pose—on the bed, on the floor, sitting on the kitchen table. But despite assurances from the gynecologist and baby books, neither of them dared have sex for fear of harming the baby. And, they avoided foreplay, knowing that they couldn't stop themselves if they got started. Their rule was look but don't touch.

Mark's teachers blocked his applications for early discharge because they didn't want to lose him. They enjoyed his facility at conversation, the humorous quips he came up with and his surprising ability to quote ancient haiku that was appropriate for the topic under discussion; even his ability to sing the haiku with never-before-heard and memorable tunes. They wanted him to re-up, with the near certainty that he would get an assignment in Occupied Japan. With his talent for the language and the experience of an extended stay there, he could build a career in foreign service, business, or academia. But he and Ruth had their sights set on Southern California, acting in movies together, maybe Mark getting a job as a cartoonist at Disney. The war was over, and opportunities were everywhere. With the GI Bill, he could go to college for free. Ruth wanted to go, too, once he had finished and had a good paying job, and little Davey was in school. Still sure it would be a boy, that was the name they had chosen. That was the plan. The sky was the limit.

Ruth had lost her safety net when all her friends left. She asked herself how would she get to the hospital when her water broke? And how would she cope when she came home with their son?

Mark called Uncle Adolph, hoping that Margery might be able to come and help. But Adolph had just had a run of bad luck at the racetrack, and the trip would be too expensive.

Emily was willing to come, but it would be expensive for her, too, and she couldn't get time off from work. Besides, she knew nothing about pregnancy and birth or caring for newborns.

They would have to cope on their own.

When her water broke, on February 23, Ruth called for an ambulance, as Dr. Jones had told her to. She couldn't reach Mark in class, and he couldn't have helped anyway. He didn't have a car, so he couldn't provide transportation. And at the hospital, he wouldn't be allowed in the birthing room.

Dr. Jones was out of town, so the baby would be delivered by a stranger.

When she was under anesthesia, she felt like she was in a different world. "Does this world have a nuclear bomb?" she asked. She fell asleep before she got an answer.

When Mark came home after class, he saw the note she had left him. He called a taxi. By the time he arrived at the hospital, she was still in the recovery room. All he could do was stare wide-eyed at his son, on the far side of the newborn nursery, among dozens of others. He wouldn't be able to see Ruth until regular visiting hours the next day, and she'd be in the hospital for the standard nine-day post-natal stay.

Mark called to proudly tell Uncle Adolph about the birth, in lieu of telling his parents—he was still miffed that they had opposed the wedding.

When he arrived at the hospital in the morning, he found Margery and Judy walking up and down the hallway. Judy had the baby in her arms, and Margery was talking to the baby non-stop.

Ruth was delighted that they had come. "You can stay in Rachel's old house," she told the newcomers, "right next to ours. It hasn't been claimed by anybody since they left, and it isn't likely to be. Everybody's moving out and nobody's moving in. They left all their furniture, even their linen. They just wanted to get out as quick as they could. The key is under the mat."

It was Saturday so Mark could stay all day at the hospital, sitting by Ruth's side. Margery, who could get the nurses to do anything for her, brought the baby into the room and gave Ruth and Mark a crash course on how to hold and change and bottle-feed a newborn. The hospital frowned on breastfeeding and, much to Margery's annoyance, made it virtually impossible for a mother to try.

Both Ruth and Mark listened to Margery as if she were the Mother of God delivering the ten commandments of parenthood. Ruth had had a little experience with Rachel's daughter, but this wasn't just any baby—this was Davey, their Davey. Mark was a total novice. Every bit of advice was precious.

After nine days, when Ruth and Davey could finally go home, by hospital policy they had to ride in an ambulance. Then Ruth had to stay in bed for another two weeks, not because there was any problem, but because that was the way things were done.

If Margery and Judy weren't there, Mark and Ruth wouldn't have been able to cope without paid help that they couldn't afford. They no longer had any close friends to turn to. They should have foreseen this issue and planned for it, but there were so many other things that they needed to deal with like buying a secondhand crib, a baby carriage and diapers, and hanging wallpaper with elephants and giraffes in Mark's former office that would now be the baby's room. They hadn't realized that Ruth would be confined to bed and hadn't planned how to handle it.

The day after they got back home, Ruth was still groggy—not so much from the trauma of childbirth as from the extended stay in the hospital maternity ward, with nurses and screaming babies waking her repeatedly. She had a moment when she wasn't sure where she was and what was going on. Then she remembered she had a baby son, but she didn't know where he was. She got up quickly, and her legs couldn't support her weight. She fell, then pulled herself up by holding onto the drawer handles on the bureau. Leaning on the walls, and supporting herself with any furniture in reach, she stumbled through the house. Davey wasn't in his room. He wasn't anywhere. She didn't know where to look for him. She thought someone had stolen him, and she didn't know what to do. She grabbed a broom to use as a walking stick, went outside and wandered down the street in her nightgown.

The MPs picked her up and figured out who she was.

Mark was in class, reciting his part in a dialogue, when an MP walked in, grabbed him by the arm, and led him away. In the hallway the MP explained, "You've got to go home immediately. Your wife is frantic. She claims your baby has been kidnapped."

"Kidnapped? Who the hell would—"

"She suspects two women named Margery and Judy."

At home, she blurted out, "It had to be them. It couldn't be anyone else. They loved him so much, they must have taken him. I know that sounds crazy, but as helpful as they are, they're also unreliable and morally questionable."

Her fear and her suspicions were contagious. His new-found sense of responsibility for his infant son made Mark over-protective and suspicious of everyone. Davey was gone. What other explanation could there be? He loved Davey so much he could easily imagine someone falling crazy in love with him and carrying him off. He wouldn't put that past Margery and Judy. And Davey had been missing for hours by now. They could be anywhere. By bus, train, or plane, they could have gone anywhere.

After spending several frustrating hours with the MPs, Mark and Ruth returned home. They found Margery ready to serve spaghetti dinner, and Judy and Davey were on their bellies face-to-face on a blanket on the living room floor.

"Where have you been?" asked Margery.

Ruth and Mark ran up to her and hugged her and begged her forgiveness for ever doubting her. Margery laughed when she heard what had happened. "A fit of post-partum craziness," she concluded. "Par for the course."

They held the christening at the multi-denominational chapel on the base. The Protestant minister had been mustered out, so a Catholic priest filled in for him. Judy stood as godmother. Adolph was the absentee godfather, connected to the ceremony by telephone. Other than them, the chapel, which had been built to hold three hundred parishioners, was empty.

When he saw the baptismal fount, Davey screamed and tried to slither out of Margery's arms. She explained, "He thinks we're going to give him a bath. He hates his bath." She settled him down by singing softly to him, "Hush little baby, don't you cry, Margey's goin' to buy you a pie in the sky. Hush little baby don't say a word, Margey's going to tell you the best story you ever heard." With that final burst of too many words, she rubbed noses with him, and he laughed.

Over the coming weeks, Ruth read the Spock baby book half a dozen times. She felt guilty that she hadn't breast fed—the nurses at the hospital hadn't given her a choice. Now, she wanted to be sure to handle the potty training just right. Margery laughed and told her that all that mattered was love. Babies responded to love like flowers growing toward the sun.

25 ~ California Dream

May 1946, Venice, CA

When Ruth was pregnant, she didn't want to have sex for fear of hurting the baby, and the sleeping pills seemed to take away her desire. When the mandatory bed rest was over, they tried, but she was sore — it was taking longer than expected for the episiotomy to heal. Then the lack of sleep took its toll. Even after three months, Davey didn't sleep for much longer than three hours. By May, when the discharge papers finally came through, they hadn't had sex in eight months. They needed to start fresh. They needed a third honeymoon. Everything would be different when they got to California.

They set their sights on Venice. A classmate of Mark's had told them that Venice wasn't far from Hollywood, and it was much cheaper. There was an amusement pier and a great beach. A cousin of the classmate worked at the front desk of the Venice Hotel and could get them a special rate. Just say Carlos had sent them.

They called ahead and reserved a room, delighted there was a vacancy. They had heard that Southern California was swarming with ex-GIs and that housing of any kind was hard to find. If they could get a hotel room this easily, maybe it wasn't all that hard to get permanent housing.

They decided to fly because the train would take too long, and it would be a nightmare trying to sleep on a train with an infant. They flew standby to keep the cost down. Mark had been accepted in UCLA's drama program, courtesy of the GI Bill, but that was for the fall. They had three and a half months to get settled, to find summer work for Mark, and to enjoy the beach. Neither of them had been to the West Coast before. It would be an adventure.

The weather was fine, but they kept getting bumped from the flights they planned to take. Instead of getting to Los Angeles in two hops, they flew from Minneapolis to Chicago to Indianapolis to Kansas City to Albuquerque, and eventually to Los Angeles. Each stop meant a long wait for the next flight. They slept in airports for four nights, changing and washing diapers in restrooms, then sitting outside until the diapers dried. Fortunately, it didn't rain. Unfortunately, Davey was fussy and slept little. Fortunately, they packed enough baby formula for a week. Unfortunately, it was a struggle at each airport to find an eatery with a waitress willing to warm his bottle and alert enough to get the temperature right. If the formula was too cold, Davey would get colicky. If it was too hot, it would burn his mouth. Ruth carefully checked each time, and often the waitress lost patience, and they had to find another eatery where they could beg for help.

When the last plane finally landed in Los Angeles, they splurged on a taxi to Venice, desperate for a good night's sleep in a hotel.

Venice was not what they expected. The amusement pier had closed the week before they arrived and was scheduled for demolition. They hoped to relax on the beach with the baby. But when they said that to the desk clerk, he laughed and told them that Venice was where the raw sewage from Los Angeles poured into the ocean.

They went to their room and talked about what they should do. They agreed that they needed to do something frivolous and fun to get in the spirit of starting a great new adventure. They would go to Paramount Studios, to Central Casting, and try to get a gig as extras in a movie—all of them, as a family. For their first night, they were too exhausted to do anything.

Lying with her head on Mark's shoulder, Ruth realized how long it had been since they had made love. Abstinence had made medical sense when she was pregnant, and then soon after the birth, and then because they were both exhausted, taking care of Davey and not getting sleep. She had assumed that Mark wasn't pushing for it out of consideration for her; it was a sign of his love. She had assumed that he would want to resume activities as soon as possible but he hadn't even talked about it—not even here on their first night in California. It was his role, his job to make the first move. That's the way it had always been between them. But she wanted it now and he just fell asleep. She wondered if something was wrong, if he was tired of her or if he took her for granted now that they were an old married couple.

She got up and took a critical look at herself in the full-length mirror in the bathroom. Circles under her eyes. Varicose veins. Stretch marks.

Excess flesh around the waist. The extra weight of pregnancy hadn't disappeared as she had expected. Where the hell was that beautiful, young, sexy body that Mark had fallen in love with? she thought. Was it gone forever? Was she over the hill at the age of twenty-six?

***

They had no idea how Central Casting worked, or how likely it was that either or all of them would be picked. But that didn't matter; they were star-struck. This was Paramount, where movies were made. This was like when they watched the Broadway rehearsal. They didn't care if they made money; they'd gladly pay to be here.

Miraculously, they were picked for a crowd scene in a western, and Davey behaved well enough. His occasional fussing and low-level crying felt natural to the director — an unexpected touch of realism. They made more money in four hours than Ruth would have made in two weeks at a secretarial job. Then Ruth was picked, alone, for another scene. Mark took Davey back to the hotel to feed and change him. Ruth would join them when she was done.

Her second gig lasted just an hour, so she went back again to Central Casting, delighted to be making easy money. She asked Janis, the young woman sitting next to her, "Is it like this every day?"

"No way. You got beginner's luck. When school's out in another week, this place will be totally mobbed. Even when school's in session, I'm lucky if I get picked for something one day out of five. Mostly I sit and read. I do a lot of reading and star watching. Paramount has the best." She pulled out a notebook with autographs of stars: Cary Grant, Betty Grable, Ray Milland, Gary Cooper, Bing Crosby, Mary Pickford, William Powell, Marlene Dietrich, Olivia de Haviland, Douglas Fairbanks, Bob Hope, Mae West, W. C. Fields.

"You actually saw all of them?" Ruth asked in amazement.

"I got close enough to get them to sign for me."

"Why, I'd sit for days on end for that. I'd pay for that. Do you think we might see someone like that today?"

"It's random. A star might stroll by on the other side of the street, and you wouldn't notice. But all of us here have our eyes peeled, and the tourists, too. When someone recognizes a star, there's a rush, and everyone has their autograph books out."

No such luck today. But as everyone was leaving, a young man approached Ruth. He introduced himself, "I was a cameraman working on that western scene you were in this morning. You stood out from the crowd. You're photogenic. You have *the look*." He handed her his business card. "I do this movie work at Paramount part time, as a fill-in when one of the regulars can't make it. I'm really an artist, a professional photographer. I'm putting together a portfolio of still shots to advance my career. If you would pose for me, I would give you a set of head shots for your portfolio. As you must know, you'll need head shots to get anywhere in Hollywood. Normally, you'd have to pay a lot for good ones. Pose for me, and I'll give them to you for free."

She was flattered. It felt good to be admired for her looks when she was having doubts about herself. And the attentions of a younger man made her feel younger. He had a winning, innocent look like Jimmy Stewart in *Mr. Smith Goes to Washington*. But she knew enough not to trust strangers, especially in Hollywood. So, she turned away from him and didn't respond.

Janis, who had witnessed the encounter, vouched for the guy. "He does good work," she said. "He was at UCLA when I was. He's a go-getter, an up-and-comer."

Ruth turned back. They made eye contact. He had a hopeful look on his face. He looked even younger than Mark. Maybe she had a thing for younger men. His eyes drew her to him. It seemed like he was memorizing her every feature. If any other man had looked at her that way, she would have walked away, quickly, finding that creepy, even scary. But she felt a shiver of excitement. Without meaning to or even thinking, she said, "Yes" and took his business card.

Then he was gone, in the crowd.

She read the business card, "Kent Boswick."

The next day she went back to Paramount alone. Mark would take care of Davey and start the hunt for housing. She brought a book, *Mrs. Minever*, and sat down next to Janis again. When lunch break came and neither of them had been picked, Ruth took out the business card and looked at it again.

"Nothing's going to happen today," said Janis. "Why don't you give him a try? His place is just a few blocks from here—studio space in an old warehouse that he shares with a bunch of other artists and photographers. I did it," she added, taking a handful of headshots from her pocketbook. "I bring these with me when I come here. You never can tell when you might need them. It's random, and I don't want to miss my chance if I ever get one."

"Why not?" Ruth replied, surprising herself.

When she arrived at Kent's studio, he was doing portraits of a family, patiently posing three young and restless boys. He had an array of camera equipment and lights. He had a professional manner. The photos displayed on his walls showed a wide range of subjects from weddings to proms and bar mitzvahs, to shots of products for advertising, to artsy pictures that looked good enough to hang in a museum. He did good work. He was legitimate. She was impressed. Her gut was right; she could trust him.

When he finally settled the boys down and finished their portraits, Kent turned to Ruth, "Are you here for head shots? I'm booked for today. But I could fit you in tomorrow."

"I'm Ruth," she said. "You saw me at Central Casting, at Paramount." She was miffed that he didn't remember her.

"Ruth, yes, of course. It's been a busy day. Forgive me. You're totally unforgettable, dear lady. Can you come back in the morning? Nine o'clock?"

"Yes. Of course," she answered without thinking, taken by surprise.

"I'll look forward to seeing you then," he said, opening the door for her to leave.

26 ~ Lead Me Not Into Temptation

June 1946, Venice, CA

At dawn, before Mark woke up, Ruth squeezed into her one-piece bathing suit, a far more difficult task than she had imagined, and went out on the beach intending to get her feet wet in the Pacific Ocean, no matter how polluted the water might be. Some kids were playing on the beach. No, not kids, it appeared that this was the aftermath of an all-night high school graduation party. They looked very young to her. A year ago, when the war ended, they were probably seventeen, too young to be drafted. They were another generation for whom the war would never have been a direct threat. She was eight years older than them, matronly, a mother with the battle scars of childbirth. Even in her bathing suit, they wouldn't give her a second look. No one had told her what would happen to her body—that that was part of the price for having children. Of course, she'd willingly pay the price. But she hadn't realized that trading in her body for an older one, with flaws, was part of the bargain. Her friend Rachel had never said a word about that.

She ran back to the hotel room and changed. She told Mark she was going to Central Casting. She didn't mention Kent and his studio. That was strictly business. She'd be getting head shots, which were important for getting acting work, so she wasn't exactly lying—this was, indirectly, about Central Casting. Kent didn't have any interest in her as a woman, otherwise he wouldn't have forgotten her. It was good that he had forgotten her. She didn't want him to have an interest in her. All she wanted was head shots. And, yes, it would be good to bask in the attention of a handsome young photographer. Her ego could use a harmless boost. But Mark might not see it that way. She had never known him to act jealous, but she had never given him reason to. No need to upset him or, even worse, for her to find out that he wasn't jealous, that he was taking her for granted. Maybe he needed a reminder that she was a very attractive woman, that men turned to look at her when she walked by—they always had before, and once she got back her pre-motherhood figure, certainly they would once again.

She put her engagement and wedding rings in her pocketbook. Kent wouldn't want those to appear in his photos and she wouldn't want to misplace them.

She would tell Mark about this photo shoot when she had the head shots and was well on her way to a career in acting and modeling. They would have a good laugh over it when she mentioned that the photographer, who had come on strong to her when he first met her, didn't recognize her when she took him up on his offer and showed up at his door.

***

The day before, Mark had called the housing office at UCLA, but they wouldn't give him information over the phone. He had to go there in person and check the files himself. He took Davey with him on the bus. There were long lines just to get to the file drawers full of index cards. He couldn't find anything they could afford, not even a studio.

The next day, when he thought Ruth was returning to Central Casting, Mark checked the LA Times, then made phone calls to likely sources of housing help—Travelers Aid, Red Cross, the Lutheran Church, the Veterans Administration. They laughed at him. There was nothing available in their price range within a hundred miles of Los Angeles.

He had no more options on his to-do list, and it was still early in the day so he hiked up the beach to Santa Monica with Davey in a papoose pack on his front and a backpack full of baby gear. He bought a sketch pad and pencils at a shop along the way. There was no way they could find housing here. His California dream had crashed. He needed a distraction.

Several miles from the pollution at Venice, the beach at Santa Monica was mobbed with college-age swimmers and surfers. He started sketching girls who were sunbathing nearby. Between Davey and the quality of his sketches, he drew lots of attention. He gave away the sketches to the girls he drew. There was no way he could take those drawings back to the hotel where Ruth could see them. She might get the wrong idea and get jealous. He had never seen her jealous—had never given her reason for it. He should get back into sketching her. And they should get back to making love—it had been far, far too long. Maybe she didn't feel that way about him now that he was a father, an old man of twenty-three. Maybe, with parenthood, they both had gone through a metamorphosis. Maybe this was a new sexless and responsible stage of their lives together. He hoped not.

Here and now, it felt good being the center of attention of good-looking young women who, while waiting their turn, were happy to play with Davey, even to feed him and change his diapers. This gave him a much-needed boost to his self-esteem. And these women were a joy to behold. It was a delight to stare at their thinly clad forms, close up, as he drew them, especially a stunning blond who reminded him of Ruth when he first met her. She was wearing a bathing suit that showed her midriff, like a Betty Grable pinup. When he gave her the sketch he had drawn of her, she leaned forward as if to whisper, but, instead, she handed him a note with her name, Cheryl, and her phone number, her address, and the words, "If you can get away tomorrow, without the kid, come to my place, and I'll model privately for you."

She smiled as she walked away.

Mark was speechless.

That night he told Ruth that the housing search was a bust, but he wanted to try his luck at Disney. If he could get a job there, that could change the range of the housing they could afford. Maybe he didn't need to go to college; maybe he could learn on the job. He wanted to go to Disney Studios and fill out an application and see if he could schedule an interview for a job as an artist. Could she watch Davey for a day?

***

Back at Kent's studio, after working on headshots—some standard and some in extreme close up—Kent had asked Ruth to try on a bathing suit. He had bought three for her, correctly guessing her size. "I'm an optimist," he explained. "I cleared my calendar today for you. Please stay."

The cowboy twang in his voice was disarming. She didn't say yes, but she didn't say no, either. She walked toward the door, then did an about-face, picked up the red bathing suit, and went behind a screen to put it on.

Posing for him reminded her of posing nude for Mark in Minnesota. It felt good being looked at with appreciation and desire. Soon, she was on a roll, coming up with her own ideas for poses and expressions.

At the end of the day, Kent asked, "Have you ever posed nude?"

"Yes. Many times," she answered, delighted to see his surprise.

"For film?" he asked, incredulous.

"For art. Life drawing."

"Then you have no problem with nudity?"

"Of course not," she answered, throwing him off-guard.

"Could you come back the day after tomorrow?"

"Maybe," she answered, flirtatiously, with no intention of seeing him again. She was enjoying playing this role, and then riding off into the sunset.

***

The next day, Mark went to Cheryl's apartment instead of Disney Studios.

She told him where and how to touch her and kiss her. Then she said, "That's enough foreplay."

He apologized, "But I didn't bring a condom. I never expected we'd get to this point."

"No matter. I prefer a diaphragm. You don't need to think about a thing. I've got it all under control."

While she was in the bathroom, his erection vanished.

Obviously, she did this often. No matter how well this went, she would be with someone else soon. For her, this was amusement. That way of looking at the world was foreign to him.

But, God, it felt good to be desired by someone so desirable. How could something that felt that good be wrong? They were consenting adults. No one would be hurt. This was a victimless crime.

No one except Ruth would care, and she didn't need to know.

But whether he told her or not, Ruth would know. She would sense the change in him.

God! Why am I doing this? he thought.

Then his mood swung the other way and he wondered why his equipment wasn't working? Why was his normal bodily function not functioning?

When Cheryl came out of the bathroom, prepared for action, she immediately saw that Mark wasn't ready.

"Maybe tomorrow," he said, optimistically.

"I don't think so," she said.

Mark got dressed and left.

He hadn't gone all the way with her, but not by conscious choice, rather by physical incapacity. He felt embarrassed at his failure, and guilty for having gone as far as he did and for wanting more. He considered confessing to Ruth. Maybe she would interpret the fact that he couldn't go through with it as proof that his true self couldn't betray her, despite temptation. But telling her about Maxine hadn't gone well. Better that he tell a white lie. As Adolph would say, what Ruth didn't know wouldn't hurt her.

When he got back to the hotel, Ruth was tired and irritable after a long day with a tired and irritable Davey. He told her that he had sat all day in a waiting room at Disney. Then, when he finally got a chance to talk to a personnel guy, it turned out that an artist should never go job hunting without a portfolio. He should have brought dozens of examples of his work, but all he had was the nude drawings he had done of her back in Minnesota, and he would never show those—he wouldn't want anyone else to see her naked body. When he said that, he wanted to sound like that was a sign of his respect for her; but the tone of his voice didn't ring true.

***

Ruth didn't intend to ever see Kent again. She certainly wouldn't pose nude for him. But when Davey finally fell asleep, Mark once again showed no interest in getting physical with her. He was acting strange. When he talked, the muscles of his jaw were tense. She sensed that something was wrong.

When she got up to go to the bathroom, she noticed a new sketch pad lying on the chair near the door. She took it into the bathroom with her. There were no sketches, but dozens of pages had been torn out. And when she held the top page up to the light, she could make out pencil impressions of a reclining figure, with prominent breasts. He had lied to her. He didn't go to Disney. He had spent the day with this other woman. How did he dare do that?

She wasn't sure how to deal with this. Yes, she was angry. She was sure that he had betrayed her. And this wasn't his first slipup. There had been Maxine, and there might have been others as well. That might be why he hadn't been coming on to her, why they had gone so long without sex. How long had it been? She took out her pocket calendar to count the months.

Then she realized that today was June 5. With all the hassles of moving out of Fort Snell and the long, frustrating multi-flight trip to get here, and dealing with Davey, never getting a good night's sleep, one day had blurred into another. She had lost track of time. Today was Mark's twenty-third birthday. How could she have forgotten? And it was their second anniversary as well. How could he have forgotten that? His forgetting was far worse than hers. That was the last straw.

She didn't want a confrontation, not yet, not now. She wasn't ready to give up on her marriage. She still loved him. Somehow, she'd find a way to move beyond his infidelity. But she needed revenge. She needed to make him feel as bad as she felt. She needed him to realize how close he was to losing her, and how bad that would be.

In the morning, she went to Kent's studio. And the first thing she said when she walked through the door was "Do you have condoms?"

He hesitated, with a look of shock in his eyes. "Yes," he mumbled.

"Then use two of them, one on top of the other. I don't want an accident."

27 ~ Losing Davey

June 1946, Venice, CA to Chicago, IL

By the time Ruth got back to the hotel room, Mark was already asleep.

After her time with Kent, she had gone to a movie, a new release—*The Postman Always Rings Twice*. Sex and betrayal and guilt—many flavors of guilt. Then she caught a bus to Venice, but turned around before opening their hotel room door, and went out again, and walked, for hours, along the beach, from Venice to Santa Monica and back.

She didn't know what to say to Mark—angry at him for his betrayal and feeling guilty about her revenge sex. Staying away until late at night gave her ample time to think and gave a clear signal to Mark that she hadn't spent the day at Central Casting, that she was up to something else. She wanted him to confront her, not the other way around. She wanted him to suspect her and accuse her, to fly into a self-righteous, jealous rage. Then she'd throw his own guilt back in his face, and tell him that, yes, she had had sex with another man, but only because of what he had done, to get back at him. And how did that make him feel? And how did he think she felt about what he had done to her? What goes around comes around. In the theater of her mind, they broke out in tears, fell into one another's arms, had passionate make-up sex, forgave one another, and lived together happily ever after.

When she finally opened their hotel room door, he was asleep, for God's sake, no doubt dreaming about that floozie who had modeled nude for him. She opened the door again and slammed it to wake him, but only succeeded in waking Davey, who she picked up and held tight and rocked in her arms, singing "Hush little baby don't you cry. Momma's goin' to change you and make you dry. Hush little baby don't say a word. Momma's goin' to tell you what just occurred." Making up new words for the old song, like Margery had when he was a newborn, was a welcome distraction. By the time she put Davey back in his portable crib, she had forgotten what she was about to say and do.

When her eyes met Mark's, she turned away without a word and went into the bathroom. There she undressed and started the shower, then turned it off. No, she wouldn't wash up. She would go to bed with the smell of sex and Kent on her.

She lay down on the edge of the bed, as far from him as possible, with her back toward him. He reached out and moved close to her, pressing his nakedness to her, and caressing her. She thought, He wanted sex? At a time like this? By reflex, she recoiled, and fell out of bed. When he tried to help her up, she spat at him, like she had when he told her about Maxine.

She whispered harshly—loud enough for Mark to hear her but trying not to wake Davey. "How could you? I saw your sketch book. I know damn well what you were up to."

"But we didn't go all the way," he whispered in defense.

"But you went, for God's sake. You wanted her, and you went to her, whoever the hell she was."

"I was tempted, but I couldn't go through with it. My equipment wouldn't work. My conscience wouldn't let me do it. I love you."

"A fine way you have of showing love."

"And where were you today?" he finally dared to ask.

"Doing what you couldn't, and it serves you right."

She slept on the sofa that night.

In the morning, without blaming and without confessing the details of their trespasses, never raising their voices at on another, Mark and Ruth agreed that they should leave California as soon as possible.

Sensitized by their own guilt, each was certain of the guilt of the other. Each was both hurt and remorseful. Maybe they could move on. Maybe they could forget. But there would be a long tight rope walk from here to there.

They wouldn't fly this time. A train would take longer, but they could book berths in a Pullman car.

They got tickets on the Super Chief—Los Angeles to Chicago in thirty-nine hours and forty-five minutes. All trains stopped in Chicago. They would switch there, then on to New York. They hadn't decided where to go once they reached New York. Philadelphia? Washington? Miami? They found it difficult to look one another in the eye, much less decide on a destination and talk about the rest of their lives; and whether they were going to stay together or go through the horror and shame of divorce.

The Super Chief was a Diesel-powered train with Pullman sleeping-cars. The meals were reputed to be "gourmet." Because the meals were costly and they couldn't afford to splurge, they brought sandwiches and drinks. But they underestimated how hungry and thirsty they would be. They ran out of food and drink ten hours before they reached Chicago.

Four-month-old Davey, who seemed to sense something was wrong, had a hair-trigger temper, and cried frequently. His outbursts prevented both Mark and Ruth from sleeping, which added to the stress.

On their first day on the train, Mark lost his wallet, with all their money. It fell out of his pocket in a restroom. The person who found it turned it in to a conductor. The conductor compared the ID with the passenger list and returned the wallet to Mark in his Pullman berth. Miracle of miracles, all the money was still in the wallet. After that, Mark was tense and nervous about everything. He pulled out their suitcases and checked to make sure they hadn't left anything behind. He stood up and sat down and stood up again. He was upset that they had missed lunch in the dining car, and it would be three hours and twenty minutes before they could get dinner at any price. When they got off in Chicago, Mark reluctantly hired a porter. He thought he could handle the luggage on his own—he had managed in Los Angeles, but he needed someone to guide them through the maze of tracks to the next train. This was one of the biggest and busiest train stations in the world. He wanted to make sure he didn't screw up.

Ruth carried Davey, and the bag with his formula and bottles, and a little blue teddy bear they had picked up in Venice, and that Davey had taken a liking to. Ruth called it "Catfish Snail," the name she had given to a stuffed bear she had as a child. She could get Davey to laugh by rubbing his nose with the bear's nose and saying that silly name.

In short order, they found the train and their seats, and stowed their two large suitcases in a tightly packed overhead rack. Then Mark spoke to the porter, "Can you do us a favor, please? We haven't eaten in ages.

We'd like to grab a bite and buy enough sandwiches and drinks to last until New York. Could you please watch our son, little Davey? We'll only be gone a few minutes, and I'll make it worth your while."

"I don't know, mister. I do luggage, not babies. I don't know a thing about babies."

Mark handed him a five.

"That's generous, very generous for handling your bags, but there's no way I'm babysitting for you."

The porter started to leave. Mark offered another five. The porter stopped but shook his head. Mark was desperate and determined. He didn't have much money, but, in his mind, this was an emergency, and he didn't have time to negotiate or to find someone else. He put a twenty on top of the fives, and the porter smiled and said, "I guess I've got me a new career."

Ruth hesitated. "Why are we doing this?" she asked. "You go. I'll stay with Davey. There's no way I'm going to leave our Davey with a stranger."

Mark looked her in the eye. "It's not just the food. We need to be alone together, even if only for five minutes." He took her hand and squeezed it. "We need to talk. We can't go on like this."

Ruth squeezed back, without thinking, then pulled away, glaring at him. All the things she meant to say to him, that she had rehearsed over and over, raced through her head, but not a word came out of her mouth.

Meanwhile the porter was warming up to Davey and vice versa. He rubbed Davey's nose with his finger, and Davey smiled back. "He reminds me of my grandson—a real charmer. He'll be no problem at all, no problem, I'm sure."

Mark grabbed Ruth's arm and pulled her off the train with him. She looked back, then looked at Mark and squeezed his arm—the first sign of affection she had given him since the disaster in California.

They ran down the walkway between tracks, then ran even faster, following signs to the "Great Hall," the concourse where the restaurants and food stands were. The big clock overhead showed 12:10. Their train was due to leave at 1:15. They slowed down; no rush.

The ceiling was over a hundred feet high, a vaulted skylight. They looked up and around in awe.

"Norman Rockwell," said Mark.

"What?"

"This station is an architectural marvel. A Norman Rockwell painting of it was on the cover of *The Saturday Evening Post*."

"We're starving, and you think of Norman Rockwell?" Ruth laughed. "That's what I get for marrying an artist, an artist with a talent for drawing nudes."

Mark took her arm, and started running again, forestalling that line of conversation, heading for a deli-style sandwich shop. They needed to talk, but that was the wrong way to start.

The line was long, but it was a relief to be out of the claustrophobic space they had been confined in for so long, to stretch their arms and legs, to get away from the screaming baby. Thank goodness Davey wasn't screaming when they left him with the porter. There's no way the porter would have agreed to it. Mark hoped that this brief excursion would relieve the tension between them. Otherwise, they might explode at one another and say things that they could never unsay. Any conversation at all—even mentioning Norman Rockwell—could trigger thoughts of their double infidelity. The less said the better. If they said out loud what they were thinking, that would make their anger and pain even more real; there would be no going back. So maybe they didn't need to talk—not now. But they certainly needed a few minutes alone together, to begin to reconnect.

He had restrained himself on the train, not wanting to scream in front of Davey, much less strangers. Though they hadn't talked about it, he believed that she thought the same as he did—that they both hoped that this could be patched up although they had no idea how. At the same time, he had doubts, and she probably did as well that maybe they were living a lie. Should they ever have gotten together in the first place?

When they reached the front of the line, the woman at the deli counter was Swedish or some other flavor of Scandinavian and had trouble understanding their orders, delivering white bread instead of rye and mustard instead of mayonnaise. Mark would have taken anything, but Ruth insisted they get exactly what they had ordered. Then the coffee was intolerable—they both agreed on that—and they both needed coffee. They were still groggy from lack of sleep. That was making them irritable, and they couldn't afford to be irritable—their future together depended on that. He checked his watch:12:20. They were doing far better than he had thought. It must be the tension between them that made it feel like they'd been wasting lots of time. So once again, they waded into the swarming crowd in the concourse, looking for another place where they could get coffee, eating while they walked.

Periodically, the loudspeaker barked indecipherable announcements.

Mark laughed, his mouth full of pastrami. "It's amazing how they do that," he commented.

"What?"

"Talk so nobody can understand them. It's that way everywhere—airports, bus stations. There must be a special school for loudspeaker people to learn how to do that."

"That's your trouble, you have no empathy," Ruth snapped back. "Everything's a joke to you. There are people here who need to hear and understand that message, otherwise, they'll miss their train, and their lives will be changed."

Mark took another bite, a big one, to muffle another laugh that would have irritated Ruth even more.

The next food stand also had a long line. But when they finally got coffee, it was very good—well worth the wait. It was so good that they got back in line for seconds. Mark was calm now, and Ruth was, too. They even smiled at one another as they sipped and savored their second coffees. They were making progress.

Then he checked his watch—12:20; still 12:20. He looked again. He tapped the watch with his finger. The second hand wasn't moving.

"What's wrong," asked Ruth, reacting to his alarm.

"My watch stopped. I must have forgotten to wind it."

"God almighty!" she screamed. People around them stopped talking and stared at them.

Nevermind

"Calm down. There's no need to panic," Mark insisted, trying to sound calmer than he felt. "The station clock up there says 1:05. We still have ten minutes to get back to the train. We can make it, but we have to run."

They tossed their half-full coffee cups in a trash can, grabbed the bags with their sandwiches and drinks, and battled their way through the crowd back to Track Fifteen.

***

On the way back, Ruth saw another couple walking in the other direction with a cute baby. The baby was close to Davey's age and dressed just like Davey was. And they were carrying a bag just like the one they kept Davey's stuff in. And the woman had a little blue teddy bear in her hand.

Ruth stopped abruptly and stared at them, as they disappeared into the crowd.

Mark tried to pull her forward, "Come on. There's no time to waste."

Ruth pulled back and yelled, "Davey! That was our Davey. That couple just stole our Davey!"

"Pull yourself together, Ruth. You're hysterical. No one stole Davey. This is like at Fort Snell when you thought Margery and Judy stole him. Don't make a scene. We need to get back to the train before it leaves."

It was 1:12 by the station clock when they reached Track Fifteen, but there was no train.

They sprinted toward a uniformed railroad employee and asked frantically, "The train. The train to New York. Where's the train?"

"Didn't you hear the announcement? There was a track change, nearly an hour ago. They needed to switch engines. You can still make it if you hurry. It's over on Five; no, maybe it's Seven." He pulled a notebook from his back pocket, flipped through the pages, then announced. "It's Five. I was right in the first place

They arrived in time to watch the train pull away.

They stood and stared in disbelief as it went out of sight. Then they collapsed on a bench.

Ruth blamed Mark, "If you had listened to me, we could have caught up with that couple who stole our Davey."

Mark blamed Ruth, "If you didn't have to have rye and mayo, if you had been satisfied with the coffee at the first place, we'd have gotten back in plenty of time. You're never satisfied."

"Well, you never satisfy me."

"That's a cheap shot. Let's stop bickering. The sooner we find someone in authority here, the sooner we'll get Davey back."

"You want to talk to railroad people?"

"Of course."

"We shouldn't waste our time on that," Ruth insisted. "He's not on the train. We saw the kidnappers. We should go straight to the police."

"Sure. We screw up and miss a train and for that, you want to go to the police."

"Correction—you screwed up. And of course, we need to go to the police. Our baby was kidnapped."

"You live in a strange world, lady."

"Well, while you chat with your railroad people, I'll go to the police."

"And you'll get to Scotland before me. Never mind."

"Don't say 'never mind.'"

"That again, at a time like this. Well, you do it your way, and I'll do it mine. Where shall we meet?"

"I wish we had never met," She shouted at him as she walked away.

All the phone booths in the concourse were busy and had long lines. Ruth spotted a policeman and ran to him.

"My baby's been stolen!" she blurted out.

Instinctively, he touched the gun in his holster to make sure it was there. He had never used it on duty, but there was no telling with something as important as a kidnapping. He pulled out his notebook and pencil to take down the details.

"When did this happen, ma'am?"

"Ten, maybe fifteen minutes ago."

"Where?"

"Right here in this concourse. I saw them—a couple, early thirties, I'd guess. He was in a brown suit, with a brown hat, a fedora. She was wearing a dress, black with white spots. He was carrying a suitcase, and she was carrying the baby, my baby, with a canvas bag over her shoulder and a blue teddy bear in her hand."

"And they took your baby right out of your arms and ran with it?"

"Not it, him. Davey, four months old, in a blue sleep suit. They took the bag with his formula and bottles, too. And his teddy bear. His bear is named 'Catfish Snail.'"

"Catfish Snail," he repeated, looking askance, but writing this down. "They took the baby and the bag right out of your arms, and you couldn't stop them?"

"No. They took him from the train and ran right by us—my husband and me. But we couldn't react quickly enough to stop them, and they disappeared into the crowd."

"The train, you say. You were on the train when they took your baby from you?"

"No. We were eating lunch at a food stand. The porter was watching Davey on the train while we stepped out to get some food. It was a long train ride from Los Angeles, and we hadn't brought enough food."

"So, the porter was in on this baby snatching. What's the porter's name?"

"I don't know. He helped us with our luggage, and then we paid him to watch Davey for a few minutes."

"And you didn't get his name?"

"We didn't think we'd need it. We were only going to be gone for a few minutes."

"So, you got back to the train after a few minutes, and the baby wasn't there. Was the porter there? Did he have any explanation?"

"No. It wasn't like that. You see, we lost track of time and were gone for over an hour."

"So, you left your four-month old baby on a train for over an hour with some stranger, whose name you don't know. Maybe you should be talking to a lawyer, lady, not a policeman. That could be negligence or child endangerment or both."

"Please, officer, please. Don't be ridiculous. It hasn't been long yet. They might still be in the station. They might have stopped to get something to eat."

"You seem to think a lot about food, lady. Are you okay? You look flushed, and you're sweating heavily, but it isn't a hot day. Maybe a glass of water would help you settle down and get your bearings."

"I am settled down," she screamed.

People passing by stopped and stared, like they had when she yelled at the kidnappers.

She grabbed a chair, sat down, and started sobbing uncontrollably.

"Okay, lady, okay. Where's your husband? Maybe he can talk sense, and we can get this all sorted out. He probably knows where your baby is."

"I don't know where he is."

"Yes, you don't know where your baby is. That's the problem. I understand."

"I don't know where my husband is, either."

"So your husband took the baby? Then this is a custody issue?"

"No! No! No! My husband has nothing to do with this. He isn't my husband, not anymore."

"You're divorced?"

"Not yet. But we will be, soon, believe you me. Leaving our baby on the train with a stranger, and then missing the train."

"You missed the train? And the baby's on there?"

"We missed the train, and some strange couple ran off with him, through the station, took him home to make him theirs. And it's all his fault."

"Your husband's fault?"

"Yes, my dear unfaithful husband, who picks up strange women on the beach and has sex with them; My soon to be ex-husband. My X-rated husband."

The policeman put his notepad back in his pocket, tipped his hat, and walked away.

Ruth blanked out. When she became conscious again, she was on a bench in the lost-and-found office. A nurse was pressing an icepack against her forehead. A first-aid box was on the floor at her feet.

Ruth sat up quickly and asked, "Where is he?"

"Who?"

"My baby. No, my husband. No, both of them."

"Do you live in Chicago, ma'am?"

"No. We were on our way from Los Angeles to New York."

"Do you have family here or friends?"

"I don't know a soul in this city."

"Well, do you have your train ticket to New York?"

"My husband has the tickets."

"Do you want to buy a new one?"

"A new husband?"

"A new ticket."

"No. I need to find my baby. My baby was stolen."

"You seem to be confused and under stress. I suggest you get a hotel room and try to sleep. I'm sure everything will be clearer in the morning."

Ruth had enough cash for two nights in a hotel. She had the bag with sandwiches and drinks. She would call Emily and ask her to wire her money. She would pay her back. She would hire a private detective. She could get secretarial jobs at a temp agency. With her skills, that shouldn't be a problem. She needed to think rationally, long range. A detective could find Davey, and Mark, as well. In movies and novels detectives find everything and everyone. This would all work out. It had too.

***

On his first day on the job, Jack Pearson, the detective, had no luck tracking down Davey, but he did find Mark in another Chicago hotel. Ruth called him. He hadn't had any luck either. He asked where she was. "Never mind where I am. That's none of your business. I'm none of your business. Stay put, and my lawyer will get in touch with you."

"Lawyer?"

"The sooner we start divorce proceedings, the sooner we'll be free of one another.

"And where are you going to get money for a divorce lawyer?"

"None of your damned business!"

She switched from hotel to rooming house and did two shifts of secretarial work five days a week so she could afford to keep Jack on the job and pay the lawyer as well.

28 ~ Process of Elimination

As Jack explained three days later, "Your porter wasn't a Pullman porter who stays on the train, makes the beds and performs other hotel-like services for passengers. Your porter was one of the hundreds who work at Union Station, helping passengers move luggage on and off trains. More than three hundred trains and a hundred thousand passengers go through Union Station every day. Your porter wasn't assigned to your train from LA or to the train going to New York. He was someone who just happened to be around to help with your luggage when you needed help."

"Did you find him?" she insisted.

"That's not the way to go about this, ma'am. I could try to find and interview every porter who was on duty that day and try to figure out which one you left your baby with. That could take weeks and probably wouldn't lead anywhere. These porters get paid very little except for tips. They come and go. Many work part-time or as temporaries. And if I found him, what could he say? If what you say is true, he gave the baby to another couple—not for personal gain and with no malicious intent. He wouldn't know their name or where they came from.

"Instead, I started with what you told me—that a couple who took Davey got off the train for New York shortly before it left the station. If this was a crime of opportunity, not premeditation, and not involving violence, the couple talked the porter into handing them the baby, and then they left in a hurry. When you saw them, they had the bag with the baby's gear and one suitcase. Chances are that, in their rush, they left at least one other suitcase behind. In any case, I needed to track down the two suitcases you and your husband left on the train. When I called the baggage claim office in New York, they confirmed that they had yours—with your names on tags but no address. And they told me that they had another suitcase as well from that same train. The address tag on that one was illegible, but it wasn't like the ones on yours. I went to New York and collected yours, and claimed the other one as well, generously tipping the clerk so he had no objections."

"Well, what was in it? Why didn't you bring it here with you?"

"There was nothing inside but cheap clothing—nothing that would indicate name or address, no laundry marks, nothing. The only thing of interest was this address tag." He handed it to her.

"But it's torn and smeared. I can't make out a word."

"Oak."

"What?"

"I looked at it with a magnifying glass, and all I could make out was the word 'oak,' capitalized. From the position of the word on the tag, that's a town rather than a street name. But it might be the first word or the last word of that name. I'm sorry, ma'am, but that's too much of a puzzle for me to solve. I'm afraid we've reached a dead end."

"No!"

"It probably happened the way you figured. But we have no idea who those people are or where they live; and we have no way to figure it out. It makes no sense for me to stay on this case. You'd throwing your money away, ma'am. I've done everything that I can do, everything that anyone can do. You're just going to have to accept the fact that your son is gone and move on with your life."

He brought up the two suitcases that she and Mark had left behind. They hadn't written an address on the tags because they didn't know where they were going.

"Okay, ma'am. Are we all set now?" he asked, folding his money, and putting it in his wallet.

"Well, what would you do if you were me, and money didn't matter?

"You mean if I had world enough and time? Well, I'd go one state at a time."

"And how would you do that?"

"Brute force process of elimination. All you have to go by is the word 'oak.' I'd start with Illinois, then do the states bordering on Illinois, then the states bordering on those. For each state, I'd get a road map. They give them away free at gas stations. There's an Esso around the corner from here. Then I'd go to the library and check a large format atlas of the U.S., probably Rand McNally. First, I'd look in the index for every town in Illinois with a name that begins with 'oak.' Then I'd look for every town in Illinois with the word 'oak' anywhere in the name. I'd mark each of those towns on my road map. Then I'd go to each of those towns, starting with the ones closest to Chicago and moving outward. And in each town, I'd go to every park and every other place where mothers often walk their babies in carriages. I would sit and watch for hours and days. And I'd go through that same process state by state. But that would be a waste of time because I would never be able to recognize your Davie."

"But I have the baby book I've kept of him, with dozens of photos."

"Seriously, ma'am, lots of babies look alike, and they grow and change fast. It could take months or years to chance upon your son. Photos would be meaningless. You're the only one who could recognize him if anyone could. It wouldn't be by his looks, it would have to be by some mother-son affinity, a mother magic."

"But here, see." She showed him in the book. "Here's his birth certificate with his fingerprints and footprints. Just look at those precious little feet." She wiped away her tears and tried to smile.

Jack shook his head. "I can just imagine what that would be like— you confronting a mother and claiming that her infant is yours and trying to get hand or foot prints of her baby so some police expert could compare them and prove she stole your baby. There's no way that's going to happen." He laughed ironically. "I'm afraid, ma'am, that you have to accept that what is done is done and can't be undone, without serious magic. And the last time I checked, there was no magic in this world."

Despite the odds, she went through that task herself, alone, religiously, one state after the other—Illinois, Wisconsin, Iowa, Missouri, Michigan, Indiana, Kentucky. She worked as a temporary secretary a few days a week to make enough to pay for food and lodging. She spent the rest of her time travelling to towns with "oak" in the name and sitting in parks and watching for babies in carriages, hoping for a miracle.

By the time she got to Tennessee, the state her father had come from, she had been doing this for six months, and she had been yelled at and humiliated dozens of times. Twice she had had the police called on her. She had reached the limit of her capacity; she couldn't keep doing this anymore. It was December now and, most days it was cold and windy in the parks of small towns in the Midwest.

Over and over, she replayed in her mind the scene in the train station—the moment when she saw the kidnappers with Davey.

Davey was gone. Her son was a lost boy, like the Lost Boys of Peter Pan in Neverland.

"Never mind," she thought. "Never mind," she said aloud. "Give me now my nevermind, happily-ever-after time," she said that over and over, until the rhythm of her heartbeat matched the rhythm of her words. And when she finally fell asleep that night, her heart continued to pray those words.

She dreamt about the last time she saw Davey, in the arms of the woman who stole him. The woman was wearing a black dress with white spots. But as the dream repeated, she saw the dress from closer and closer, like looking through a movie camera and zooming in, and she saw more than she had noticed before. Those white spots were acorns and near the shoulder blades there were two trees. She thought "Twin Oaks," the name of Ashley Wilkes' plantation in *Gone with the Wind*. And in the background, she heard *The Tennessee Waltz*, the first slow song that she and Mark had danced to at the Stage Door Canteen. And now, in her dream, she was dancing to that song with Davey in her arms.

When she woke up, she checked her map of Tennessee and near the Mississippi River, north of Memphis, she saw the town of Twin Oaks.

PART FOUR ~ On Her Own Again

Chapter Twenty-Nine—Ruth and the Kidnapper

December 1946, Twin Oaks, TN

A lady pushing a carriage stopped at the bench where Ruth was sitting, lifted out a near-toddler, bundled in a blue snow suit, and stood him up. He stood straight and tall, holding onto the bench, delighted to be standing.

"Such a big boy," Ruth said to him. He smiled back. All she could see of him was his face and his smile.

"Big indeed," said his proud mother. "They grow so fast. Why if I hadn't seen him for a few months, I probably wouldn't recognize him. Six months ago, he was bald and now he has a full head of hair. And first his eyes were blue, and now they're dark brown."

"My son's eyes are blue, bright blue. I don't think they'll ever change," Ruth added whimsically, trying to imagine how much Davey would have grown by now.

The mother had red hair, green eyes, light skin, and freckles.

"Does he have red hair like yours?" Ruth asked. "I can't tell the way he's bundled up."

"No. He doesn't look a thing like the McDougals. More like his father's side, the Whiteheads—not that his hair is white," She laughed.

"His hair came in dark black when he was about six months old. I'm Angela," she added. "Angela Whitehead. This is Jaimie. And you?"

Ruth hesitated. Married, she was Ruth Hocker. But she wouldn't be married much longer, and she didn't want her name to be a reminder of the man she wanted to forget. Before marriage she had been Ruth Ames Yates. But even "Ruth" felt wrong—part of the inseparable couple of Ruth and Mark. On impulse she said. "Amy. Amy Yates."

"Why you must be from Tennessee folk. There are lots of Yates around here. There's even a town named Yates, just fourteen miles from here."

Angela took a baby book out of a pouch on the carriage. "I take this with me everywhere in case he does something new that I should record. Today he got his second tooth and said a new word—bam bam. That's what we call his teddy bear. That's what my husband Cal called his teddy at that age. Bam bam," she said, and Jaimie echoed, "Bam bam." Angela took a blue teddy bear out of the carriage and handed it to him.

"He can say dada, baba, mama. 'Baba' was his first word at seven months. That's early. He's very bright. Now that he's ten months, he can make little sentences like 'Give baba' when he wants his bottle."

Jaimie said, "Hug mama," and squeezed his mother's leg.

Ruth cringed at the sound of "mama."

Angela opened the baby book and recited her son's measurements and accomplishments. "He's ten months old, twenty-six inches tall and nineteen pounds. At seven months he could sing-along not the words, but the tunes of nursey songs. Also, at seven months, he could sit up. And now, he can pull himself up to a standing position all alone by grabbing hold of something. At five months, he started crawling and in no time, he was crawling everywhere. At nine months, he could pick up a cup and drink by himself. And as of today, he has two teeth. The teething is difficult. It makes him fussy, much fussier than normal. But you must know that, having one of your own."

Ruth nodded in acknowledgement and wishing that she did in fact know from experience.

Angela continued, "He's an amazingly good baby. We were very lucky to get him."

"May I?" Ruth asked, reaching toward Jaimie.

"Of course. Jaimie takes well to strangers and loves being held."

Ruth picked him up, held him high, then brought him close to rub noses with him. Jaimie laughed and reached for her. "Mama," he said.

Ruth got teary eyed. She had never heard that from Davey. By four months, she had never heard anything but crying and random noises. It was bittersweet to hear this stranger's baby call her that.

"My boy was named Davey," she said, handing the baby back and wiping her eyes.

"Past tense?" Angela asked hesitantly.

"Lost."

"Horrible!"

"I don't mean dead. Someone, we don't know who, took him. We haven't seen him since. He was four-months old."

"Unimaginable! What agony that would be." Angela hugged Ruth and held her tight. "Ours was just the opposite."

"How's that?"

"We found him."

Ruth cringed—there was a chance that this could be Davey. She didn't dare say it out loud. How could she accuse this proud and loving mother of being a kidnapper? This could turn into another incident with the police. She needed to be careful, not to alert this lady, not yet. Let her talk—please talk.

"Found him?" Ruth asked, as if out of ordinary neighborly curiosity. That phrase begged the question. This lady wanted to talk about it. She had a story to tell. So please tell it. Please.

Angela continued, "Jaimie was a gift from God, the answer to our prayers. I had had a miscarriage, and the doctor had told us that I couldn't bear children of my own. We were planning to adopt. And here was this baby whose parents had abandoned him on a train in Chicago. How they could have done that I have no idea. He was in the arms of a Pullman porter who didn't know what to do. Some local porter, who needed to get off the train, had passed the baby on to him. The Pullman porter guessed that we were the parents and handed him to us. We had a split second to decide, and we both knew this baby was meant to be ours. With just a glance between us, not a word, we knew we both had that same thought.

"The train was about to leave for New York. If we did nothing, the baby would wind up in social services and foster care or in an orphanage. And we so very much wanted a baby, and we couldn't have one of our own. So, we took him and his baby stuff and got off the train as quickly as we could. Then we headed home, by train and bus. We didn't need a vacation in New York. We needed Jaimie, our Jaimie. We had picked the name before my miscarriage. And there he was—our Jaimie."

Ruth felt an over-powering surge of elation—this was Davey! Despite the impossible odds, she had found him. He would be hers again and forever. She tried to control her facial expression, her body language. This was the acting role of her lifetime. She imagined what this woman would feel to lose her Jaimie—this well-meaning woman who had lovingly cared for him for months. It would be brutal to take her child away from her, but she had to. She absolutely had to. And she had the proof—she had the birth certificate with his foot and handprints.

"My Davey is ten months old now, too," Ruth ventured to say. She took out her baby book and opened it. "He was born on Saturday Feb. 23 at four p.m. He was seven pounds. and four ounces. We were in Minneapolis. Mark, my husband, was stationed at Fort Snell, at the language school."

"How long ago did you lose him?" asked Angela.

"Six months ago. June 10. In Chicago."

Angela cringed. From the quivering of her lower lip, the tremor in her hands, it was clear that Angela realized that this woman sitting beside her could the real mother.

"It was our fault, all our fault," Ruth tried to explain. "We had been on a train for two days from Los Angeles. We were switching trains to one bound for New York. We were hungry and cranky. We asked a porter to watch Davey for a couple minutes while we got some food. That was so dumb, so immature. Mark insisted. I didn't object enough. One of us should have stayed behind with Davey, or we should have taken him along with us. Then one thing after another happened to delay us. Mark's watch stopped—of all times for that to happen. In the meantime, our train was switched to another track. By the time we got to the right track, the train was pulling away in the distance."

"Couldn't the railroad company call ahead to the next station?"

"That's what Mark thought. But I knew better."

"What?"

"As we were racing back to the train, a couple passed us carrying a baby who looked just like Davey."

"Babies look so much alike. That might not have been him."

"He had a blue teddy bear, like the one I had as a child, like the one Jaimie has."

"They sell those everywhere."

"Yes, you're right, of course. But there was one other detail that I remembered and that led me to come to this town in hopes of finding him."

"And what was that?" Angela asked softly.

"The woman was wearing a black dress with white spots. And if you looked closely you could see that the spots were acorns and on the back were two trees like twin oaks."

Angela sobbed uncontrollably, then admitted, "I have a dress like that. A seamstress in town makes them. We wear them for Founder's Day each year." Then she picked up Jaimie and hugged him with one arm, and hugged Ruth with the other arm, and they both sobbed, and Jaimie/Davey cried, too. "How did you find us?" Angela asked. "How could you possibly have found us?"

"Magic," said Ruth, smiling and crying at the same time—her joy tempered by her sympathy for the woman who loved Davey and had taken good care of him for so long. "It was magic."

They stood and hugged again, then together walked through the park, in silence, each with one arm pushing the baby carriage.

Ruth thought that in a perfect universe, there would be two babies, and they could each have one. But the universe was unjust, heartless. Call a spade a spade—God was heartless. And it dawned on Ruth that Mark had been going through the same agony that she had having lost Davey. Mark would be ecstatic when he found out that she had recovered Davey, that Davey was healthy and safe and happy. But no, they never would have lost Davey if it weren't for him, if Mark hadn't left Davey on the train. Let him suffer. He deserved it for his infidelity as well, which had prompted hers. She hated him now as much as she had loved him before. Men are evil. Maybe not all men. Certainly not Davey. But Mark, undoubtedly. She never wanted to see him again, and certainly didn't want to go through the hell of a custody battle and have to share Davey with him and let him corrupt Davey with his noxious influence. No. Never. She would raise Davey alone, raise him the way he should be raised. She wouldn't go back to the Aunties, either. She was a grown woman. She didn't need or want protectors. She could make her way on her own and build a new life. Her office skills were in high demand. She could find work, at a decent wage, anywhere in America. She could afford to hire help to take care of Davey while she worked.

Angela broke the silence. "Where do you live?"

"I don't live anywhere now, nowhere permanent," Ruth replied. "My husband and I broke up. The divorce will be final soon. I'm not in touch with him. I don't think I'll tell him that I found Davey. I don't want a custody battle, and I don't want my life to be tied to his life. I don't want us to have to live near one another. He was unfaithful. It was his fault that we lost Davey. I don't want to have anything to do with him. If I don't say anything about this, the divorce will go through without a hitch, leaving us with no connection, to live our separate lives. I've been staying in Chicago and doing temp secretarial work. I haven't given any thought to where I would settle down after finding Davey. I had pretty much given up hope of finding him."

Angela hesitated. "Then where will you be going with Jaimie?"

"I don't know. I need to build a new life, without Mark and now with Davey. Suddenly, I'm a single mother, and I've never played that role before, and I don't have a script. I'll have to improvise."

"Well, you're welcome here," Angela suggested, hopefully. "While you're deciding on a permanent place and getting yourself together, you and Jaimie—I mean Davey—are welcome to stay with us, as long as you like. I could help with Davey while you learn how to be the mother of a ten-month old, and I could babysit if you need it, when you need it. You could get secretarial work here in town. There's always a need for that."

"I'm good at shorthand and typing—stellar speeds," she said proudly.

"Then here. Let's get you set up here. Maybe you'll like Twin Oaks. Cal and I certainly do. We both grew up here and wouldn't live anywhere else. You'd be doing us a favor, a big favor if you decide to stay. It would give Cal and me a chance to see ... Davey."

And hence, for a while, Ruth stayed in Twin Oaks, Tennessee, so this well-meaning and loving woman who had cared for and bonded with Davey, could continue to see him. There weren't two Daveys, but Ruth could share the one there was with Angela.

As it turned out, a few months later, Angela became pregnant, to the amazement of her doctor, who claimed this must be some kind of magic. She had a son, a big one—ten pounds five ounces. And Ruth was there to help with him during the first, most difficult months. If it wasn't for this new Jaimie absorbing all the attention of Angela and Cal, Ruth might have felt obliged to stay in Twin Oaks forever. But once Jaimie started sleeping through the night, Ruth started thinking about moving—not far, maybe to a nearby town, maybe to Yates, the town with her family name. She was curious about that.

30 ~ Finding Gran

1949, Yates, TN

Ruth didn't have an address or any name other than her father's, Philip Yates. He had never talked about his family or his childhood home. But asking around, she soon found the family farm which once had been a plantation. She went alone. Davey, now age three, was in nursery school weekday mornings.

Her father was there, alone on the front porch.

At first, she didn't recognize him—an overweight old man in a wheelchair. But this man had the long legs of someone over six-feet tall, and dark brown eyes, and a mustache, white now, not blond. He was puffing on a cigarette instead of a pipe, but with a similar rhythm—inhaling, taking the cigarette out slowly and elegantly, then blowing smoke.

"Hello, sir," she addressed him.

He didn't respond at first—maybe he was hard of hearing or maybe he was absorbed in thoughts or dreams.

She stepped closer and asked louder, but politely, "Are you Philip Yates, sir?"

"Yes, yes, that's my name," he finally replied. He tried to get up to greet her, then realized he couldn't and settled back in his chair. "And you? Who might you be?"

"Your daughter."

"Daughter? Yes, yes, I have a daughter. But it's been many years since I've seen her."

"You have five daughters and two sons. I am the one you named Ruth. Now, people call me Amy."

"Amy, yes Amy. My long-lost Amy. Come up on the porch, please, and have a sit so we can talk."

She was taken aback by how easily he accepted her name change from Ruth to Amy. "How long have you been back here, Father?" she asked.

"Three years. Yes, I remember that well. After the war. It was good to come back home."

"So, you were in prison for fourteen years. That must have been difficult. I see it took its toll on you."

"Yes, all together, I was away for fourteen long years, doing business out of Vienna, and then caught up in the war. I knew it was coming, everyone did, but not so fast. It took me by surprise. And then they seized my property bit by bit for one reason and another, and they said I was under suspicion as a spy, and they took my passport. I couldn't get out. And then they shipped me to an internment camp in Germany."

Ruth looked askance. Was this the story he had told everybody? And had he told it so often that now he believed it himself? She decided to indulge his fantasy, rather than challenge him. "And why were you in Vienna?"

"I was working for an investment firm out of Philadelphia. They transferred me to New York. That's where you were born. Your mother, Mabel, died soon after your birth. Mabel's sisters took you to Philadelphia where they cared for you, out of sympathy and kindness to you and also to punish me, I'm sure. They thought that your mother might have been saved if I had called for a doctor sooner. But that wasn't so, that wasn't so at all. It was good that they took care of you. I couldn't cope with an infant alone. But blaming me as they did, they wouldn't let me see you. I believe that they told you and everyone else that I had died, though hearing you now, maybe they said I was in prison. It would be just like them to say that. When the company I worked for opened an office in Vienna, because of my experience and because I had no family, they picked me for the job. Such was my luck." He shook his head.

Ruth was amazed by the complexity of this wild story and its self-consistency. He ignored what she told him about her sisters and brothers. To him, she was an only child. In his mind, not only had he never abused Emily—Emily never existed.

She played along with this strange narrative and asked, "Why in all those years, and especially since you got back, why didn't you try to contact me?"

"I felt guilty about your mother because of the doubts your aunts had sowed, and I felt guilty, too, for not having tried sooner. I kept telling myself that I would get around to it soon, and I never did. But now you're here, and I'm delighted to finally meet you. Come give your father a hug, a big hug."

Then they went inside, and he introduced her to his two unmarried sisters Edith and Violet—another pair of Aunties. He called her "Amy," and said she was his only child. They knew the story he had just told her and knew her name as "Amy." That story wasn't something he had made on the spot.

There, too, she met the other members of the household— descendants of slaves from the days when the farm, much larger then, had been a plantation. Mammy White had nursed Ruth's father when he was a baby. She was now in her 90s and lived with these Aunties, often gossiping, and reminiscing with them in rocking chairs on the porch. Her grandsons Pete and Lew ran the farm and shared the profits. They were the ones who later taught Davey how to ride, swim and fish.

Ruth, now Amy, told her new-found family that she had a three-year-old son, Davey and that she was no longer married. They presumed she was a war-widow, and, out of consideration, didn't press her for details. She could have left it at that, but instead she found herself spinning a story that these good and friendly people—these long-lost relatives—could accept and empathize with in the context of what they already believed. She borrowed facts from the story of Emily's husband, the pilot shot down over Sicily. She modified that tale to take away any hint of heroism. She said that she only knew her husband for a few weeks before marrying him and his shipping out. But instead of a pilot she made him a mechanic. And instead of being shot down in combat, she said the plane crashed due to engine failure during a training exercise. It was a short and boring story. She wanted it to be easily forgotten. She realized that that's the story she should tell Davey when he was old enough to understand. She didn't want to motivate him to look for a long-lost father or to idolize a heroic dead father, either.

When Ruth brought Davey to the farm, he was more interested in the wheelchair than in his grandfather. The old man welcomed him on his lap and took him for a ride down the ramp from the porch to the yard. Then Ruth, directed by her father, pushed them on a tour of the property. They followed the trail past the woodshed and the barn down through the pasture to the pond, which was big enough and deep enough for both swimming and fishing. They had a cow, a mule, two work horses, and a few dozen chickens. Soybeans and corn were their money crops. And they also grew their own vegetables.

This wasn't your archetypal many-columned southern plantation mansion out of *Gone With the Wind*. Such an edifice once stood on this ground. But it had burnt down long before. The farmhouse had a living room, dining room, and kitchen, plus a study that now served as her father's bedroom. Upstairs were four bedrooms: one for Edith, one for Violet, one for Mammy White, and one shared by Pete and Lou. There were two empty bedrooms above that in what used to be the attic. That's where Ruth and Davey moved in a few days later. And a week later Father bought a pony named Dusty for Davie.

Ruth tried to teach Davey to call her father Grandfather. Davey shortened that to Gran, and soon that was what Ruth called him as well, even when Davey wasn't around. That change was easy for her because in his physical condition he looked to her more like a grandfather than a father. And the new name helped her think of him in new ways as if he were a new person.

This man was her father, yet he wasn't. Something was off—off in a good way. This wasn't Father who had physically hurt her mother, and who had done whatever he had done to Emily, for which he spent fourteen years in prison. This man was empathetic and caring. How could all that prison time change a person for the good? That made no sense, but such he was. She wanted to hate him, but she couldn't. This was the father she had always wanted. Renaming him Gran was an aid to forgetting, forgiving, and starting fresh.

31 ~ Gran and Davey

Ruth needed to talk to someone about what had really happened. Under promise of confidentiality, she went to the family's minister, Reverend Schroeder, a Lutheran.

"He was brutal to my mother and he did horrible things to my younger sister; things bad enough to be sent to prison for." She had silently rehearsed the words many times, and spoke them quickly, unburdening herself. She hadn't talked to anyone about this since she broke up with Mark, not even Angela.

"Does he acknowledge these sins and ask for forgiveness?" Reverend Schroeder asked.

"He denies he ever did such things. He even denies that he served time in prison."

"But I understand he was in Europe. He was in Austria on business when the war broke out and spent much of the duration in an internment camp. He acknowledges that prison. In fact, he takes pride in it, as if his suffering there were heroic."

"That's all lies or fantasy—lies he tells us and that he tells himself, as well. I don't know what to do, what to say."

"Whatever the truth may be, he has found peace with himself. With you and Davey around, he's happy like I've never seen him before. He's had a hard life before now. He's frail. He isn't likely to live much longer. My advice is for you to let him live in his own world. Share that world with him as best you can. Let his stories become your stories."

Her father used to smoke a pipe—probably not because he enjoyed smoking, but rather for the image it projected, as if he were a wealthy man of the world, rather than the manager of a general store. Now he chain-smoked cigarettes all day. Ruth guessed he got the habit in prison. She had heard that some prisons gave away cigarettes as rewards for good behavior, as a way to control the inmates and keep them content. It was like including cigarettes in the ration kits of soldiers. Cigarettes were considered an inexpensive treat. In those days, the retail price of a pack of cigarettes, including taxes, was about 18 cents.

Concerned about her father's failing health and the danger of him smoking so much, Ruth visited the family physician, Dr. Allan Jenkins, who lived a quarter mile away. "Smoking is the least of your father's problems," the doctor observed. "He enjoys it. Let him indulge himself. Stopping now, if he could, would be painful and probably wouldn't make any difference. He doesn't have long to live."

"And why is that?" she asked.

"He's sixty-nine, but to look at him, I'd guess he was twenty, even thirty years older than that. Premature aging, I'd call it. Probably due to malnutrition all those years he was interned in German prison camps."

Ruth didn't contradict him. Dr. Jenkins was a family friend as well as a doctor. If she told him about her father's real prison time, everyone would know in short order. She didn't want to do that to her father. He had done a good job of covering up his past, and she didn't want to destroy that.

"What about his memory, his mind?" she ventured to ask.

"He's sharp as can be, and damned clever for his age."

Ruth cringed. She'd have attributed his not remembering her sisters and brothers, his crime and his punishment to some memory illness—something like dementia or senility.

"Savor the time you have left together," Dr. Jenkins advised. "And give him large doses of Davey—that's my prescription. I've seen them together. Davey's good medicine for him."

As far as Gran was concerned, Davey could do no wrong. Gran followed him around and took photos of him doing everything, even deliberate mischief—like crayoning the walls and tearing papers found on his grandfather's desk—which Davey didn't hide, but rather showed off, enjoying the attention. Gran shot two or three rolls of film a day. Davey loved being the center of attention and hammed it up, striking silly poses. When the photos were developed, Gran taped them to the walls. Soon every wall of the house had photos of Davey, taped at spots that Davey himself picked out.

Gran had lots of old picture post cards from Italy, France, Austria, and Germany that he said he got when he was in Europe. Davey loved to play with them. When Davey was four and could write a few words, he wrote on one of those postcards with the help of his mother who told him the spelling.

Hi Gran

Wish you were here.

Love

Davey

She addressed it for him, put a stamp on it, and mailed it. Gran was delighted when it arrived. He taped it to the wall above his bed where he already had taped dozens of photos of Davey.

Gran also connected two tin cans with a string and ran the string from his room to Davey's so they could talk at a distance. Davey loved that. Every night they "signed off" together that way.

When he was four, Davey started asking Gran to read him stories over that tin-can phone. He called them "phony" stories, and he mixed up the words phony and funny, and called everything that made him laugh "phony."

Once a week, Pete and Lew would drive to the center of town to buy groceries and farm supplies. They'd take Davey along so he could go to the Five and Dime and spend the pennies that Gran gave him. For one cent he could buy a bag of candy. For ten cents he could buy an ice cream cone, or a plastic cowboy or Indian or horse, or a comic book. Gran gave him nine pennies a week so Davey would have to save to afford one of the ten-cent items. That meant he'd have to go for a week without buying anything. All week long the question of how to use his money was a subject of conversation with Gran. Gran listened carefully and respectfully as Davey weighed his choices but didn't try to sway him toward one thing or another—it was entirely Davey's choice. First Davey went for penny candy week after week. Then he saved for ice cream. By the time he was five he realized that while candy and ice cream tasted good, they were gone as soon as he ate them. So, instead, he focused on the toys and comic books that he could enjoy repeatedly. Gran was delighted when he chose that way and played with the toys with him and read him the comic books.

For Davey, Halloween was the most important holiday of the year. When he was four, he wanted to be a pirate; at five a cowboy. Gran put together homemade costumes for him, and Ruth pushed his wheelchair as he went along with Davey to the neighbors for trick or treat. Gran himself wore a long-nosed carnival mask he said he got in Venice when he was in Europe. Davey called it his Pinocchio mask.

Gran died a little before Halloween when Davey was six. Davey was going to be a Roman soldier that year, with a wooden sword, a helmet, and a shield that Gran had put together for him during his last days when he was failing. Using a pen knife, with Davey watching intently, Gran had hand-carved the sword out of a slat from a wooden box, then painted the blade silver and the hilt black. The shield he cut from plywood with a coping saw. The helmet he made from cardboard, covered with aluminum foil.

Remembering the trauma that she had felt when her mother died, Ruth didn't let Davey see the body, and didn't take him to the funeral. She told him that Gran had been called away suddenly. He was needed on an important mission in Europe. And though he loved them very much, he probably wouldn't be able to return—not for a very long time.

Hearing that, Davey changed his mind about his Halloween costume. Now he wanted to be Gran. He put that costume together himself. It consisted of the long-nosed mask plus Gran's brown jacket with elbow patches, and Gran's big black belt. And when he said, "trick or treat," he did so with a deep voice that sounded like Gran.

Two weeks later, Davey took the postcard down from the wall by Gran's bed and used that as a model to write and address another postcard:

Hi Gran

Miss you. Miss you. Miss you.

Wish you were here.

Love.

Davey

He put that in the mailbox out by the road.

Ruth removed it when he wasn't looking, wanting to keep it as a remembrance of Davey's love for her father. But Davey checked the mailbox a few hours later, and seeing that the post card was gone, he concluded that it had been picked up by the mailman and would be delivered to Gran wherever he was now.

Then Ruth took one of her father's old blank European postcards and wrote on it:

Dear Davey,
Having wonderful time in Venice.
Love.
Gran

She addressed it to Davey and stamped it and mailed it.

After that, she sent similar replies every time Davey sent a postcard to Gran.

So, until he was old enough to stop believing in Santa Claus and the Easter Bunny, Davey exchanged postcards with his Gran, getting back messages from all over Europe that he taped to the walls of his bedroom.

32 ~ A Marriage of Convenience

1952 to 1963, Yates, TN

After her father died, Ruth slid into the role of caregiver. With Pete and Lew running the farm, it was up to her to deal with the needs of her new Aunties and Mammy White, as well as Davey. The pace was exhausting, and there was no end in sight.

Sometimes a neighbor would stop by with a casserole or a salad, but that meant she had to spend an hour or more rocking on the porch and talking about matters that she had no interest in. She preferred to be left alone so she could do what she had to do.

Then Dr. Jenkins started visiting often, staying long, and helping with chores. He was ten years older than Amy, not particularly handsome, but not bad looking either. This was his way of courting— he was explicit about that.

"I always intended to get married and have children," he explained. "But there aren't many eligible women in the town of Yates, and I don't go elsewhere very often. Even when I do, I'm not good at meeting people. I always believed in 'true love,' but never felt that way about any woman, and apparently no one ever felt that way about me. Now I'm 42, and if I don't find a mate soon, I never will.

"I see you here—young, beautiful, single, and stuck in a difficult situation. Let's face it—you could take care of these old ladies for years until you're old enough to need taking care of yourself. That's a hell of a life. Have you ever thought of getting married again and having more children?"

Ruth rocked silently, staring off toward the pond where Davey was fishing with Pete and Lew. Finally, she answered, "My husband was Rh negative, and I'm Rh positive. We knew from the beginning that we could only safely have one child. So, I got used to that idea, and I cherish Davey all the more since he's the only one."

"Well, let's think about this practically," Jenkins pursued. "I'm Rh positive, like you, so we could have children. There would be no natural limit to how many we could have together. And my practice is successful. I'm not hurting for money. I could afford to hire visiting nurses for the ladies here—all day every day. They'd be taken care of and you wouldn't have to feel guilty about leaving them. And I live just a quarter mile down the road, so Davey could come back here whenever he wanted, to ride his pony, and swim and fish. Consider this a proposal. Ours could be a marriage of convenience, a pleasant partnership, with all the benefits of companionship and parenthood, and none of the drama and heartache of passion."

She mused, "A friend of mine once told me that romantic love is a myth; that we delude ourselves. She thought that life was easier and better in the old days when marriages were arranged by parents and were business contracts, when emotion had nothing to do with it."

She stood up and started to walk away.

"Can I take that as a yes?" he insisted.

She stopped, turned, and nodded.

He got up and walked toward her, with a big grin on his face.

She braced herself for a hug and kiss.

Instead, he shook her hand.

It was a deal.

Jenkins was a kind, intelligent, unambitious man. He went out of his way to do things with and for Davey—to play ball with him and go fishing with him. But Davey didn't take to him, preferring to do those things with Pete and Lew, and with Jaimie, too, who was a little over a year younger than him, and who Angela often brought from Twin Oaks to visit.

For two years, Ruth and Jenkins tried diligently for her to get pregnant. They timed their efforts to the rhythm of her periods, having sex whenever she might be ovulating. She wasn't physically attracted to him, so sex with him was a chore rather than a pleasure, especially since he was so clinical about it, and didn't seem to enjoy it, and didn't expect her to enjoy it. But she wanted more children. She would have been happy to have a half dozen, like her mother had.

When nothing happened, not even a late period, they went to a specialist in Memphis, who told them that Jenkins' sperm count was too low. There was no way they could conceive. Ruth was angry that he hadn't had himself tested before they married.

Davey was a handful. Between him and the housekeeping, Ruth was busy. She was disappointed about not having more children, but her life here was better than it would have been playing caregiver at the farm.

Then Ruth found out that Jenkins was having an affair with his married secretary. Knowing that he couldn't have children made the secretary willing to do it with him. Apparently, sex between them was a habit—a pleasant diversion with no consequences. There was no love between them and neither of them wanted to divorce their spouses. They liked their arrangement and didn't want anything to change.

Ruth confronted him, "I don't give a damn what you do. But it's high time I got on with my life—with the life I want to live. If you'll support me in that, I'll keep up appearances—no scandal, no divorce. These are my terms, my non-negotiable terms. I go to college, and we hire a nanny to watch Davey. When I graduate, I'll get a job as a teacher."

"College—I can see that. But," he objected, "it wouldn't be fitting for a wife of mine to work for wages. People would think I couldn't afford to support you."

"Nonsense," she replied. "Our getting married was a practical matter, a contract between two rational people, not a matter of passion. Well, we need a new contract. You can have your comfortable arrangement with your secretary, and I won't make a fuss about it—no scandal, no divorce. We'll keep living together civilly, respectfully. I have my room, and you have yours. I have my car, and you have yours. And I'll do what I want when I want, as will you."

Hence, she had a room of her own and, until college started in the fall, she had the leisure to write. So, she sat at her desk, looked out over the pasture and the pond, and wrote short stories that she submitted to magazines big and small. She taped the rejection slips to the wall near her bed. It dawned on her that maybe she was working in the wrong genre.

Most of the classic short stories she liked best were based on the premise that a life can have a defining moment of decision and revelation. Others presumed that lives were static, and a snapshot taken at any time could show what mattered about a character. She felt that growth and change were what mattered in life and couldn't be shown in the confines of a short story.

She kept returning to the puzzle of her father. She found it hard to believe that we are what we do. There must be more to us than that. A person shouldn't be defined by a single mistake. We aren't just what we do. We have the potential to do this, that, and another thing—all contradictory. We have the potential for other lives, in addition to the life we find ourselves in. There must be the possibility of redemption and renewal. And for redemption there must be forgiveness and forgetting.

Did that same principle apply to Mark? She wondered where he was now, what he was doing, what their lives would have been like if she had been able to forgive him, if they had stayed together.

She put her writing efforts aside when school began. She commuted to the University of Memphis and earned a bachelor's degree and a teaching certificate. Then she got a job teaching English at the regional high school where Davey and Jaimie went. The teaching kept her busy during the school year, and she put her wages in her own bank account, so she never had to ask Jenkins for money.

Summers she took more college courses until she got a master's degree in literature, which meant an automatic boost in her teacher's pay. Then she continued taking courses subsequent summers, not working toward another degree, but rather following her interests and doing it out of habit and to keep busy.

33 ~ Davey Grows Up

Meanwhile, Davey grew up.

Angela's son, Jaimie, was a year and a half younger than Davey. They became close friends, like brothers. Jaimie was big for his age and Davey a bit small. By the time Davey was twelve and Jaimie eleven, they looked a lot alike and would introduce themselves to strangers as brothers.

They got together often because Angela visited Ruth often and because Jaimie loved the farm where they could ride Dusty together, and they could go swimming and fishing, or they could get Pete or Lew to hitch up the mule to a wagon so they could play with that. Summers the two of them went shirtless and barefoot in their bathing suits, or they'd dress up in cowboy or Indian costumes and ride Dusty through the pasture and around the neighborhood. Ruth told them stories about Tom Sawyer and Huck Finn, and they acted out those stories or others of their own making with Pete or Lew, whichever of them happened to have spare time.

Gran had proudly told Davey that his great-grandfather, Joel, ran against Davey Crockett for the state legislature. Joel lost the election, but it was an honor to have run against such a man, to be in the same league with him. Joel was Davey's great-great-great grandfather. And that's how Davey got his name, Gran said, though Ruth and Mark had picked the name out of a book of names. When Davey was ten and Disney made Davey Crockett famous with movies, Davey proudly wore a coonskin cap to school.

By the time Davey was twelve, Ruth's connection with him was strained. When she took him for walks when he was a toddler, she had sung with him, "Step on a crack, and you'll break your mother's back," and together they had avoided the cracks in the pavement. Now, when they walked together, which was rare, he would deliberately step on as many cracks as he could. She reminded herself that rebellion was normal and good. He needed to build his own world of friends and interests, his own fantasies and ambitions and faults. But she missed the days when he would let her hug him, and they could be happy together, even doing nothing.

Over the years, Jenkins tried repeatedly to bond with Davey, but never succeeded. In 1962, when Davey was sixteen and got his driver's license, Jenkins bought him a new car to win his gratitude and respect. Ruth thought that was extravagant and unnecessary. She would've been happier if the driving age were thirty or even forty. Davey was far too young to drive a car, and it was far too expensive a gift. They were well off and could afford it, but you shouldn't give something that valuable and dangerous to a sixteen-year-old.

The car Davey asked for and got was a Pontiac Grand Prix. He pronounced the word "grand" without the "d," the way the French did. So, it was his Gran Prix, his Gran car. He took good care of it, kept it immaculate inside and out, quite different from his room or anything else in his life. Ruth was sure the cleanliness was meant for the girls he was taking out in it, whoever they might be, because he would never talk to his mother about such matters.

Later that same year, Davey caught mononucleosis. He missed nearly two months of school and had to repeat the year. Ruth blamed the gift of the car, with its large comfortable back seat. That led to Jaimie and Davey being in the same grade at the same regional high school—the school where Ruth taught—cementing their already close ties.

Junior year of high school, for the Halloween dance, they both dressed up in World War II uniforms and got army-style crew cuts. It was hard for Ruth to believe that Mark had been not much older than that when she met and married him.

Davey and Jaimie both went to college at Vanderbilt, where they were roommates. Davey who, from his experiences on the farm and his love of animals, had planned to become a veterinarian, followed Jaimie's lead, and got into computer programming instead. Ruth's main source of information about him was Angela who occasionally got a letter or a call from Jaimie, who said little about himself but rambled on about Davey's doings. That was how Ruth first heard about Hanna, Davey's future wife, who he met standing in line in the computer lab with a stack of punch cards.

Davey had been the center of her life, and now she only merited a few short visits a year. Vacations he either had a school project that he needed to finish and could only do on campus, or he had a programming job that paid too much for him to pass up. "Such is life," Ruth conceded. Angela suffered the same fate. So do most mothers.

Davey and Hanna married shortly after graduation and moved to Silicon Valley. Hanna was Japanese American, third generation. Her name meant "one love." Her parents, as children, had been detained in an internment camp in California during the war. She had big anime eyes and would probably always look like a schoolgirl. They intended to have one child, a boy who they would call "Hiro." But they were in no hurry to get started. They foresaw vast opportunities in computing — from videogame design to robotics to artificial intelligence. They were going to be on the ground floor and help make a whole new world. They would deal with child birthing and rearing when the excitement slowed down.

34 ~ Ruth Grows Up

After Davey left for college, Ruth tried to reread Virginia Woolf's novels and essays. But her eyes got tired, and even when she set aside several hours to devote to reading and settled in a comfortable chair with good lighting, she fell asleep after only a few pages. Then it dawned on her that maybe she was going through another metamorphosis, and her eyes weren't as strong as they used to be.

She went to an eye doctor. Her distance vision was still good enough, though not perfect, as it used to be. She wouldn't need prescription glasses to drive. But she did need reading glasses—3.0 magnification.

She picked up Virginia Woolf again. This time her eyes didn't get tired, but the text didn't hold her attention. Her tastes had changed. The rhythm of the prose and the images no longer resonated with her. It was as if she suddenly didn't like the taste of ice cream, or she could no longer digest milk.

During the school year, Ruth immersed herself in work and school-related activities. Summers she kept busy taking courses toward another master's degree, and then taking creative writing classes and going to writers' conferences and workshops. She wrote dozens of story-length personal memoirs with the idea of one day putting them together as an autobiographical novel. She wasn't sure what the balance should be between fact and fiction. As she explained to Angela, who remained her closest friend, "I understand so little about myself and the people I've known that if I tried to write fact, I'd end up writing fiction. Also, the direction of our lives is shaped by the lies we tell ourselves and the ones we tell others, often with good intent, to alleviate pain, to avoid embarrassment, and to be kind. And if you lie frequently and consistently, as I have, at some point you come to believe your own lies."

"Maybe that should be the theme of your book," Angela suggested. "Well-meaning lies."

"Yes, maybe it should." Amy laughed. "Truth is over-rated."

She was impressed by the work of a historian, Perry Burr, who wrote about a similar theme—the role of lies in history. She sent him a fan letter by way of his publisher, but, of course, he didn't reply. She tried to sign up for a conference where he would be speaking and teaching, but it was sold out.

***

Ruth's writing had been stalled for years when, in 1972, she read *The Optimist's Daughter*, a Eudora Welty novel which had just won the Pulitzer Prize. On the final page of that book, she saw the words "never mind," and thoughts of her mother came rushing back, and memories of her anger about social injustice and the Japanese, and the time in Chicago, when she invoked the nevermind magic with all her heart and mind, and then, against all odds, she found Davey.

At the time, she had considered it a coincidence, a wildly unlikely coincidence that she prayed nevermind and then found Davey. But now she wondered.

Finding her father had been wildly unlikely as well. And when she found him, he told a life story that was completely different from what she knew had happened, and everyone believed him. It was as if his abuse of Emily had never happened, and he had never spent fourteen years in prison for that crime—as if that had been undone, magically, and as if the same powerful magic that had led her to Davey had changed the world.

That's when she realized that the book she had in her, that had been gestating for years and that now needed to be written, was driven by her need to make sense of her life. She felt compelled to drive to Jackson, Mississippi and sit in her car in front of Eudora Welty's house and begin her book there. So that's what she did. She parked there for a day and a half and filled three notebooks with handwritten notes, seeing Welty herself three times—collecting her mail from the box at the end of her driveway, working in the flower garden beside the front door, and pulling out of the driveway, wearing a bright red hat, with a broad smile on her face.

When Ruth got home, she quit her teaching job and wrote twelve hours a day for six weeks and finished her novel. At first, she thought that draft was brilliant. She pored over directories in the library to decide what agents and what publishers to send queries to. Then she reread it, was disappointed, and set it aside.

A few months later, she returned to the project, and slowly, carefully, over the course of a year, she rewrote it.

After letting it sit again for months, she started another rewrite. At this point, writing the book of her life was the business of her life. It was her identity. And she was in no hurry to finish.

Meanwhile, her father's sisters died and left the farm to Pete and Lew who both had married and lived there with their growing swarm of children. Ruth thought of finally leaving Jenkins and moving but procrastinated—first she would need to finish the novel that she didn't really want to finish.

Then when Jenkins died in 1980, after twenty-seven years of marriage, Ruth, age sixty, collected her husband's life insurance, sold his medical practice, sold the house, and took off. She settled in Venice—California, not Italy—intending to start a new life. There she would be closer to Davey and Hanna, but not so close as to disrupt the rhythm of their lives, or for them to interfere with hers. There she would finish her novel and maybe, for the fun of it, she'd audition for parts in movies.

35 ~ The Love of Granny

1980 to 1990, Venice, CA

When she arrived in Venice, ready to start a new life, she went to a psychotherapist once a week for six months, talking about her childhood, her father, her romance and marriage with Mark, the disaster in Chicago, her anti-romance and marriage with Jenkins. It felt good to unburden herself; that helped her as she rewrote her novel yet again, and it also motivated her to undergo a complete personal makeover—through exercise, diet, cosmetics, new wardrobe, plus new hair color.

Her hair was mostly gray now; no stranger would guess that it had once been bright blond, a color that would look phony at her age. She decided on dark brown and short. With that change alone she could hardly recognize herself in the mirror.

The therapist, Elaine Casper, a woman her age, became close friends with her. When Ruth ended the therapy sessions because she had finished telling the complete story of her life, they still met once a week for dinner. Elaine sometimes set Ruth up with blind dates, friends of her current boyfriend, whoever that might be. In 1984, four years after her move to Venice, joking with Elaine over dinner, Ruth came up with the idea of starting a sex therapy business.

Ruth stuck a sign in the sand and held her sessions on the beach. The sign read:

"Granny knows best

I'm a self-proclaimed sex therapist.

Guaranteed to have no credentials.

I help you help yourself."

First, she charged just $5 an hour. Everyone was welcome to sit nearby, listen in, and even express opinions. But if someone abused that privilege, she'd insist that he or she pay a share of the fee or leave. Her business uniform was a bikini, a floppy straw sun hat, sunglasses, and beach shoes. Clients, too, had to wear bathing suits. She'd counsel men or women, individuals or couples, straight or gay.

At first, most of her clients were young men in groups—high school or college age—daring one another to open up in public about intimate prurient matters. She would begin by telling the client, "Imagine how your partner will look when she's in her sixties, which I am now. Will you want to caress her and hold her, to have your way with her? If so, let's talk—there's hope for you. If not, don't waste your money—you're not in love. What you call love is mutual friction, science friction. Buy a good lube and get on with it.

"You and your partner will inhabit many different bodies over the years—young and old, thin and fat. If you can truly connect with one another, those changes won't matter. You'll want one another as much as you do today when you're both as old as I am now."

Her clients presumed that she was speaking from experience, sharing what she had learned from a long life of love. They came away convinced that true and lasting love was possible, and motivated to work through their problems with their partners. Many believed they benefitted from her sessions and spread the word. As demand grew, she raised her price, in stages, and eventually charged $100 an hour.

When counseling a couple, she often advised that instead of dressing up, using makeup, and doing all they could to look their best for one another, they should do the reverse and try to look their worst. She said, "Don't try to be prince and princess. See how well you get along, how much you attract one another and enjoy one another when you are Mr. and Mrs. Frog. Forget about what your friends would think. You aren't looking for trophy partners that your friends will envy you for winning. This is about the two of you, and how you connect, and how you enjoy being with one another when you are at your worst as well as your best. Both of you should dare to be the worst you can be—not just in looks but in temperament and behavior. Then you'll be able to decide if what you feel for one another is real and lasting."

When she was asked, as she often was, "How long have you been married?" she replied, "We got married the day before D-Day."

When she was asked, "Do you still love one another?" she replied, "Beyond belief."

Someone nicknamed her "The Love Granny," and the name stuck. A shop near the stretch of beach where she did business sold T-shirts, caps, towels, and bathing suits printed with that slogan. Soon hundreds of people on the beach and the walkway all the way from Venice to Santa Monica were advertising her business through their attire. She could no longer handle walk-in customers—there were simply too many of them. So, she booked them in advance, with timeslots from noon to five on weekends and holidays, no sessions during regular business hours. She wouldn't let her business interfere with her reading and writing, and she enjoyed sleeping late.

At first it felt strange calling herself "Granny," since technically she wasn't one and probably never would be. She was the right age for it and looked the part, but Davey and Hanna still hadn't had the one child they had planned and promised. He and Hanna, now thirty-eight, had been married for sixteen years and seemed in no hurry for parenthood, blissfully immersed in their careers and technical accomplishments.

She found it titillating to talk about sex and imagine it, though she hadn't experienced it in decades. And hearing about her clients' problems, feelings, and fears, she realized how inhibited she herself had been when she was as young as they were now. She laughed at herself, recounting her experiences to Elaine and realizing how much she had changed—Uncle Adolph could have dispensed advice like this. She was having fun doing this and from the way the business grew, she must be helping people. She readjusted her judgment of Mark's failings—his infidelity with Maxine and with the unnamed woman he sketched in the nude. And it was good for her writing to better understand her own hang-ups, limitations, and mistakes.

As her seventieth birthday approached, one of her clients asked, "What are you going to do now that you're rich?"

"A world cruise," she replied, surprising herself with her answer. "I've always wanted to go on a world cruise." She remembered saying something like that to Mark long ago.

PART FIVE ~ Love at Second Sight

Chapter Thirty-Six—The Love Boat

March 1990 on board The Pacific Princess

Ruth was tempted to disembark at the next port—Fort Lauderdale—and cut short her world cruise.

She had boarded the Pacific Princess in San Pedro two weeks before. She had signed up after watching the made-for-TV movie *The Love Boat: A Valentine Voyage*, just three days before the cruise began. She had window-shopped for such a cruise after the thought cruising occurred to her on the beach. The show had triggered the actual decision, cutting short her procrastination. It helped that she got a generous last-minute discount. Someone must have cancelled.

In fact, she appeared for fifteen seconds, as an extra, in that very *Love Boat* movie. She had watched the series religiously, enjoying the fantasy of romance while stuck in a marriage of convenience. The show stirred her memories of bygone days when she believed in true love and spent her Saturday nights at the Stage Door Canteen, meeting and dancing with soldiers and sailors, until she finally met the man who, for a brief while, was the love of her life.

Standing on the Lido Deck, by the outdoor pool where a band was playing the theme song of *The Love Boat*, she couldn't help but shiver with the thrill of being on the very ship that was used in the TV series, even though she was having second thoughts about this trip.

She took a brochure from her pocketbook and reread the itinerary, re-igniting her enthusiasm for exotic destinations—Aruba, Barcelona,

Rome, Athens, Aqaba, Abu Dhabi, Kuala Limpur, Singapore, Hong Kong, Bora Bora, Sidney, Auckland. She had spent all her childhood and teen years in Philadelphia. She had stayed put in a small town in Tennessee for her entire second marriage. And for the past ten years, with no responsibilities and plenty of money in the bank, she hadn't left the Los Angeles area.

She should be ready for new experiences. But this was a hundred-and-eleven-day cruise, and already she was bored. She should bail out now, get a refund for the balance of the trip, and go back to Venice and her comfortable life as the Love Granny.

Over the last two weeks, she had read and swum and had gone ashore at the ports-of-call for the beaches and the shopping. But the beaches were no better than the beach in Venice—which had been cleaned up decades ago—and the stores sold the same merchandise as stores back home. There was dancing, shows, and fine dining. But she was alone. She was the only adult without a partner or family group.

How different it was in the TV series where the ship was packed with singles mingling and falling in love. Maybe it was that way on three-day cruises and even week-long cruises, full of young people taking a break from work to party and play. But genius that she was, she had chosen a cruise that would last three and a half months, filled with people as old as she was or older and retired, with time and money on their hands. Elderly couples.

Maybe that was the problem—not the cruise itself, but the fact that she was doing it alone. Maybe that was the problem with her life, as well.

She had trip insurance. If she quit now, she wouldn't get all her money back, but she would get most of it, and she could escape the torture of three more months of loneliness in an environment designed for romance.

Before she reached the purser's office to settle her account and end her cruise, the ship docked at Fort Lauderdale. She heard over the loudspeaker that tomorrow night they would be showing that same *Love Boat* movie under the stars. She went out on the Promenade Deck—like Jimmy Durante, tempted to leave and tempted to stay—and watched the gangway as passengers went ashore, and new passengers came on board.

She did a double-take. Someone who was walking up the gangway, alone, looked very familiar. She knew him, but she couldn't remember his name. She took off her sunglasses to get a better look but put them back on again—the sun was painfully bright.

He was tall and had black hair with streaks of gray. His hair was long, tied in a ponytail. He looked self-confident, relaxed. He, too, was wearing sunglasses. He paused several times to take in the panoramic view of the ship, the harbor, the ocean beyond. He was the only incoming passenger carrying a book.

Ruth raced to the library. She felt a primal need to remember who this man was, and she knew there was a connection between him and books. He was an author whose works she had read. She hoped the ship's library, with a collection much smaller than her own at home, would have a book of his, and she'd be able to solve this mystery. She hated "senior moments," and liked to fill memory gaps quickly. She kept notebooks with lists of names that could trigger her memories of related names. This instance felt more important than the everyday forgetfulness she was used to. She needed to know who he was.

She was determined to look at every book in the library, until she found one by him, or until she was certain the library didn't have any of his books. Fortunately, his name began with B—Burr. He was Perry Burr. The book in the library was one she had read years before, the one that established his reputation—*Red, White, and Blue Lies*, the first of a series of non-fiction books about the effect of lies on historical events. There was a photo of him on the back cover. That was him all right, even to the ponytail and the sunglasses, which gave him an aura of mystery. In the photo, he was in his fifties, but she knew he was as old as she was. From her brief glimpse of him on the gangway, he had aged well, like Sean Connery.

She read the blurb on the back-cover. He had started this book as a Ph.D. dissertation, but got immersed in the research and missed his deadline. He continued working on the project for another two decades while getting on with his life in the workaday world. The scope of this book was wide-ranging: from the Trail of Tears, to Communist scares, to myths propagated by white supremacists, to the Gulf of Tonkin Resolution. His thesis was that lies have frequently shaped American policy, and that lies are an important part of our daily lives—lies that we tell ourselves to motivate us to do what we feel is necessary, and lies that we tell others, even our children and often with good intent, to get them to do what we feel they should do. That theme resonated with her own literary ambitions—the autobiographical novel she had been working on for decades was entitled *Well-Meaning Lies.*

She wanted to talk to this man. In the best of all possible worlds, he'd read her book and give her an introduction to his agent. She needed to stop obsessively rewriting and polishing and try to get the book published. Regardless of whether she made any money from it, publication would be a cathartic moment, a validation, a personal triumph.

Perry and she would be on this ship for three months. They might be the only two unattached adults on board. Surely, over the course of that time, she would meet him and summon the courage to talk to him.

She took his book back to her cabin, dressed for dinner, and fussed over her makeup. Then she went to the International Cafe in the Atrium and found a seat with a clear view. She remembered that that was one of the first places she went when she came on board, orienting herself and getting a sense of what was available where. Besides, in a few hours they'd start serving dinner, and most passengers going to the dining rooms would pass through there.

At 5:30, soon after the dining rooms opened, Perry walked by. Apparently, he was on "anytime dining," not assigned to a particular table at a particular time. That was good. She followed him, but not closely, not wanting to seem like a stalker. He was alone. Standing in line, nobody was paying particular attention to him. He was still wearing sunglasses—a celebrity incognito. She put hers on as well since they made her feel less self-conscious.

She might be the only one on the ship who recognized him. She might also be the only one on the ship who had read his book.

She tipped the maître d' and, embarrassed but determined, she asked to be seated at the same table as the gentleman who had entered shortly before her. He smiled knowingly and gestured for a waiter to lead her there.

It was a round table for eight. Ruth was seated directly across from him. She tried not to stare at him and when everyone at the table introduced themselves, he just said , "Perry," and didn't volunteer anything more about himself. The other people at the table were couples from Florida and Australia. Perry was polite in answering the small-talk questions directed at him. But he was far more interested in eating than getting to know these strangers who seemed to delight in swapping travel stories and one-upping one another about how many cruises they had been on, and what future cruises they had booked.

After dinner, she followed him in the corridors as he made his way to the auditorium for the show—a stand-up comedian. It was crowded, and there were no empty seats near him. She stood in the back, near one of the exits. But when the show ended, she didn't see him. He must have left through a different door.

The next morning, she got up early and stationed herself on the Lido Deck just outside the buffet. After a couple of hours with no sign of him, she gave up and got her usual Wheaties and grapefruit.

She checked the schedule and headed to the ping pong tournament on the off chance he might be there. He was playing and losing when she arrived, then he left abruptly, and she followed at a discreet distance. He headed to the adult, enclosed swimming pool. He had his trunks on under his trousers and started swimming laps. By the time she went back to her cabin and changed into her swimsuit, fussed over her looks, and waited for the elevator back up, he was gone.

After another change of outfit, she stationed herself in the Atrium again. He showed up for line-dancing lessons. She joined in, but the dance floor was crowded, and she couldn't get close to him.

Then Perry disappeared. She sat and waited, drinking coffee, and nibbling on pastries. She didn't see him go to the dining room for lunch or supper. Maybe he went to the buffet on the Lido Deck instead.

She couldn't help but laugh at herself for trying so hard. She fetched his book from her cabin and grabbed a hamburger. She settled in a deck chair to reread his book and wait for the under-the-stars showing of the *Love Boat* movie.

37 ~ Ulterior Motive

March 1990 on board The Pacific Princess

A lady leaning on the railing a couple decks above was staring at him. Perry Burr stopped on the gangway and pretended to take in the panoramic view as other incoming passengers squeezed past him, annoyed that someone would be so rude as to block the way on embarkation day.

He checked her out with the corners of his eyes. She was about his age—65. Tall and slim, with short perky dark-brown hair. He took a couple steps forward, then stopped to check her out again. She was leaning as far forward as the railing allowed. She took her sunglasses off, for a moment—to get a better look at him, he presumed.

He turned and looked straight at her. She ducked back, probably embarrassed to have been caught and disappeared. Something about her was hauntingly familiar.

At dinner, the woman sitting across from him was the same woman who had stared at him when he was on the gangway. She was still wearing sunglasses, as was he. He tried not to stare at her. It was a big table, and the room was noisy. He couldn't make out her name when she introduced herself. He was curious, but it would have been awkward to strike up a conversation and flirt with her from such a distance and surrounded by strangers. It would be easier when he chanced upon her alone, which he was sure he would since it would be a long cruise.

She followed him to the auditorium. She was right behind him, and he was guessing that was deliberate. Maybe she was a fan. There were far too few of those. He had received a few whacky and flirtatious letters forwarded by his publisher. He was flattered and intrigued by her interest in him, and it was a pleasure to look at her. If she weren't stalking him, he might want to stalk her.

His wife of 40 years had died three years ago. He was ready to move on, but out of practice in dating or even talking to single women his own age. He had gone out on blind dates with half a dozen women that friends set him up with. But that never prompted a second meeting. He had hoped he might meet someone on this cruise but, in the boarding process, it had looked like they were all couples.

His uncle, still active and brimming with life at 89, had warned him that the odds of his meeting a single woman on a world cruise were astronomically small. He replied that he wasn't doing this to meet women. He had booked this cruise on November 9, 1989, the day the Berlin Wall came down. To him, that marked the end of the Cold War. And this cruise was how he wanted to celebrate that landmark in history. He hoped the cruise would provide inspiration for his next book, the fourth in the *Red, White, and Blue Lies* series.

His uncle had encouraged him to make the most of the situation. If he wanted to do a world cruise, he should bring someone along to have fun with. He should post personal ads for a cabin mate and should interview prospects and maybe even test drive them, offering the trip of a lifetime, for free. And it wouldn't cost much of anything to make such an offer, because the cost for two sharing a cabin would be the same as the cost of going alone, except for gratuities and port fees.

He had replied that if he chose the wrong woman, it would be three months of hell. He didn't trust his judgment. It was hard to tell what made for compatibility and, at his age, chemistry was rare. It was different with the woman he had loved and lived with for a lifetime. He always saw her as younger than other people did, her present looks overlaid with his memories of her. Now as a widower, women young enough to physically attract him were so young he could be their father, and they showed no interest in him.

His uncle had suggested that he play the celebrity card, the sugar daddy card. "Be the guy with deep pockets," he said. "Don't waste your time with forty and fifty-year-olds. Go for broke. Get a twenty-something who's drawn to you for your fame or your money."

But Perry knew he would have nothing in common with such a woman. What would they talk about? He'd bore her, and she would bore him, and sex without a connection would get stale fast.

His uncle had concluded, "What a waste."

He didn't see the mystery lady the next day. Maybe she had lost interest in him, or maybe it was hard to find someone without knowing his name on a ship with thousands of passengers.

Then, after dinner, he spotted her stretched out on a deck chair watching the *Love Boat* movie, with his first book open and lying on her lap. As he had suspected and hoped, there was no ring on her ring finger.

***

The author was standing right beside Ruth, but she wasn't about to make the first move. In the dark and without sunglasses, he looked different from the photo on the back cover, but familiar. He looked at her with what might have been a flash of recognition, but still he didn't speak. He knew she had been following him. He went out of his way to walk over here. And now he just stood here, without saying anything, pretending to watch the movie? How long was it going to take for him to speak?

He smiled and she smiled back, and she knew that despite her efforts at a poker face, he knew that she had been following him, and he knew that she knew that he knew, and there was no reason to pretend otherwise.

"Admit it. Fess up," he finally spoke, mockingly. "That's my book you have there. You've been stalking me. I don't mind. I'm flattered. It wasn't an accident that you were leaning over the railing staring at me as I went up the gangway. You knew I was going to be on this trip, and you were looking for me. Somebody at Doubleday let you know I had booked this cruise. Don't get me wrong. I'm delighted to meet you.

"And here you let me ramble on like this with that quizzical look on your face and not a word in response. Who told you that I'd be here?"

"No one told me," she insisted. "I recognized you."

"Really? Not many people would remember what I look like from my book covers. But I suppose you did because you happened to be reading a book of mine."

"First I recognized you. Then I got the book from the library to make sure. I read it years ago."

"So, it wasn't an accident that we ended up sitting at the same table last night."

"Guilty as charged," she admitted.

"Okay, I can buy that with your superpower photographic memory you matched me, sunglasses and all, with an old dustjacket photo. But why were you staring my way when I walked up the gangway? No one else was leaning over the railing. There were only a handful of people like me boarding in Fort Lauderdale. It wasn't a big-deal embarkation with fanfare and celebration. I'm a researcher. I understand that details matter. I'm used to following up on details that don't feel right. And this is one of those details. Why were you looking for me?"

"But I wasn't looking for you. I had no idea you were coming on board. I was thinking about leaving the cruise. I got on in San Pedro two weeks ago, and the cruise wasn't turning out the way I had imagined. I was bored, can you believe? I was lonely on a ship with thousands of people. I didn't know anyone here and hadn't seen anyone I wanted to meet. And I couldn't imagine another three months of the same."

"So, do you plan to get off in Barcelona?"

"No. Not now." She smiled flirtatiously.

He chuckled. "I apologize. It isn't like me to poke and probe an attractive woman like you at first meeting. I'm sure that rude behavior like mine would chase away anyone else, and I'd never see her for the rest of the cruise. But there's something about you, something that makes me feel we're already connected."

Now she was the one who chuckled. "So first you accuse me of being a stalker fan, and now you imply that we could be soulmates, fated to meet, magically connected to one another. That's too much. Has that line ever worked for you?" She continued in a mock dramatic voice, "From the first time I looked deep into your sunglasses, I knew that you were the one."

"We aren't wearing sunglasses now. But the lighting is bad. I can't even tell the color of your eyes."

"Night has a tendency to do that."

"Seriously, let's step back into the light of the walkway. You can afford to miss a few minutes of this silly made-for-TV movie."

"That's my movie you're talking about."

"Yours? Are you the producer or the director? Or are you such an avid fan that you feel you own it? You seem to have this fan thing."

"I'm in it as a nameless extra."

"Aha! An extraordinary lady. Congratulations. You'll have to show me where you appear. Your scene hasn't come on yet, has it?"

"Not yet. Not for another half hour. My fifteen seconds of fame. You'll have to watch closely, or you'll miss it. I missed it myself the first time I watched it. I'll show up on the left side of the screen, in a red evening gown, dancing the cha cha."

"No wonder you look familiar," he said. "You're a famous actress."

She enjoyed his attention and didn't mind him knowing she enjoyed it and letting him know that she knew. She hadn't flirted like this since she was in her twenties.

"Your interest in me is flattering," he continued. "But I can't buy the story you're telling me. A woman your age—who is my age, I'm sure—took one glance at me, then raced to the library and matched what she saw of me from a hundred feet away with an old photo on a book cover. She guessed that that was me, and then followed me all over the ship. And for what purpose? Because I'm irresistibly handsome? That doesn't ring true. Women don't respond to me that way. I don't have a harem of groupies following me around, certainly not attractive sophisticated women my own age. You were intent on meeting me, and you knew who I was. But I'm not that well known. People don't stop me in the street and ask for my autograph. So fess up—why was it so important to you to meet me?"

"My book," she admitted.

"*Your* book? You're an author?"

"Unpublished."

"So, you're hoping I'll read your manuscript and help you get an agent?"

"It sounds crass to put it that way."

"But it's true?"

"Yes, true."

"So, then you aren't a crazy person? That's a relief. I honestly wouldn't know what to do if you were a real stalker, like the fan in *Misery*, that Stephen King thing. You're an author—that makes sense to me. We have that in common. And you've probably been working on this book of yours for years?"

"Decades," she admitted.

"So thinking I might be able to help get it published, you wanted to seize this chance to fulfill your lifelong wish—not to connect with a brilliant handsome man who might be the love of your life, but rather to be published. The ulterior motive. That I understand. Before my first book was published, I would have done the same. I'm delighted to meet you, and I'll be delighted to read your manuscript. Not that I do that often. Normally, I turn down such requests. I have no time for it, and it's tedious reading a book in typescript. It's hard on the eyes. Even a good book is difficult to read that way. But here you are. I'm intrigued by you, I must admit. And having seen you and recognized that you are alone, I would have gone out my way to meet you and to get to know you. And here's my perfect opportunity—you're an author and you want me to read your book and help with it. The perfect ploy, the perfect come-on line, and you hand it to me as a gift. I'm delighted. But you have me at a disadvantage. You know my name, but I don't know yours."

"Amy. Amy Yates," she replied.

"Yates? I once knew a lovely lady named Yates; not so lovely as you, of course."

They chuckled at the lame compliment.

"And what's your book about?" he continued.

"It's called *Well-Meaning Lies*."

"So, we have that in common. We're both into lies. Non-fiction? Perhaps a work of psychology?"

"Fiction. Autobiographical. If I knew myself well, it would be non-fiction. Since I don't, it's a novel."

He smiled. "Do you intend to watch the rest of this movie? I gather you've seen it before."

"Half a dozen times." She smiled.

"And I'd rather see the true you than your celluloid image, and rather see you for hours or days than fifteen seconds. Do you dance?" he asked. "There's a band playing old-time dance music in the Atrium."

"Give me a moment," she said. "I'll run to my cabin and get shoes I can dance in. These sandals won't do. I'll meet you in five, no fifteen minutes in the International Cafe."

At her cabin, she changed out of shorts and blouse to a knee-length dark blue dress. She brushed her teeth, washed her face, powdered her cheeks, fussed over her eye lashes and eyebrows, brushed her hair. She decided against high heels—that would be too much.

Then she smiled at herself ironically in the mirror. She was making mistakes her Love-Granny clients typically made—trying to look her best, trying to impress, not daring to show her true self. But it felt good doing so. She felt exhilarated like when she was twenty-three, getting ready to go to the Stage Door Canteen. She liked being twenty-three again.

Just yesterday, she was making a mental checklist of everything she had to pack and how to do it so it would all fit in her two suitcases. She was in near-panic mode then, aware of the need to close her account before the purser's office closed, and anticipating waiting in lines for passport control, then customs, and finding a cab, and a hotel with a vacancy. Her head had been crowded with concerns that were connected in sequence, where one forgotten detail could have annoying consequences.

Now her mind was a blissful blank. She was untethered. There was nothing she needed to think about but her makeup and her shoes.

Half an hour later she found him—pacing, sipping a drink, scanning from one side of the vast Atrium to the other, looking for her. His face lit up when he saw her. It had been good to make him wait.

The band was playing "The Boogie Woogie Bugle Boy from Company C", and the singers were Andrews Sisters look-alikes in World War II army uniforms. Perry and she danced every dance—fast and slow, swinging wide while instinctively avoiding the other fast-paced dancers crowding the floor and then clinging close like high schoolers at their prom, with no notion of what others might think of them. Hearing the familiar oldies played one after another, it was easy to forget who they were, where they were, and how old they were; to forget everything but the music and the motion that came naturally to them, that was part of their being, a being they had long lost and now found. "Swinging on a Star," "Sentimental Journey," "Buttons and Bows," "I'll Never Smile Again," "You Are My Sunshine," "The Tennessee Waltz."

They danced until the band stopped playing at midnight. Then they nibbled coconut almond croissants at the International Cafe.

They agreed to meet for breakfast at nine in the morning, at the buffet, on the port side, amidships.

38 ~ True Love, The Sequel

March 1990 on board The Pacific Princess

Ruth slept soundly and woke with a buzz of anticipation, high like she hadn't felt in over forty years. She didn't know how far this would go, but she was determined to enjoy the ride while it lasted. There had been an electric tingle when their fingertips first touched. He had continued to hold her hand when they sat during the band's breaks. She gave a gentle squeeze, and he squeezed back. She almost giggled, like a seventh grader holding a boy's hand for the first time. She was embarrassed, self-conscious, but delighted. This was outlandish—a seventy-year-old woman holding hands with a stranger on a cruise ship.

After they started dancing, they hadn't spoken much. She hadn't felt the need to talk, nor had he. They enjoyed one another's company. She hadn't danced since she had with Mark, long ago. But dancing with Perry, the moves came back, her muscles remembered what her mind had forgotten. They had parted with a quick, but not too quick kiss; just enough and not too much for strangers with three months ahead of them on a cruise around the world, plenty of time to get acquainted and more than acquainted, to let their mutual attraction grow naturally, however far it might grow.

If she ever played Love Granny again, she would change her pitch. She had told her clients to put their worst foot forward, to act like their inner frog, rather than pretend to be a prince, to be honest and hence attract a mate who loved them for who they really were. But now, attracted to Perry, she realized that that advice was dead wrong. It would be foolish for her to look and act her worst. Truth was overrated. A would-be lover was a liar; a sincere, passionate, considerate, and well-meaning liar. Such is life.

Should she feel guilty for having dispensed bad advice? No way. She had wanted to provoke her clients to question the standard wisdom and think for themselves. And even when she was wrong, she had succeeded in that.

She wouldn't wear sunglasses today. She wanted to look Perry straight in the eye in full daylight.

At the buffet, she only wanted coffee. She wasn't hungry. It was hard to think about food. Walking to the table where he was already sitting, their eyes locked. He, too, wasn't wearing sunglasses.

His eyes were green. She had seen those eyes before. She tried to remember—where, when, who? Distracted, she tripped. She grabbed the table to steady herself. She didn't spill her coffee, but the table moved, splashing his coffee onto his lap.

"Never mind," he said, wiping off his trousers with a napkin.

"What?

"Never mind."

"Give me now my nevermind," she responded without thinking.

He smiled, then broke out in laughter. "This is too much. This can't be happening."

"You had a crew cut."

"Your hair was long and blond."

"You put on weight."

"You didn't." He smiled.

"Perry Burr?"

"My pen name. 'Perry' from Perry Mason, and 'Burr' from Raymond Burr. Writing about lies and lying, it seemed natural that the name on the book should be a lie."

"And you use that name in everyday life as well?"

"I wanted a fresh start. I wanted to become a new me."

"Me as well."

"You want me to call you Amy?"

"No, I want you to call me Ruth, one letter shy of truth."

"I missed you."

He stood up, took her hand, and led her to the top deck, to the jogging trail, which was empty. There they hugged and kissed, and she nestled in his arms quietly. She felt echoes of the time when they had been close and crazy in love. The pain of their breakup felt like it hadn't happened to her, that she had seen it in a movie long ago.

There was much to say, but she preferred to postpone mentioning Davey. What she had done in lying by omission, by keeping their son from him was unforgivable. But she needed him to forgive her and she didn't want anything to get in the way of their having a happily-ever-after together. Their finding one another again after all this time and being drawn together again as strangers—it was a miracle. She didn't want to lose him again.

She laughed remembering her test for love, then explained her laughter. "Believe it or not, once upon a time, I was a sex therapist."

"A sex therapist? You? You have changed, my dear." He joined in her laughter.

"I was known as the 'Love Granny.' And the first thing I told my clients was: 'Imagine how your partner will look when the two of you are in your sixties. Will you still want to caress, hold, and have your way with one another? If so, let's talk—there's hope for you.'"

"So, we should talk," he said, holding her tight.

"And we have so much to talk about."

"But me first," he insisted.

"You're not going to say you're married, are you?" She looked at him askance. "You wouldn't go on a cruise like this alone if you were married?"

"I'm widowed."

"Sorry for your loss," She hugged him closer, not knowing how fresh and deep the pain might be.

"Three years ago. It's time to move on."

"I'm widowed, too. Ten years ago."

He rubbed noses with her and kissed her on the forehead, the cheeks, the ear lobes. A pair of joggers came their way. Ruth and Mark stepped aside to let them pass.

Ruth whispered in his ear, "Come to my cabin. It will be easier to talk there."

He lifted her and she wrapped her legs around him, and they kissed deeply.

When the joggers approached again, having gone the full circuit of the boat, nearly half a mile, he let her down so they could step aside again.

"Yes." He agreed. "Let's go to your cabin so we can—"

"Talk."

39 ~ Which Davey?

March 1990 on board The Pacific Princess

From the door to the cabin, they could see that the steward had made up Ruth's room, leaving on the bed a towel cleverly folded in the form of a swan, and half a dozen chocolates wrapped in gold paper. The sliding door to the balcony was open. The temperature was in the mid-seventies. No wind. No clouds. Aside from the ship's wake, the ocean was smooth like a pond. For another three months there'd be no need to shop for groceries or cook or do laundry; no need to do anything but enjoy themselves. It was the perfect setting for a honeymoon.

Ruth hesitated at the doorway and gave Mark an expectant look.

"Like I said, I need to tell you—" he started to say.

She stopped him. "No, silly. We're standing on the threshold. Where's your sense of tradition?"

He smiled, picked her up, and carried her to the bed.

"Now, I have to get this off my chest," he continued.

"I can help with that." She started to unbutton his shirt.

To her surprise, he stopped her. "What's wrong?" she asked.

"I'm sorry. Oh so sorry."

"For what? Are you still blaming yourself for leaving Davey on the train? That was as much my fault as yours."

"I found Davey," he blurted out.

"You what?" She stared in shock.

"I found Davey, after we lost him in Chicago. And I never told you. I made no effort to contact you. The divorce was going smoothly, and I didn't want a custody battle."

"Davey? You found Davey?"

"Yes. He's safe. He's happy. He's married. He has a life of his own. And you never had a chance to know him, much less raise him. I robbed you of your son. I never should have done that. I'm so, so sorry. I was selfish. I was cruel. I don't know how I can ever make that up to you."

Ruth pinched herself. She glanced in the mirror. This couldn't be happening. This made no sense.

"Why aren't you screaming?" he continued. "You should be furious. I stole your son. I stole a whole lifetime of raising him and loving him and having him as part of your life. Why aren't you mad as hell?"

"I have nothing to be angry about. I'm just as guilty as you are."

"What do you mean?"

"I did the same thing," she told him.

"You what?"

"I found Davey, and didn't tell you, and raised him and he and his wife are doing just fine. Whatever you're guilty of, I'm guilty of, too."

"But that's impossible. There can't be two Daveys." Mark insisted.

"Of course not."

"We both couldn't have found and raised Davey. There's only one Davey, and that's my Davey."

"Yes, of course there's only one, and he's mine."

"If there are two, then one of them isn't real," Mark said.

"Don't say that."

"One of us must have made a mistake and raised the wrong child, like a mix-up at the hospital and parents going home with the wrong babies."

She reached in her pocketbook and pulled out a snapshot.

He took out his wallet and flipped to a snapshot.

"They could be twins," Mark said.

"They could be the same person."

They both laughed, nervously, then reached out to hug again. They were relieved, unburdened of their guilt. This wasn't going to break them up. But they needed an explanation.

"What happened?" she asked. "How did you find your Davey?"

"You insisted that Davey wasn't on the train, that you had seen him, that he had been stolen. I was sure that he *was* on the train, that nobody had done anything wrong—we just hadn't gotten back in time. I went to the ticket counter and from there found the security office. I wanted them to stop the train, or at the very least to send a message, to make sure that Davey was all right, and to arrange for him to be taken off in Cleveland, the next stop. They told me that there weren't any telephones on trains because telephones require wires. And they didn't have two-way radios on trains. This wasn't the Army, they insisted. That kind of radio was expensive, and there was no need for it. They did call Cleveland, and police met the train when it got in. But Davey wasn't on board."

"So, I was right."

"No. It's more complicated than that. He had been on board when the train left Chicago."

"What did the porter say?"

"The porter we gave him to wasn't on the train. He was an ordinary porter who works at a single station, helping move luggage on and off. That kind of porter doesn't ride on trains. When the train was getting ready to leave Chicago, our porter, the one with Davey, panicked. We hadn't come back, and he had to get off. He handed Davey to a Pullman porter, with little or no explanation, and ran for it. He didn't want anything to do with that mess."

"You spoke to him?"

"Later, yes. The police quickly tracked him down at the station in Chicago. But all he knew was that he gave Davey to a Pullman porter. Whatever happened after that wasn't his fault."

"And what did the Pullman porter say?"

"Normally, he rode back and forth on that same train between Chicago and New York. The police took him off the train in Cleveland and got the whole story, at least as much of it as he knew, and what he said matched what the porter had said. Suddenly he had this baby in his arms and the baby was screaming and the parents apparently had missed the train. He didn't know who the parents were. He wasn't even sure that the couple who had left the baby were the real parents. 'What parents would do such a thing?' he asked. Maybe the baby had been kidnapped and the felons had panicked and ditched him. The Pullman porter didn't know how to deal with babies since he had never had children of his own. And he had his job to do. He was relieved when a passenger offered to help, took hold of Davey, and rocked him and spoke to him, and Davey stopped crying. This kind gentleman offered to watch Davey while the porter did his work.

"Davey was asleep in the man's arms when the porter returned. The porter figured that everything would be okay now. This passenger could babysit until they got to Cleveland, and then the authorities—

either the railroad or the police—could deal with the matter. He would be off the hook. Then the passenger said that it would be a shame for this kid to wind up in social services and then foster care or an orphanage. He said he had a friend who handled adoptions, who could take good care of this kid and find him a good home, fast. The conductor hesitated because that didn't sound legal. Then the passenger offered him money—$500 cash, on the spot. The conductor took the money, and the passenger got off the train in Cleveland with Davey before the police came on board to find him. When the police asked about an unaccompanied baby, passengers pointed to the porter, and when his answers were dodgy, they took him off the train and interrogated him until they had a credible accounting of what had happened, and a full description of the man who took Davey."

"So how long did it take for the police to track him down?"

"They got nowhere. I hired a private detective who found him later."

"And then what did you do?"

"I went to Florida, to my Uncle Adolph, who had generously wired me the money I needed for the divorce and the detective. He was living with his wife Margery and her daughter, Judy."

"The two of them were great with Davey at Fort Snell."

"And they were great again, especially Judy. She bonded with Davey, and I bonded with her. A couple years later, I married her. We were married for 40 years."

Ruth pulled Mark to the bed and lay down with him, her head on his shoulder. She didn't want to look him in the eye. She didn't want to look at him at all or say anything more to him. Their finding each other was wonderful. Period. She was guilty of not telling him, and he was guilty of not telling her. That there were two Daveys made no sense, except if one of them was the "real" Davey and the other not. But how could that matter at this point? She loved her Davey, and Mark loved his Davey. No physical evidence was going to change that. What mattered was the life they had lived and the emotions that they felt. The question wasn't, "What is the truth?" but rather, "Why should the truth matter?" She was shocked at how mellow she felt, how quickly she accepted that the impossible was possible.

"So that's it?" Mark asked. "All these years I've been carrying the burden of that guilt, and it turns out no-fault, no-guilt; it doesn't matter?"

"Let's call it a draw," she suggested. "We did the same thing to one another. And it doesn't matter anymore. We forgive one another and start fresh. Let's enjoy the moment. Someday we'll swap stories and laugh about the foolish things we did in our youth. But not now. Please."

"But how do you explain the two Daveys?"

"Not now. We'll talk about that later. I can't get my head around this. It makes no sense. Rain check. If we talk about it now, we'll give each other headaches. Let's move on."

"I must admit that I'm relieved," said Mark. "This has weighed on my conscience. It was such a terrible thing I did to you. But however it happened, you had your Davey. You raised your Davey. There were times when I was tempted to track you down, to get to know you again, to be friends. What we had together was special. But I couldn't bring myself to confess and try to make things right, even after Davey had left the nest and there was no longer a question of custody. I had lied so long it was hard to stop lying. I guess, that's a character flaw of mine."

"Enough, Mark. Please. It's over. What we did back then makes no difference now. Both our Davies are forty-four years old now and married. They have their own lives and don't depend on either of us. Whether natural born or accidentally adopted, we raised them like our flesh and blood. And, I dare say, we did a good job of it. That's enough about them for now."

"But details matter to me. I'd like to sort out this puzzle. I told you how I found my Davey, now you need to tell me how you found yours."

"No, I won't tell you," she insisted.

"What?" he sat up, held her by the shoulders and looked her in the eye.

"I don't need to tell you. It's in the book, my book—everything. You can read it. Then you'll have the whole story and the context. You can read it any time you want. It's on the desk. But there's no need to do that now."

She gently pushed him down and cuddled again.

"You're determined to get me to read that, aren't you?"

She shut him up with a kiss, which led to more kisses. Then she suddenly got out of bed.

"What's wrong?" he asked.

"Nothing's wrong. All's right with the world," she replied and hung the do-not-disturb sign on the door.

40 ~ A Novel Situation

March 1990 on board The Pacific Princess

When Ruth woke up in the morning, Mark was sitting at the desk, reading her manuscript. He was involved, intent. He looked like he wanted to swallow it in a single gulp. Maybe he loved her writing, or maybe he was involved in what the book revealed. She didn't want to break his concentration. Ravenously hungry, she ordered room service—pancakes, eggs over easy, coffee, cranberry juice, three Danish. What she didn't eat herself, she put on the desk for Mark. He kept reading, without a pause.

She showered, cleaned her teeth, brushed her hair. When she stepped out of the bathroom in her all-together, he was so involved in reading her book that he didn't notice. She smiled. He couldn't have paid her a higher compliment.

From her pocketbook she took out a jewelry box she had been carrying around for decades, out of habit—the engagement and wedding rings—a sign that she wished they had never broken up. She put them on and looked at herself in the full-length mirror on the bathroom door. She felt good about what she looked like and who she was now. She put on a sweatshirt and sweatpants and went jogging on the trail on the top deck, breathing deep and savoring the view of the uninterrupted ocean extending to the horizon on all sides.

When she returned to the cabin, Mark was still reading so she changed to her bathing suit, went up to the adult pool, and swam laps for an hour.

When she returned, Mark didn't even raise his head. She ordered lunch from room service—turkey club sandwiches, chips, and soda; enough for both of them. He hadn't touched his breakfast.

She changed into a skirt and blouse and went to the Atrium for line-dancing class.

When she returned to the cabin, Mark was still reading so she changed into shorts and went to the gym for a workout on the treadmill and elliptical.

When she returned, he was more than halfway through the stack of pages and had eaten a couple of sandwiches. She was impressed at his attention span. She would have needed to take breaks no matter how good the book.

She ordered dinner—surf and turf: steak and lobster for two. Once again, she ate alone, leaving his meal on the desk beside him.

She changed into her blue dress and went to the eight o'clock show—an Elvis Presley impersonator. When she got back, she undressed and crawled into bed, exhausted, and fell asleep, with the lights on, as he continued to read, uninterrupted.

When she woke up, the room was pitch dark. He wasn't reading anymore. He was on a recliner on the balcony.

The night air was cool. She put on a bathrobe and slippers and stretched out on the other recliner. They held hands, looking at the horizon rather than one another. A full moon was rising.

"How does it end?" he asked.

"It's the story of my life. I'm hoping it doesn't end."

"So, you're not exactly a realist."

"I'm a magical realist."

"So, this is a magical realist autobiography?" he chuckles. "Seriously, how do you want the book to end?"

"They meet again, forty-four years after they broke up and they fall in love again and live happily ever after."

"You should do more research so you can tell that convincingly." He nuzzled her neck and kissed her ear lobe.

"I plan to," she replied. "I'm not going to let you out of my sight for the next three months."

"That's a good place to end a book."

"And a good place to start a new life." She dared to ask, "So you think I can write?"

"It's a good story, well told. Even if you were a stranger, I'd do everything I could to help get it published. But I do have some concerns."

"What concerns?"

"For starters, what you say about Hanna," he said.

"Hanna? Yes, in my world, she's Davey's wife."

"Yes. And she's my Davey's wife as well."

"She's a lovely girl," Ruth commented.

"Indeed," Mark replied. "But there are two different Hannas."

"What do you mean? My Davey married Hanna, and your Davey married Hanna. Weird though that is, it's consistent."

"In your life story they met by chance, waiting in line in the computer lab at Vanderbilt. But in mine, they met because I exchanged Christmas cards with Jane and George Hayashi. That was how I found out that their daughter was at Vanderbilt."

"Jane and George had a daughter? I lost touch with them. Are you saying that Hanna is Jane and George's daughter?"

"No, the Hanna that I know was their daughter's roommate. She and Davey became friends in college and met again years later and fell in love and married."

"That's odd ... that they met in a different way."

"And your Davey married Hanna twenty-two years ago, right after college, but they never had children and given their ages, they probably never will. But my Davey married Hanna four years ago, and they have a two-year-old son named Hiro."

"A grandson? I have a grandson? Out of all this craziness, I end up with a grandson? That's fine with me." She laughed and sat on his lap.

"There's more."

"Nothing bad, I hope," she added hesitantly.

"Your father—the two different versions of your father's life."

"You mean that business about him being interned in a prison camp in Germany? That was nonsense. He was losing his memory. I have no idea why so many people believed that story."

"And he claimed that you were his only child."

"That was bizarre.

"Did you ever use the nevermind before Chicago?"

"No."

"And your mother never used it."

"As far as I know. She might have tried before I was born, or she might have done it without telling me."

"And did she say anything about previous generations using it?"

"No."

"So, the only instance you know of was when you did it in Chicago, and soon after that you found Davey?"

"Yes. Coincidence. Wonderful coincidence."

"What I didn't mention before was that I did, too."

"You what?"

"When the police gave up, the detective was getting nowhere. In desperation, when I was ready to give up, I tried your nevermind thing. I said it. I prayed it repeatedly all night. And the next day, the detective called to tell me that he had found Davey. One of us doing nevermind and finding Davey would be a coincidence. Both of us doing it—maybe even at the same time—that's something else. There being two Daveys, who look like twins and who we both believe are the real Davey, neither of them a mistake—that's something out of science fiction, like the multi-verse explanation of reality."

"What the hell is that?" she sat up and took notice.

"Some physicists and many science fiction writers believe that there are an infinite number of parallel worlds with the same people in them, as if those worlds had branched off from decision points, as if more than one decision was made and each decision led to a different chain of events, a different world."

"What are you getting at?"

"This two-Davey thing, if real, isn't just an unsolvable puzzle. It could be a symptom that parallel worlds are entangled, and that could have dangerous consequences."

"Can you say that again, in English?"

"Imagine we were trains in a railroad station, and we could shunt to different tracks."

"You'll have to do better than that—I know nothing about railroads."

"Say you were in a play and you were who you were, and you were also the character you were playing—two worlds overlaid, one on the other."

"Okay."

"Now imagine that your everyday life is a play, but you don't know that it is. When something terrible happens, you nevermind it away and you continue with your life. Having edited that scene out, the rest of your script changes in ways you couldn't have foreseen. Now imagine that someone else is shocked by that same terrible thing that shocked you, and he also neverminds it away. He then plays out his part in his script. You don't see one another for decades. Then when you do get together again, you realize that your scripts don't match, that your worlds have differences that don't make sense. Remember the moment at the end of *The Matrix* when Neo realizes that the life he thought he was living was a fantasy, that he is part of some huge organic battery.

"This is also like the moment in a play or a movie when a character steps out of his role and addresses the audience. They call that 'breaking the fourth wall.' The character realizes that he's in a play or movie and is shocked by that revelation. That can be effective theater. But imagine it happening in real life, exposing that real life isn't real at all? Imagine the consequences of that?

"Imagine that we stopped believing not in Santa Claus or in God but rather in the reality of our own lives, and we let others around us know that, pointing to the telltale anomalies as evidence. The story couldn't continue. You and they couldn't keep acting out your parts if you realized that those were parts, not what you did from free will. Your world depended on your belief, and that belief popped like a balloon. That would be an emperor's-new-clothes moment; a Buddhist realizing that the everyday world is a Veil of Maya.

"I'm not saying that this is so. If I absolutely believed that the real world is a fantasy, I would go mad. I don't want to believe that. But I want to get rid of these contradictions. I want to make them go away."

"Are you well?" She puts her hand on his forehead to check his temperature. "You're scaring me."

"I'm scaring myself. This is a form of vertigo. You've felt that. I've felt that. Standing still on the edge of a cliff or sitting on a moving train, you can lose your sense of balance and feel drawn where you dare not go."

"You've got to be kidding. This is a side of you I've never seen before. Are you into aliens and conspiracy theories? Parallel worlds? The obvious truth is that we are both here, together finally, in this one very real world." She tried to laugh off this absurd suggestion.

"Bear with me, please. Suspend your disbelief and try to get a feel for the possibilities. When we did the nevermind, we focused on finding

Davey, but we must have also, in the back of our minds, imagined a long-term outcome—our happily-ever-after. That future included us getting back together as we have now. Our worlds diverged back then, but now they are converging toward this wished for outcome. I'm concerned that that convergence might have unintended disastrous consequences."

"Hold me. Please hold me and shut your eyes. Stop thinking about this—please. Think of me. Think of us. Believe in us and your anxiety, your panic attack will go away. It has to."

"Never mind."

"Of course I have to mind. I love you, and that way lies madness."

"Yes, madness lies. I'm sure it lies. But never mind."

"You mean the magic—that nevermind?"

"Yes, of course. It's real, and we need to use it. Let's do a nevermind together and focus on our Daveys, and try to imagine a world without contradictions, a new world for us together. Say it with me. Pray it with me."

PART SIX ~ HAPPILY-EVER-AFTER TIME

Chapter Forty-One — Back to Some Flavor of Reality

April 1990 on board The Pacific Princess and in Petra, Jordan

"Did anything change?" Ruth asked the next morning, stretching lazily in bed.

"How would we know? The only other time I tried nevermind, I needed to find Davey and I got a call from my detective."

"And when I tried nevermind, I had a dream that led me to Twin Oaks."

"But this time, we don't have a clear and simple question," noted Mark.

"What should we do?"

"Let's presume that the magic worked and stop worrying about the two Daveys. Let's celebrate and honeymoon."

"I love you, Mr. Crazy Person."

"And I'm crazy about you, too."

Ruth and Mark didn't leave her cabin for weeks. The ship crossed the Atlantic and landed in Barcelona, Rome, Athens, and passed through the Suez Canal. They watched the changing seascape and landscape through the sliding glass doors to the balcony or from the balcony itself, where Ruth sometimes posed nude for Mark to draw her. But mostly they lounged lazily, with no need to do anything other than luxuriate in one another's presence. They got all their meals by room service. Periodically, they got fresh towels and sheets from the cabin steward. There was no need to give him their laundry because there was no need to wear clothes. They lost track of time as they made time together, over, and over, getting reacquainted, making up for the lost forty-four years.

At Aqaba in Jordan, when they finally ventured forth from the cabin, they asked at the purser's office if they could save money if Mark vacated his cabin and officially moved in with her.

"Sorry. No way. Imagine what such a policy would lead to—strangers meeting on board and deciding to shack up together to get refunds."

"But we're married."

"You signed on for this cruise as single."

"It's complicated. We hadn't seen each other in forty-four years. We thought we were divorced, but we're still married."

The purser laughed, "Come on. How gullible do you think I am?"

Ruth wanted to go on the bus excursion from Aqaba to Petra.

"Why Petra?" asked Mark. "You don't have Jewish or Arab ancestors, do you?"

"I have Indiana Jones."

"What?

"They shot scenes for *Indiana Jones and the Last Crusader* at Petra. I was an extra in that movie. They shot my part on the back lot at Paramount. I got autographs from Sean Connery and Harrison Ford. The movie came out last year. Did you see it?"

"And who were you? A sexy German spy?"

"I was a grandmotherly Arab, wearing a burqa and selling souvenirs to tourists."

"We'll have to watch it together when it comes out on videotape. So, they shot Indy at Petra? Delightful. The bonding of ancient history and modern myth—lies of every size, layered upon one another. That could become a chapter in my next book, another flavor of lies and parallel worlds. Here's this ancient site attracting tourists from all over the world. There are people here imagining what it was like walking here 2000 years ago. And right beside them are fans of Indiana Jones, for whom walking here makes tangible the fictional world of the movie. The same sights, the same rocks, the same cliffside sculpture, but different realities."

"You promised not to talk about that stuff, remember? We're going to be happy."

"And honeymoon," Mark agreed.

"Yes, my love, celebrating nearly forty-six years of married bliss."

"Did you notice that June 5 is our arrival date in San Pedro?"

"Another coincidence?" she asked, half-jokingly.

"Remember. We promised not to talk about such things."

At Aqaba, the ship was docked beside an oil tanker, near beaches, with the city and reddish sandstone cliffs a few miles away. Here was the impregnable fortress that Lawrence of Arabia took with his band of rebels by attacking from the desert instead of from the coast where all the defenses were aimed.

Mark and Ruth raced through immigration and boarded the air-conditioned excursion bus. The heat was worse than Miami and Vegas in mid-summer. How could people have lived here before air conditioning? How did the Bedouins survive, wrapped in their woolen robes? they wondered.

On the two-hour bus ride from Aqaba to Petra, if not for the road signs in Arabic, they could have believed they had been magically transported to the American Southwest, where they both, separately, had taken Davey when he was ten, and both had ridden mules down the steep slopes of Bryce Canyon. Here they saw the same rugged treeless terrain, the same sandstone vistas shaped by wind and rain over millions of years. Their destination was in the country of Jordan, east of the Dead Sea, not far from biblical scenes. But without prior knowledge, they could have guessed the Bedouin sheep herders on distant hilltops were Navajo. They could be near the Arizona-Utah border, where the terrain looks like an alien world and which had served as the set for dozens of movies.

The bus stopped at the visitors' center in Wadi Musa. They bought matching Indiana Jones hats at one of the dozens of gift shops. Then they proceeded down the mile-long gulch cut through the sandstone by flash floods, leaving a narrow passageway, with uneven footing. The heat pounded down on them, making the windless walk feel like ten miles or more. They stopped at short intervals to rest on a ledge in the shade. The steep rock cliffs on either side of them extended thirty to forty feet high. And they needed to stay alert for mule- and donkey-driven carts careening down the narrow path, driven by young boys who seemed to enjoy giving their tourist passengers and the pedestrians in their path a scary thrill. They also had to watch for tourists on mule-back or camel-back who had never ridden such beasts before and had little control over their mounts.

Then, around the next bend of the curving gulch, they saw what all these hordes of tourists had come to see, the reason they are willing to walk through this hellish heat: the Treasury—a building carved into the sandstone cliff two thousand years ago.

Mark bought Ruth a hand-made stone necklace from a pre-teen vendor and they guzzled warm bottled water bought from another vendor for twice the price of the necklace. They watched other tourists lining up to mount a camel in front of the Treasury and hanging on, with difficulty, as the camel tried to dislodge them, like riding a mechanical bucking bronco in a bar in Texas.

Finally, they sat quietly on a stone bench, in a shady corner of the Roman theater, amid both history and fantasy.

42 ~ Third Life Story

April 1990, on board The Pacific Princess

They got back from Petra when dinner was being served in the dining rooms.

The maître d' recognized Ruth. "Ah, Ms. Yates. We missed you. I see you found your gentleman. Very good."

She smiled and confirmed, "Yes, I found him. And it is very good."

They asked for a table near a window. They wanted to watch the sail-away from Aqaba as they ate.

It was a table for eight.

The waiter was Japanese. His name tag read "Akihito Hayashi." They smiled at the familiar last name and greeted him in Japanese. Both Ruth and Mark were rusty but could still handle standard greetings and polite small talk. They bowed, and he bowed in return. No Anglo passenger had ever greeted him in Japanese before and he was delighted.

At the end of the meal, Akihito gave them a cartoon that he had doodled while they were eating.

From then on, each night they went to the dining room when it opened, at 5:15, and asked for table 63, with Akihito and he drew a cartoon for them. The cartoons were from a series of illustrations he was working on for a manga graphic novel he was writing. Mark reciprocated, giving Akihito caricatures of people he had seen on the ship.

Akihito was working on two stories. In *Comic Kamikaze,* a reincarnated WWII pilot became a superhero whose power was to disarm his opponents by making them laugh. And in *Bunny the Marine,* a meek teenage girl who had been arrested for shoplifting, joined the Marines as an alternative to a jail sentence and became a kick-ass fighter. She, too, had a superpower—when she opened wide her innocent eyes, everybody believed whatever she said.

Ruth asked, "How do you come up with these stories?"

He replied, "One think leads to another. That's a pun," he added, proud that his English was good enough to make a joke.

At Akihito's table, they met dozens of passengers from around the world. Some people appeared one night and didn't return after that. Others become regulars, going out of their way to show up at 5:15 and ask for table 63, with Akihito.

One couple said that they got engaged before they had a first date. His best friend and her best friend got married. They met at the wedding. He gave her a ride home. She invited him in. He proposed immediately, and she accepted without hesitation. They had been married for forty years.

Another couple married one another's best friends, then moved to distant parts of the country and lost touch. They each divorced. Then, years later, they met each other by chance and fell in love and married.

Another couple lived together for fifty years before they got married. This cruise was their honeymoon.

One passenger claimed to be the great-grandson of the man who was the model for Passepartout, the resourceful valet in Jules Verne's *Around the World in 80 Days*, the true hero of that story. He said that his wife was a niece of H. Rider Haggard, author of *King Solomon's Mines* and that they lived in Kenya, near the border with Ethiopia, where they conducted research as independent scholars, free of the control of universities or grant programs. This was their first vacation in twenty years.

Another passenger, named Heinrich, said that he was both a rabbi and a former Nazi, and that his wife, Miriam, was a Holocaust survivor. Heinrich was a Hitler youth as a preschooler, signed up by his father, an SS officer. After the war, his mother divorced his father and moved to America. After he graduated from college, Heinrich converted to Judaism, became a rabbi, an expert in Yiddish literature, and married Miriam.

Mark leaned over and whispered to Ruth, "How can they tell such lies with a straight face?"

Mark told the truth when he shared their story with the others at the table—that they fell in love and married during the war, lost their infant son on a train, divorced, and never saw or heard from one another for forty-four years. They met by chance on this cruise and fell in love again.

Everybody laughed in disbelief and asked for the real story.

"Okay," Mark said with a smile. "What I said is the story we're acting out for this cruise—our romantic role play. We actually got married the day before D-Day and have been together ever since."

The rest of his story rolled off his tongue, as if he were remembering, not inventing, "After the war, I went to Gettysburg College, as a seminary student, under the GI Bill. I became a Lutheran minister. But in the first month, I had a crisis of faith. A parishioner, a man in his twenties, who had survived D-Day and the war in Europe unscathed, died, suddenly. He left a widow with three small kids. I said comforting things with supporting biblical quotes. But I didn't believe what I was saying. This was inexplicable, senseless, random. I couldn't lie to those people, but that was my job. I couldn't believe in heaven and hell and divine justice. I quit. I went back to college and majored in history, focusing on historical and political lies and their consequences.

"Ruth and I scrambled to pay the bills while I went to school. At one point she juggled three part-time jobs—working for an answering center, a pharmacy, and a video rental store. I worked nights and weekends, driving a cab, selling encyclopedias door-to-door, selling life insurance, even selling my blood. Going for a Ph.D. was more than we could afford. I got a job writing the company newspaper for a computer company. Then Ruth went to college nights and earned a degree as an English major.

"We've been very fortunate. Ruth was the sixth of seven children. Her mother died when she was ten, and her father, who couldn't cope, let his wife's sisters raise the kids, while he wallowed in grief and rum. Then one day, as he was coming out of a liquor store, he chanced upon Emily, Ruth's baby sister. She was five years old, and by accident she was all alone in downtown Philadelphia. Her aunts had taken her and her siblings shopping, and in the rush-hour crunch getting onto the trolley to go home, Emily didn't make it on board. She didn't know where she was. She didn't know her address or phone number. She had no idea what she could or should do. Then she spotted her father, who she hadn't seen in months. He picked her up and hugged her and threw the bottle of rum he had just bought in a trash bin. He took her home to her aunts, who were frantic, having finally realized that she was missing and having no idea where they could have lost her. He stayed and helped with supper and came back the next day and helped around the house. He became a regular visitor. He got a job as a draftsman, and helped pay the bills, and helped discipline and motivate the kids. Eventually, he and Aunt Olive fell in love and married. So instead of being raised by a pair of old maid aunts, Ruth had a mother and a father, and her father was more involved in her life than he had ever been in the past.

"That's what I meant by fortunate. Bad things happen, but then good things happen, and life goes on.

"Later, Emily married a fighter pilot, and he was shot down over Sicily. Everybody thought he was dead, but three years later he came home, healed of his wounds and his amnesia. Tragedy turned to joy.

"Meanwhile I got shipped to Okinawa. Everybody expected the war would end soon. What terrible luck to have wound up there and then. Over fifty thousand Americans were killed or wounded in that battle. And I was nearly one of them. I stepped on a mine. Everyone in my platoon heard the trigger click and ducked for cover, but it was a dud. I came home without a scratch.

"As I told you before, our only son, Davey, went missing on a train in Chicago when he was four months old. That was no lie. He was gone for an hour, the worst hour of my life. It turned out that the train had been shunted to a different track to repair an unforeseen problem. When we found him, he was playing patty-cake with the porter. He never knew we were gone.

"We've had one lucky twist of fate after another.

"Davey went to Vanderbilt and majored in computer science. There he met and married a Japanese girl, Hanna, which means 'one love.' She has big wide anime eyes and even now, at the age of forty, she still looks like a schoolgirl. Davey and Hanna are in high tech, in Silicon Valley. They have a two-year-old son, named Hiro. His first words were, 'Me! Me!'

"While Davey was at Vanderbilt, and we were feeling empty-nest pangs, we gambled. Since the birth of Davey, we had been careful to avoid getting pregnant for fear of Rh complications with a second birth. We wanted another child, and, at our age, time was running out. We gambled and won. We had a baby girl eighteen years younger than Davey. We named her Skylark, 'Lark' for short.

"All the while, I kept researching the ideas that I had intended for my dissertation, before I dropped out of the doctoral program. Those notes became a series of books you may have heard of—*Red, White, and Blue Lies.*

"With the success of my first book, Ruth was able to quit her job teaching English in high school and focus on finishing a novel she had been working on for decades. *Well-Meaning Lies* is the title. It was published a few years ago and sold well. In fact, it will soon be a movie, produced and directed by Kent Boswick. The premiere will be held in Hollywood soon after our cruise ends in San Pedro on June 5, which is my birthday and also our anniversary."

When the meal ended, Akihito spoke to Mark, quickly and enthusiastically. "Kent Boswick? That's amazing. I love his movies. If only I could get a chance to show my work to him. That's my dream."

Mark didn't know what to say. He had never heard of a director or producer named "Kent Boswick." He only knew the name from Ruth's story, and it had popped into his head unexpectedly, as he was improvising.

After dinner, Mark and Ruth lounged on the Sky Deck. The ship was south of the Equator, nearing the Great Barrier Reef, and they hoped to spot the Southern Cross if the cloud cover gave way.

"How did you do that?" Ruth asked. "How did you talk so glibly and convincingly about things you made up on the spot?"

"I have no idea. I didn't know what I was going to say until I said it. But now we have a new life story, what should have been our story," Mark concluded with a smile.

"I particularly liked that bit about my father and Aunt Olive. That was hilarious. They would have made quite a couple."

43 ~ Renewing Vows

May 1990, on board The Pacific Princess and in Tokyo, Japan

The next night, Mark explained to the others at the dinner table, "As part of our role play, we want to renew our vows."

"Will you do that on shipboard?" asked Heinrich.

"We would prefer that it be a religious ceremony, rather than one with the captain. We checked with Passenger Services and learned that there are no Protestant ministers or Catholic priests among the passengers. And you, Heinrich, are the only rabbi. We're hoping that you'll agree to officiate."

"That's unusual, since neither of you is Jewish. But this isn't a real marriage; just a renewal of vows, a statement of love and commitment so I could do that. I'd love to."

"Thank you," said Ruth. "That means a lot to us."

"Yes," added Mark, "with a rabbi joining us the second time around, we'll be married not just in the eyes of God, but in the eyes of two Gods."

"And where do you plan to do this?" asked Miriam.

Ruth replied, "At first, I thought we should do it on a Pacific island. I always had a thing about anthropology. I dreamed of doing research like Margaret Meade and Ruth Benedict. But we decided to do it in Tokyo instead."

"Tokyo?" Akihito chimed in.

"Yes," Mark confirmed. "I hear that the garden at the Emperor's Palace is open to the public, like Central Park in New York."

Akihito interrupted. "The Emperor who reigned during the war died last year. For an ex-GI like yourself, it would have been better if he were still alive. A sort of joke, I think."

"Who cares about Hirohito?" said Ruth. She added to Mark, "We'll get a kimono for me and a plastic samurai sword for you. It will be like old times."

"The time of our life."

"The second time of our life," added Mark.

The rabbi's wife, Miriam, would be the maid of honor.

The waiter, Akihito, would be the best man.

Ruth had forgotten to bring her hair dye. Her gray roots were showing, and the on-board shops didn't have her color.

She joked about the roots of all evil.

Mark pleaded, "Don't dye it, please. I love your evil."

She agreed to wear a wig instead, a green one. They could buy it in Tokyo when they shopped for the kimono and sword.

"Do you have a copy of the divorce decree?" Ruth asked.

"No. Why should I?"

"I don't either," Ruth said. "When I heard from my lawyer that it was over and I paid him, I took his word for it that the divorce was final. And when I got my marriage license, they didn't ask for proof of divorce. I just had to check a box."

"Well, your lawyer would have it."

"He died years ago."

"Then you should write to the courthouse. They'll send you a copy."

"They did that, and they couldn't find it."

"That's strange."

"What about your lawyer?" Ruth asked.

"He's dead, too."

"Then we're still married. We've been married for forty-five, soon to be forty-six years."

Mark laughed, "Congratulations."

They kissed.

She continued, "Of course, I'd like to erase that divorce from our lives, as if it never happened. But this ceremony and celebration will be the next best thing to that."

When they arrived in Tokyo, Akihito acted as their guide, taking them first to Akiba, the district that's the world capital for anime and manga, and home to hundreds of electronics and videogame stores. There they bought a green wig, a kimono, and a plastic samurai sword.

They met Heinrich and Miriam at the front gate of the garden by the Emperor's Palace.

In the ceremony, they substituted cranberry juice for wine. Mark broke a glass with his foot, and they sang and danced to Hava Nageela.

"Did you ever dream that we would end up here doing this?" Mark asked Ruth.

She laughed. "Of course. Isn't this every little girl's dream of Happily-Ever-After?"

44 ~ Making Time

June 1990, San Pedro, CA

When their fairy-tale cruise ended at San Pedro, Ruth and Mark were both on edge. They each expected to be met at the dock by Davey. They were back in the real world, where there was no magic, and despite all their wishing and willing and self-delusion, there would be two Daveys and only one of them could be their real son. What did "real" mean when they had each raised their Davey, believing he was their son, and more than forty years had passed? What difference would blood make? Maybe they should consider them both their sons, equally and never do tests to determine "the truth."

"We could tell them that they're twins, separated at birth," Mark suggested.

"Twins with the same name?"

"We were going to raise them separately so there'd be no confusion, no harm."

"You lie so glibly," said Ruth.

"The lies have it," he tried to joke, but neither of them was in the mood for laughing.

They waited for an hour while the ship cleared paperwork with the local authorities. Then they walked down a long winding gangway and rode down an escalator to the warehouse area, where the luggage of thousands of passengers was displayed. They found their bags, then dragged them through the lines of customs and immigration. The delays didn't bother them because they wanted to put off confronting the problem that they had blissfully ignored for months—Davey.

When they came out of customs into the main lobby of the terminal, Davey was waiting for them. One Davey. They both recognized him. They rushed to hug him, then realized that his wife Hanna was standing beside him, holding a toddler. When the toddler saw them, he shouted, "Me! Me!"

"My God. Hiro," exclaimed Ruth. "I have a grandson. I really have a grandson."

"It worked," Mark whispered to her in disbelief. "But how could it have worked?"

"Never mind," she whispered back. "Enjoy."

"Me! Me!" repeated Hiro.

"Very good, Hiro," said his mother. "This is Mimi and Grandfather. You haven't seen them for a long time, but you remember."

Ruth took him in her arms and held him tight.

Then she and Mark noticed a twenty-something woman standing nearby who was clearly part of the family unit, but neither of them remembered having met her before.

Without thinking, Mark blurted out, "Lark! Skylark. It's so good you could come." And both he and Ruth hugged the daughter who Mark had invented on a whim.

To Mark and Ruth everything here was weird, impossible. But these people all acted like everything was normal. They had been married for forty-six years and today was their anniversary. Everything that Mark had made up on the spur of the moment to amuse their friends at dinner was true.

Mark and Ruth held one another's hands tightly, with shock and joy in their eyes.

Davey helped with Ruth and Mark's luggage and hurried them along. Traffic was heavy, and they needed to get to Paramount in two hours, for the press briefing and photo shoot before the premiere of the movie based on Ruth's book, *Well-Meaning Lies*.

Akihito, coming through customs for a break before leaving on another cruise, spotted the family and joined them.

Ruth introduced him and Mark, once again surprised by his own words, invited Akihito to join them for the premiere.

Then Ruth recognized an elderly couple standing in the background, holding hands, and raising their arms together to wave at them with evident glee.

"No. It can't be," Ruth whispered to Mark.

"None of this can be."

"But this more so than all the rest—they've been dead for nearly forty years."

"Who?" he asked.

"That's Father and Aunt Olive."

"Hurry up, Dad," urged Davey. "It's getting late. The traffic's heavy. We have to make time."

About the Author

Richard lives in Milford, CT, where he writes fiction full-time. He worked for DEC, the minicomputer company, as writer and Internet Evangelist. He graduated from Yale, with a major in English, went to Yale grad school in Comparative Literature, and earned an MA in Comparative Literature from the U. of Mass. at Amherst. At Yale, he had creative writing courses with Robert Penn Warren and Joseph Heller.

His published works include: *Parallel Lives* and *Beyond the 4th Door* (novels published by All Things That Matter Press), *The Name of Hero* (historical novel), *Ethiopia Through Russian Eyes* (translation from Russian), *The Lizard of Oz* (satiric fantasy), and pioneering books about Internet business. His web site is seltzerbooks.com

ALL THINGS THAT MATTER PRESS

FOR MORE INFORMATION ON TITLES AVAILABLE FROM
ALL THINGS THAT MATTER PRESS, GO TO
http://allthingsthatmatterpress.com
or contact us at
allthingsthatmatterpress@gmail.com

**If you enjoyed this book, please post a review on Amazon.com and
your favorite social media sites.
Thank you!**

Made in the USA
Middletown, DE
11 December 2020

27241897R00137